GLORY
GOLD

By
John Holmes

With sincere thanks to:

Melanie Bell for editorial advice
Claudia McQue for initial cover design work
Annie Ray for technical advice

Tim, Alanna and other Brighton NightWriters for
their encouragement and constructive criticism.

Other books by John Holmes:
Mack Breaks The Case (2022)
Lily Upshire Is Winning (2021)
Legacy And A Gun (2019)

'Do my dreaming and my scheming
Lie awake and pray
Do my crying and my sighing
Laugh at yesterday

Now it's dark and I'm alone
But I won't be afraid
In my room.'

Beach Boys: In My Room

'Maybe another day
You'll want to feel another way
You can't stop crying
You haven't got a thing to say
You feel you want to run away
There's no use trying anyway.'

Karen Dalton: Something On Your Mind

Published by Daisyblue Publishing
www.daisybluepublishing.com

ISBN: 9798864565971

For B, a fellow author,

in recognition of all his encouragement and

support with the writing of this book and its predecessors.

GLORIA'S GOLD

By
John Holmes

1

'Yeah, we crushed it.' Gloria was on the phone, glancing across the table at her friend Annalisa. The two soccer crazy twenty-two-year-olds were at The Flying Loon coffee shop in Irvine and it was her dad calling.

'And the score?'

'Yeah, 5-2. Annalisa sent off.' She moved her legs to avoid the kick. Most people saw Gloria as a serious-minded social science graduate and ardent supporter of charities, but Annalisa ('Ant') could bring out her more playful side.

'Really?' her father said. 'Mr. Garcia will be mad over that. Oh dear. Still won, though. That's the main—'

'Actually, it was me got sent off.' Ant's shoe had connected.

'Oh God, Gloria. Remember—' He sounded agitated.

'Just kidding, Dad. They were a dirty team but I scored one – and made the others.'

'Oh good. That's my girl.' He chuckled happily. 'What about Annalisa?'

'Got two. They were just her usual easy tap-ins, though. Mine was twenty yards. Goal of the season.'

'It was a frickin' pass, you liar!' Ant exclaimed. 'You mishit. You fell over. It hit the goalie's ass and rolled in!'

Another kick from her landed, this time on the shin. 'Ouch!'

After the call: 'Glo, why do you tease your dad so much?'

'I don't. It's just so rare we get to have a laugh together these days.'

'But doesn't he have a heart condition?'

'No.'

'You said he did.'

'Did I? No, I didn't.'

'Well, he will if you keep talking like that.' As Gloria took a sip of her honey cinnamon latte, she looked at her friend for a moment: almond eyes, neat bangs, long black hair tied back. Slighter than her. Less dark, prettier. No, less pretty.

'Not my dad,' she said, smiling. 'He'll live to a hundred and three.'

Gloria's drive back to Mission Viejo in her blue Toyota Camry usually took twenty minutes, but there was a jackknifed rig on the 405 freeway and she was forced to take a detour.

She started thinking about her dad Frank and the last game he'd attended. She was desperate to impress him but nothing was working for her team the Hummingbirds that day. In a rare raid into the opposition's penalty area, she detected the softest touch from a defender's boot on her right foot and tumbled over theatrically. She was immediately booked for diving and her father's frustration blew out of control. He shouted angry abuse at the referee, accusing him of taking bribes. Red in the face and still protesting, he was forcibly ejected from the ground. She was substituted, the team lost 4-0, the coach was later fired, and Gloria resolved never to cheat again. Father and daughter travelled home in shame and silence that day. Fortunately, there were no highway obstructions to prolong the torment. After that he reluctantly decided it was wiser that he not attend, for the sake of his health.

When Gloria pulled up on the white gravel drive at the Spanish colonial villa on the edge of town, 'Timeless' Ray (the laziest gardener in all Orange County, according to her mother) raised his heavy head and gave her his customary wave. The arrival of the tall, athletic Latina in her navy tracksuit was an excuse for him to pause from the pretence of work and simply admire. He adored Gloria as did pretty much everyone else except for the opposition on match days. To Gloria, Ray represented calm authority, though not one she would ever wish to rely on.

Frank was upstairs in his office, his long legs stretched out under the large empty desk, on a transatlantic Skype call. He was talking, or rather mainly listening, to old Layne, ostensibly a lord or baronet or some such.

It was never clear to Gloria what he was; all she knew was that her dad was always on Skype with him. Layne was forever moaning about his situation, solitary and absurdly wealthy in his scary-looking gothic mansion deep in the English countryside. She could never understand why her dad even wanted to indulge him; Frank was always upbeat, Layne unremittingly negative.

She decided to listen for a while because the Englishman's posh accent amused her:

'In America and other, ahem, enlightened places, wealth is revered. But in this pisspot of a country I'm marooned in, it's despised. It means a few rich people can be loathed and envied by everyone else, blamed for everything, and most importantly, be required to pay for everything. Every tub-thumping halfwit wants this persecuted minority to give up all they've got in tax so the government can go and waste it.'

'I'm with you on that, Layne, although I think over here people both love and hate the rich.'

'I already pay more tax in a year than most people earn.'

'I can imagine you do.'

'Indeed, I could easily build a hospital with what I pay in a year's tax. In fact, I do. I build hospitals all over the world through my charitable foundations.'

'That must be a lot, for sure.'

'But, as you're aware, selfless charitable work is only part of what I do. I also have to manage my properties.'

'Of course you do.'

'Some people think management is just sitting on your arse and swanning about.'

'That's mean.'

'Well, as you know yourself, it *is* sitting on your arse and swanning about, but thinking and planning and organising as well.'

'Of course it is.'

'Or half-listening to someone you've paid to do all that for you, who's passed it to someone else who's not even half-bothered.'

'I'm sure that's right.'

Gloria had heard enough of the old fool for now. She wondered whether her father liked him because he helped him appreciate that his own life was not so lousy. Hearing Layne bleating despite all his riches was to her a fine illustration of how, once you'd reached a certain level of physical comfort, your mental wellbeing no longer depended on how much wealth you possessed.

She checked the morning's Facebook messages. There were three new friend requests: two creepy-looking guys from out-of-state and a coach from a rival soccer team. She accepted none of the requests.

She'd also received a direct message: 'Tough game today but what a brilliant goal! Well done!' She felt gratified.

'Didn't I tell you we could do it?' she exclaimed out loud. After seventy-five minutes of evading trips and wild tackles she'd had the best possible reward. Annalisa had been correct, however. Everyone was expecting Gloria to pass, but her foot slipped as she struck the ball which then flew high and with force straight into the far corner of the goal, beating the 'keeper who could only flap at it in frustration.

But who was it who was so quick to compliment her? She looked at the name. It was not of anyone she knew. The picture was of a forty-year-old woman who was supposedly local.

'Weird,' she said aloud. 'Sketchy, for sure.' She closed her Facebook page and listened to see whether her father's Skype call with his English aristocrat friend had ended.

They hadn't finished. For a few moments she sat following the conversation.

Layne was still carping about the burden of being wealthy, sounding like he might croak at any moment:

'Lately I've come to realise the right to accumulate wealth is a fortress that must be defended at all costs,' he said.

'Not literally, I hope,' Frank replied.

'Of course not. The way I see it, wealth must be allowed to evolve. It's organic. It's the most natural thing in the world. That's why trying to destroy it always fails in the end.'

'It does.'

'And you can have your high-minded socialists spreading the gravy about the way they do, but they soon create their own elites and *they* certainly know how to help themselves, thank you.'

'I can see that.'

'It's very stressful for us. You see, there's no one you can talk to. You can't phone up a support line – "Can you help me, I'm a multi-millionaire?" – and you can't trust anyone because they're all after your money. It's the loneliest job in the world, I tell you. And worse than that, everyone secretly hates you. I ask you, Frank: who would feel sympathy for a depressed rich man?'

'A maybe not-so-rich woman?'

'It's so unfair, what with all I do for charity and to help fight climate change.'

'It is.'

Layne gave a heavy sigh. 'But I'll just keep plugging away at my projects to keep me out of trouble.'

'Projects?'

'Animal projects. You know, I told you before: rewilding the estate with beavers, European bison, sand lizards on specially made dunes. All sorts.'

Gloria closed her door. Rewilding could wait.

Online, she noticed Trey had sent her a message. He was in Las Vegas and was telling her he'd already won three thousand dollars on the slot machines that morning. He'd been a friend until she discovered, from a routine check, that he wasn't who he claimed to be. According to his Facebook page he was twenty-three, but his real age was thirty, and he was not living in Vegas permanently as he claimed but Wisconsin. Gloria had also established that his Facebook picture was not of him but of a male model living in Malmö, Sweden and that he was not a 'sought-after music producer' but a sales assistant at Plumbing Parts Plus, and his real name wasn't even Trey. He said he was keen for her to fly out to Vegas 'so we can be together as one at last', and he would even pay for her ticket. She did not believe a word of it and replied that she had a conference to attend in San Diego, adding, with the twist of an imaginary knife, that she did not feel he was 'fully committed' to her yet.

Gloria left her laptop to check whether her father had finished his call with Layne. Opening her door, she heard nothing and so went to see him.

'How's the rewilding going?' she said facetiously.

He shook his head. 'Beavers and bison,' he sighed. 'Oh, I don't know.'

'Why do you even talk to him? Is it because he's a lord or something? What does he even want?'

'I met him at some environmental business event.'

'What's environmental business? Sounds like garbage collection.'

He gave her a helpless look. 'I mean, green. A green conference.' He sighed. 'Is the interrogation over?'

'So defensive! You sounded like his therapist just now.'

'Gloria, please. He's just a friend. I am allowed friends.'

She realised she'd perhaps gone too far but then said, 'I worry about you.'

'Well, don't.'

She returned to her room. She had no desire to hound him, only to help. Of course, he resented the very idea that he might benefit from her help.

Next she visited her mother Maria in her room and found her lying on her back in bed, her head on a cradle of black hair, a small teddy bear within easy reach on either side of her. 'Hi, Mama,' she said. She received a mere mumble in response. 'It's stuffy in here. Don't you want some air?' Without waiting for an answer she went to the window to open it. She looked out. 'The garden's going to look nice this summer with all the new planting. Ray and the boys have done a good job.' Her mother said nothing. She appeared to have just fallen asleep.

Whenever she felt disappointed at her mother's lack of reaction, she always gazed up at the painted portrait on the wall behind her bed. It was of Maria as a young woman, the stunning and successful Mexican-American actress.

Gloria then switched her attention to the face of the woman, now approaching fifty and beginning to show it. She was reminded of her own habitual sadness at her mother's decline. Her own childhood had been happy and her teenage years apparently less fractious than those of her contemporaries. Much of this was to the credit of her ever-patient mother. But by now, with the two boys having left, Gloria increasingly independent, and Frank always preoccupied with business, Maria had faded into the all-consuming depression that can arise from the sense of a lack of purpose.

On hearing the bedclothes move, Gloria said, 'Can I tell you about soccer?' Maria said nothing and her expression was indifferent. Gloria decided to speak about it anyway: ' We won 5-2 but they were a weak side. I scored.' This brought a faint smile to Maria's lips. 'Annalisa was on fire as usual. I got kicked all over.' This exaggeration was intended to provoke her mother, who frowned in response, perhaps reminded that she'd once wanted her daughter to be a teenage model as she herself had been. She'd said, 'Those eyes, that face, those legs of yours could break any man's heart. Let them.' But Frank was adamantly against the idea and Gloria was shy and had no desire to parade her looks in front of leering men.

Maria never had such inhibitions. When Gloria tried, in an attempt to ease her mother's depression, to encourage her into ceramics or painting or writing, she could not settle on any of them, and in her mind returned instead to her days of being an object of male desire. She went through a period where, it seemed to Gloria, she loved nothing more than to flirt with any young man of acceptable looks that visited the house. It was embarrassing, but when Gloria challenged her on it Maria appeared genuinely mystified, and her daughter eventually had to accept it was entirely innocent, even unconscious. But by then the flirting had stopped anyway as Maria had no more enthusiasm for it than anything else.

Gloria's thoughts were disturbed on hearing a car arrive at the house. It sounded like the Mustang belonging to Dr Mencius. Even though he never visited on a Saturday, she felt the same disquiet on hearing the car. Dapper and devious, this old man called round every week to check on her mother's wellbeing and 'prescribe' some herbal remedy or other of dubious efficacy. He would stay in Maria's room with the door closed for almost an hour and, so Gloria believed, take advantage of his heavily sedated patient. She had once thought about proving it to her father – it would hardly be difficult to install a spy camera without her mother realising it – but then she balked at the idea. Besides, she did not want to believe there was an affair.

She found Mencius odious. He always wore a strong sickly cologne and was overly solicitous towards her. He knew she played soccer and always seemed to anticipate her reporting a twinge or minor sprain worthy of his attention. She never said anything anymore, however, since the time she mentioned a muscle tightness in her right thigh and he insisted on inspecting the relevant area, immediately pulling a jar of ointment from his bag and beginning to massage her leg before she could object;

he took his time, making it obvious he gained pleasure from applying it. It made her queasy recalling this incident.

She returned to the window. It was not Mencius' car. It must belong to one of her father's corporate clients. She could breathe freely again. She looked at her mother. On concluding there would be no further reaction from her, Gloria stood up, leaned over and kissed her on the forehead, gently squeezed her hand, and quietly left the room.

Back at her desk, she noticed she'd received a message from one of her online psychology students. A student in need of her help always made her happy. She loved giving tuition to others on her favourite subject. She felt studying social sciences had left her with a greater understanding of the world, even though the conflicting theories sometimes irritated her. It was certainty she looked for in life, not ambiguity, and she was delighted when she found something that rang true to her own experience. The syllabus had now thrown up one such concept, that of the 'fundamental attribution error', and her student Marie wanted to discuss possible examples with her.

She phoned Marie, who was the kind of student who always thought a topic was beyond her even when in fact she understood it. She just needed reassurance. 'I was thinking of the example of my dad,' she said.

'OK.'

'So let's say he's going to a business meeting—'

'Right.'

'So if he's late it's because of things beyond his control. The traffic was backed up. Or maybe Mom was ill and he had to take my brother to school which made him late.'

'Yes. And what if the other person's late?'

'He often meets someone called Rick. My dad complains about him. He says Rick's nearly always late.'

'And why's that?'

'He always says his train is delayed, but Dad says it's because Rick's disorganised and is someone who doesn't care about punctuality and likes to keep people waiting, which is disrespectful.'

'So what's your conclusion?'

'If someone else fails in some respect it's because their character's flawed, but if we fail it's because of some external cause.'

'Yes. Fate or malevolent actors.' Gloria always thought of her father's business in this context. To him, when it was growing and making healthy profits it was down to his drive, determination and skilful entrepreneurship, but when it spectacularly crashed it was because of fickle customers, incompetent and corrupt authorities, and rapacious lawyers.

'Great, so you got it, Marie.'

'Thanks. Cool. I was also thinking about sports coaches. How they always blame the officials or the other team cheating when they lose.'

'Right. We have a coach who does that. He'll say, "We won because we've trained hard, we're well-organised, and we have a strong work ethic," so it's about us. But if we get beat it'll be, "The ref made too many mistakes and their blatant fouls went unpunished."'

'I see.'

'But you have to be careful. It's not a good example because in the dressing room he says something different entirely. And when he talks to the press he's always indirectly trying to motivate the team. And Barti - that's his name - is a former goalkeeper and he's always harder on the defence.'

'Yeah?'

'I probably shouldn't tell you, but I will anyway. Last season in a game, I was getting so frustrated at being fouled all the time that I just poleaxed the opposition's striker.'

'Yeah? I can't imagine it.'

'Yes and I'm not proud of it. I should have been sent off but got away with a booking and a free kick to them. They scored and won 1-0. But Barti, bless him, told the press it was a "highly dubious decision", and in the dressing room he told the defenders, "Once again, you guys at the back let the side down. Why? Because the forwards had to help you out." I wasn't too popular with them that day.'

After the call, she rested on her bed and dozed for a few minutes. During that time she had a vivid dream in which a giant excavator broke the window of her father's office and grabbed him in his pyjamas, executive swivel chair and all, thrust him into the open air, suspended him shouting and helpless with limbs flailing above the swimming pool, and then dumped him into the chlorinated water. Fear of the rage such an occurrence would induce in him woke her instantly. She heard a splash outside and thought perhaps it was the new young gardener Carlo working on the pond. She arose from her bed and went to the open window. No, it was the pair of black swans that had arrived the night before.

2

Late one afternoon, Gloria met up with Annalisa and a few other friends to go shopping at Fashion Island in Newport Beach. She bought a couple of dresses with the bright floral print designs she especially liked, but the main benefit of the trip for her was to be out of the house and socialising with friends. Afterwards, the five of them went for coffee. In a group of this size, Gloria's natural shyness came to the fore and she was subdued. This was exacerbated by the conversation which was all about the guys the others were dating. Gloria felt out of it, the only one without a boyfriend. Annalisa felt for her, and when the others had left she asked Gloria, 'What's the matter, babe?'

'What do you mean? I'm OK.'

'You're not. On match days you're full of it. But on a day like today with the others you're quiet.'

'Sorry to be a disappointment.' Gloria stood up to leave.

'Sit down,' said Ant. 'Please.'

Reluctantly, Gloria returned to her seat. 'Please don't tell me I need a boyfriend,' she said. 'I do not want that conversation again.'

'I won't talk if you don't want me to. Go if you want.'

'I'm sorry,' said Gloria. 'Let's get more drinks. Same?' She called the server over. 'Two regular vanilla lattes, please.'

'Tell me about Lily,' said Ant. Seeing her friend's surprised expression she added, 'You mentioned her once. Some deep relationship.'

'Did I? Why, are you jealous or something?'

'How could I be? Whatever makes you happy, Glo.'

'Well, I'm not gay, if that's what you're thinking.' This response surprised both of them.

'I wasn't thinking that. But it wouldn't matter to me if you were. Glo, you're my best. And you'll always be my best.'

Gloria smiled. 'Likewise. What do you want to know about her?'

'Whatever you want to tell me.'

'OK.'

When the drinks arrived Gloria said, 'You'll find it a strange story.'

'Try me.'

'I've been in love with Lily on a platonic basis for several years. She lives in England with her wife whose name is Mack.'

'What? That is weird.'

'If you're going to be like that, there's no point talking.'

'Glo, please. Does Mack know?'

'Yes. And she accepts it. But she also understands I'm no threat to her.'

'How did—'

'It's all associated with the collapse of my dad's company. When Lily was twelve she found something strange in the drink she bought made by a small subsidiary of Dad's great corporate empire. Instead of doing what so-called "normal" people would do and claim a new one or seek compensation, she wrote to the company for an apology. It was not forthcoming. So she asked again. And again. Then other people got involved - neighbours, local press, and so on - and it built up from there. A campaign made up of people claiming all sorts, and that turned into a lawsuit. All done in Lily's name.'

'Wow. So she was suing your dad's company?'

'No. She never did. She sued the people who claimed, because they were using her name against her wishes. And when this huge whale of a lawsuit settled she got some money too, and it made her rich.'

'But how did you get involved with her?'

'I looked her up when it all started, so she was maybe thirteen then. A blonde girl, just like the bitch who threw stones at me when I was a kid, called me dirty, and shouted "Get back to Mexico!" at me. So I trolled her. I sent nasty messages to her.'

'That's not like you.'

'I know, I'm not proud of it. But I soon began to admire her. We became friends. And one day I realised I was in love with her. I told her. And she told me she loved me too.'

'And she's not gay either.'

'No. I know it sounds weird. People can think what they want. I don't have to justify it to anyone.'

'Of course you don't. Relationships are not always plain vanilla. It doesn't matter. All that matters is what's real for the people concerned.'

'That's how I feel.'

'It makes me and Jimmy seem pretty boring.'

'No, it doesn't. So, anyway, she and I have met three times over the years.'

'So you write to her. How often?'

'Less since she got married. Every few weeks maybe. I thought it might die out altogether then, but it hasn't. As a matter of fact, I got an email from her a couple of days ago. I haven't read it yet.'

'Saving it.'

'That's right.'

3

Frank meanwhile was nursing a headache. He'd had a lousy day from lack of sleep and had achieved nothing. Suzie, the daily help, had been sympathetic since she'd arrived in the afternoon, making him cups of coffee whenever she noticed his eyes begin to droop. 'You don't seem really up for it today,' she said. It was a typically considerate observation from this shy, slight woman in her early forties, whose cares in life rarely strayed beyond her own family and that of Frank and Maria Salesman, for whom she had worked for almost a decade.

He didn't tell her that what had kept him awake was his annoyance with Gloria. His daughter had no right to even comment about his relationship with Layne, nor did he appreciate her constant fussing about Dr Mencius who took so much burden off the family. She was too much of a fusspot, a goody two-shoes. But what had kept him awake most was the fear that she might actually be right about Layne: that he was an ancient relic unworthy of his time, when instead he could spend it at least *trying* to communicate with his depressed wife. The unwelcome truth was that

Layne was his distraction from the issues in his life which he was unable or unwilling to address.

He'd procrastinated all day in every way he could think of, but finally had to accept that a client's latest presentation could no longer be avoided. As a consultant he was to review it in order to advise them on how they could better market themselves. Within a few seconds of turning on his laptop he had the video before him. A comfortable-looking, beef-fed Texan man began with a tiresome, redundant and over-long lecture on the importance of renewable energy, then described with overripe zeal what his company did and how vitally important it was for the planet's survival. Frank, bored, barked at the screen, 'You're making a li'l doojigger the size of my pinkie, you jerk! Not exactly solar geoengineering, for God's sake!' The man's fervour was exhausting and Frank began to yawn. When he heard 'sustainable and climate-friendly in everything we do' he fell into a stupor. Whatever was next in the video was replaced by a dream. He was back in his role as a corporate executive officer and some highly paid experts – Bluffin', Boffin, and Bafflin' or some such – were visiting. Their first speaker was all optimism, the second all doom, and the third, the boss and most ridiculous of the three, was all syrup and said he agreed wholeheartedly with the other two, even though their analysis and conclusions had contradicted each other in every respect. The dream ended with him thanking them profusely and saying their work was well worth the three hundred and fifty thousand dollars a year it cost, and the boss correcting him, pointing out it was that amount per week.

He awoke from this dream only to discover, to his horror, that the real presentation had thirty-one minutes yet to run. Someone, probably Gloria on returning from her shopping trip and hearing him snoring, had snuck in and paused the video. He was trapped by others' good intentions.

A few minutes later, Gloria was receiving a visit from Suzie. She'd made a traditional Mexican Tres Leches cake for them and had brought her a piece. Gloria didn't want it, delicious though it looked, because it was so close to dinner time, but she accepted it, exploiting this moment to say to her, 'Suzie, this is lovely. Can I ask you something?'

'Thank you,' she replied smiling, perhaps anticipating a recipe question, 'Sure you can.'

'Tell me: what do you know about Dr Mencius?'

Suzie frowned. 'He won't be here until next week now,' she said. An evasive answer that was not unexpected.

'Yes, but what do you know about him?'

'He is a good man, I am sure.' Gloria noted how self-consciously Suzie uttered those last three words, inadvertently conveying the opposite meaning.

At that moment, her father entered the room to congratulate Suzie on the 'wonderful' cake. Seeing the room's two occupants looking pensive, possibly conspiratorial, he said, 'Is everything alright?' Suzie's face indicated it wasn't, then Gloria said, 'I was just asking about Dr Mencius.'

Sensing the tension around her, Suzie then excused herself. When she'd gone downstairs, Frank said, 'You can't leave it alone, can you?'

'You don't know anything about him. Nor about what medications he gives her.'

'Unless they're hiding pills, that's hardly difficult to find out, but I don't need to know.' He immediately left the room.

Gloria resolved that she would uncover the story behind Dr Mencius.

4

Maria had sent word that she would not be leaving her room for dinner. The message was conveyed by Suzie. Accordingly, it was Gloria who took the simple meal of rice, chicken and vegetables to her mother. She found her sitting up.

Maria barely reacted to her arrival in the room, only giving a little nod when her daughter asked how she was feeling. Gloria then watched as she tentatively dabbed the food with her spoon. It was obvious she would not manage to eat more than a quarter of it. Gloria was tempted to grab the plate and force the food down her mother's throat because she felt that Maria was being the actress once more. Yes, she was depressed, but more than that she was playing the part of a depressed person. When Gloria began telling her about her next soccer match there was a flicker of interest revealed in a smile, but no words.

It was a trial of will for Gloria to sit there and endure the achingly slow process of Maria silently moving the food from the plate to her lips. Gloria started talking randomly about the weather, about news stories from the local online *Patch* newsletter, about anything that popped into her mind, but there was no response from her mother and, realising she was talking to herself, in the end she said, 'Well, I'll leave you to it, then,' and did just that, feeling disappointed with both her mother and herself.

A little after dinner, Gloria looked in on her father who was at his desk, disinterestedly looking at a brochure for an internet startup he could tell wouldn't last more than three weeks. Noticing her, he said, 'What's up with you these days? Talk to me.'

'What do you mean?'

'You seem so uptight. I mean, you've always been a little on the serious side.'

'You mean, I'm boring. Thank you.'

'No.'

'My own father thinks I'm boring. That does wonders for my confidence. If it's boring to care, then I plead guilty. I care about you and I care about Mama. I mean, why do you spend so much time talking to that dreadful man? Are you his psychiatrist or something?'

'Who, Layne?'

'Who else?'

'He interests me.'

'What, like a beetle in a matchbox?'

'No.'

'So he tells you all his problems and you pick over them like a vulture looking for good meat.'

'No.'

'Isn't it a bit intrusive?'

'He's my friend. What's with you anyway? I know you're concerned about it, but why so much?'

Gloria was all too aware of her father's fragility. Since his breakdown after the corporate collapse, she had played a protective role as regards his mental health, but maybe he could no longer cope with that. 'I'm sorry,' she said. 'By the way, have we got any papers on Dr Mencius?'

He sighed. 'Papers? No, I don't believe we do. Why?'

'We have nothing? Not even an address?'

Seeing his pained expression, Gloria did not pursue it further.

Bored with his corporate work, vexed by Gloria, and frustrated at his wife's condition, Frank was delighted to hear from Layne again, it being early morning in the UK. The old man was grumbling about his 'faithless' ex-wife and it cheered Frank up.

'So you've phoned up to complain? Good, I'm in need of a boost.'

'Of course I'm complaining. I have every right. So would you. My last wife, my third, was a grasping Yank who only married me for the prestige and the bank account. She was idle. The only thing she ever laundered in her life was her boyfriend's drug money. Now she's written a book about the aristocracy. Well, I doubt very much she wrote it herself. It's for foreigners wanting to marry into English wealth. God knows what eyewash she's put in it. It has to be all about me.'

'Does it?'

'Of course it does. So I'm going to need a lawyer. An American lawyer would be best. I assume you've got through your share of them in your career. Who could you recommend?'

'For what?'

'For fighting falsehoods, of course.'

'Libel?'

'If you like. Who would you use?'

'If I were you, I'd wait until you know exactly what she says. It may not be so bad.'

This confused the Englishman. He started muttering to himself, so Frank changed the subject to Layne's environmental work which was such a source of pride to the old man. The distraction gave a gratified Layne something else to cavil about:

'Why is it that every time I get on a plane to attend one of my important meetings on some environmental scheme or other, I invariably end up dealing with a confidence trickster?'

'I don't know.'

'Last week he was selling dodgy cars. This week he wants interest-free loans for some technology he's supposedly invented. It won't even work, but that's OK because it can be called "sustainable" and "eco-whatnot". Then you find everyone behind it's up to their necks in corruption.'

'Oh dear.'

'But I still think having an interest in green technology's worthwhile, don't you? Above all, it's good for the image of the enlightened wealthy. We certainly need all the help we can get.'

'I guess.'

'That's why, as soon as I'm back from the airport, I'm out there planting a bunch of trees on the estate to fix the carbon deficit. Well, I don't do it myself, obviously.'

'For one nervous moment I was imagining you with a spade in your hands there, Layne.'

'Someone does it for me. Except of course for the photograph where I look the part of the caring philanthropist doing his bit.'

'Ever the professional.'

'Although even posing for that puts my back out, so I don't do it anymore. They photoshop my head onto some lackey's neck.'

'Hah!'

'But the intention's there. That's the point.'

'Of course it is.'

'And these days, the reality is that someone merely tells me about someone else who's going to plant the trees. Or they put it on the list of things that the awkward cuss of a head gardener can say can't be done.'

'I see.'

'But the real problem is, I have so many of these plane trips all over the shop they could never keep up with me anyway. It'd be like a wildwood out there. I'd have to chop down trees just so I could plant all the new ones...'

And on he went happily with his patter for another ten minutes. Frank felt glad listening to him, avoiding the temptation to ask whether all his trips were necessary, and whether all the tree-planting wasn't really like buying religious indulgences in olden times.

5

Frank decided to contact his old friend, the lawyer Jack Quick. He was growing tired of his role working with what he called 'tomorrow's zombie companies'. All they did was reinforce his own feelings of failure.

They never listened to what he said anyway. Or rather, they listened but then did the opposite of what he recommended. They obviously found it reassuring: 'Well, if this loser thinks it, we know we should do anything but that.' Besides, he was bored with all the blatant greenwashing. He'd gone the 'treehugger route', as he called it, when he was a corporate boss, but now he was tired of the hypocrisy and fraud he saw everywhere. He couldn't even stand hearing the expressions 'carbon neutral' and 'eco-friendly' anymore. He'd always been a bit of a radical, a disrupter as he understood the term, and now he was ready to adopt that guise again, but in a different way. What he wanted was a lawyer he knew and could trust to work with him in a new role.

Jack Quick was his lawyer for many years, beginning when Frank's old company was just a small family low budget outfit in a friend's backyard making artisan wholegrain bread. Some deadbeat claimed they'd bitten on a stone in a loaf and broken a tooth. Frank had Jack's business card from a Welcome Wagon handout. Anyway, Jack was immediately onto it and the case was settled for fifty dollars. It never went near court. That was his style: wrap it up real quick. He certainly lived up to his name. Jack never lost a case in court; never won one either.

When, over breakfast, Frank told Gloria of his decision to team up with Jack, she said, 'A lawyer? What do you need a lawyer for? If you're so unsettled with what you're doing, why not do something different altogether, like working for a consumer group?'

'Doing what?'

'You could sit down with them to maybe find out what problems they've suffered because of different companies' products, and help campaign for them.'

'It's a possibility. I thought of working for a plaintiff law firm as a kind of consultant.'

'But that would just be for their clients. Why not do it for everyone?'

'I see your point.' His face brightened. 'And if I worked for a consumer group, maybe we could use some of the charity money to support them.'

'What charity money?'

'From the foundation.'

'Are you serious?' Gloria could not believe her ears. She was furious. 'It's not possible.'

'Why not? It would be for a charity.'

'No. No. No.' She shook her head vigorously. 'That money—'

'It's millions.'

'It's not your money. You gave it to me when you were desperate to get rid of assets. You said - and I remember it clearly - that I was to use that money to set up a charitable foundation, and you said you never, repeat, *never*, wanted to know what I did with it. I didn't want to do it. I didn't feel I had the experience. OK, I supported charities already, but this was a whole different thing. But I did it because you asked me to, and because I was worried about you, and because I love you. The business was crumbling. Your mental health was crumbling.'

'It was. But things have changed. And you can't have spent all the money. There must be some left over.'

'That's not your business. You gave me the job and I did it. And I'm still doing it. I'm meticulous about it. I choose charities that are most effective. If I find they're not I stop funding them. I don't take any non-sense. There's accountants and lawyers to deal with, and of course our beloved IRS. I never wanted the burden, but I took it on.'

Frank was taken aback by the robustness of her response. 'OK, dear.' He reached out to squeeze her hand. 'Don't worry about it.'

Frank gave up - for now. Gloria knew he'd return to the subject. She was disappointed, though. She had taken what he'd said at face value when he gave her the money. Now, it seemed, he hadn't meant it. That was dispiriting because she had worked so hard on it. She'd been brought up to be financially prudent, so when it came to the foundation's wealth she took her time in distributing it and invested the vast majority for safekeeping, principally in gold. Any major contribution to a specific not-for-profit was made with great caution to ensure all money entrusted to her was spent wisely. She did stringent checks on their management and working methods, whilst always releasing more in total than the five per cent of the foundation's assets every year, the minimum required by law.

After the argument with her father, she was glad of the solace of her room. She was almost pleased to see the new red Ferrari in the picture her fake boyfriend Trey had sent her. He wrote, 'I treated myself because a record I produced is now big all across Europe. If you ever want a taste of my truly glamorous life you can come visit me. I'm just waiting for your word, darling.'

It was pathetic. She sometimes wondered why she continued to let him send her his stupid messages about his non-existent successes. She could easily have blocked him when she first discovered weeks earlier that he was fake, but she was so upset by it she went on the offensive instead. She began teasing and tormenting him, leading him on, telling him she was always there for him and that he was the only one for her. She would say that sadly she could not send the intimate pictures of herself he wanted because her camera was broken, which was technically true although the broken camera was not the one on her laptop. She set up fake Facebook accounts under different names to send flirty messages to him, and when he expressed interest in them she'd use her genuine account to accuse him of 'playing around', saying it was clear she meant nothing to him and that she must look elsewhere. He would write back in plaintive terms. Then the fake accounts she'd set up would bombard him complaining that a 'Gloria' was claiming to have found out about them and why hadn't he mentioned her before? And in response he would claim Gloria was 'just some nut'.

It was fun to think up these things but she was uncomfortable with such chicanery, thinking it childish, mean-spirited, and potentially dangerous, even though he was a menace who deserved all the anguish he suffered. Besides, he'd once said he'd gladly die at her feet, which in her eyes made him completely contemptible.

But now she saw Trey as merely a boring nuisance. Fortunately, his messages had become less frequent, suggesting that his main interest was someone else, and perhaps he'd come to suspect that all her excuses for failing to meet up were not entirely genuine, and he was merely playing along too. She would end it soon, not from guilt at deceiving him – he deserved no less – but out of concern that she herself had become a catfish.

She noticed the latest local *Patch* online newsletter had come through. She used it to advertise her tuition service, which was how she found Marie and others, but she also liked to read it. Today's edition announced that a chapter of the Daughters of the American Revolution were welcoming new members to tea: 'Wear your best hat'. With her mother's Mexican heritage, Gloria surmised it unlikely she was, as the Daughters required, descended from a patriot who served or aided in the American

Revolution. Her dad's father, who was English, was the first of his family to set foot in the States, so they were on the wrong side anyway. Thus, she was a born two-time loser when it came to American history, all five feet nine and a hundred and twenty-three pounds, 'BMI 18.2 equals underweight', of her.

She reminded herself that she had something of her own to be proud of. For want of a suitable 'best hat' she reached into her knicker drawer, pulled out a bright red pair, and placed them loosely on her head. She stood facing her mirror, unbuttoned her shirt to the navel, raised her hand to salute and declared, 'Well, I am a daughter of the *Mexican* Revolution, so there!'

In fact, this was true. Or at least Maria maintained it was, variously claiming to be directly descended from one of Zapata's generals, or a Soldadera, or both. Maria was known to exaggerate but none of her children ever dared challenge these accounts.

Gloria removed her impromptu headgear, buttoned up her shirt, and returned to her laptop on the bed. She then opened the letter from Lily in England, which was attached to an email:

'Dearest Gloria,

I'm sorry I haven't written earlier. As soon as I get a letter from you, I want to write back immediately, even though I know I must resist that urge. And then of course I delay too long. I hope relations with your dad have improved. It must be very difficult sometimes. I'm sure he loves you, though.

'I was sorry that your last boyfriend did not turn out to be the one for you. I hope you find someone better. You haven't had much luck in that respect lately. I feel that you and I are very different in some ways. I used to always want a man, but it was really only physical desire. I have never really fallen in love with one. I now know I could not. Mack is all-consuming.'

At this point, Gloria stopped reading. It occurred to her that Lily might be taunting her a little, making her jealous with that 'all-consuming' comment. But if so, it would be unintentional because it was uncharacteristic for Lily to taunt. And surely she still loved her every bit as much as Gloria adored her, didn't she?

She returned to the letter. The remainder of it concerned Lily's business, and fancy restaurants in London she'd been to, but it ended with

'As time goes by, I find you mean more to me than ever.' She wondered if there might be overstatement or even insincerity there. No, she would take it at face value. Receiving this message from Lily had brightened her day - they always did - but she was aware that it had also reminded her of her own emotional insecurity.

6

Frank met Jack Quick at a high-end, traditional Italian restaurant called Baci in San Diego. He hadn't seen Jack in years and found him more wizened than he remembered him, though the smile and the glint in the eye were still there. Jack chose the same linguine dish he always had while Frank had scampi in lobster sauce. It felt like old times, although their relationship had not always been entirely smooth. When the major litigations had come Frank's way, he'd decided he needed a bigger law firm to defend the company, so Jack was quietly dropped. But Frank knew in his heart Jack would always return if asked. He now had a proposition for him.

'I'm doing this corporate advice work, but my heart's not in it, Jack.'

'Sorry to hear that, but why isn't it?'

'I can't stand all the posturing. They still want to make money, which is great, but these days it's not plain and simple like it used to be. Instead, they want to throw in all this environmental and social benefit baloney. It makes me queasy to listen to these hypocrites. Most of them just want to lie in the subtlest way possible. Don't get me wrong: I'm all for the critters, and the green spaces, and the dolphins, but I don't look to the corporate world for moral guidance and self-serving piety, and I'm damned sure their customers don't, especially when it conveniently hikes up their prices. So I'm thinking of closing down my consultancy work.'

'You sure? And do what? Retire?'

'I'm thinking of... I call it "going rogue", Jack.'

'Meaning?'

'Working for consumers. Helping them get their money back after being stiffed by corporations. People injured by shoddy products, that type of thing. And I wondered if you'd like to join me.'

'Me?'

'Sure. You know more about the bad side of corporate America than anyone else I know.'

'Thanks, I guess. But, no, I don't think so.'

'Why not?'

'I'm too old, Frank. I can't change now. If I said I'd turn up for the plaintiffs on a case they'd say: "Are you kidding?" Consumer groups hate me. Go and work for their side? They wouldn't allow me in the front door unless they had a knife in their hand.'

'Negative thinking, Jack. You're just like this English guy I talk to: Layne. He's a multi-millionaire, billionaire even, and all he does is moan.'

'I'm not the person you need. You want someone bigger. I'm just small fry. That's why you fired me. And I'd be even smaller fry on the plaintiffs' bar. I mean, right now I've got this case on the go: a party in full swing, everyone drunk, and a giant beach ball knocks the plaintiff into a table. I've never even heard of some of the injuries they're claiming for. That's my kind of case. I couldn't work for the plaintiffs because I'd think they were all graspers. Try someone like Ed Shills.'

'The one with all the big game trophies on his office wall? He's famous.'

'Try him.'

7

The following morning, Frank had another Skype call with Layne:

'How are you getting on, Frank?'

'Layne! Good to hear. I'm pretty chipper.'

'You're always chipper at nine in the morning. I don't know how you do it. Must be some weird Californian drug thing. It's six in the evening here, as you know. I've just had my nap and I thought I'd call you before they bring my dinner.'

'I'm always keen to hear from a limey I can trust. Besides, I don't have your money, Layne, so I don't have your worries.'

'You've had money, you old fraud.'

'Sure I have. I had money and I lost it, got it again, then lost it. Right now, I'm on a slight uptick and I'll enjoy it while it lasts.'

'But you seem to enjoy your lot even when it's gone to pieces.'

'That's me, Layne. I never stop. What's this I read, though: you're selling your superyacht?'

'Why, you want to buy it? Yours for seventy million dollars. Eighty metres. Specially designed with all the eco-conscious features money can buy. You could be in Extinction Rebellion and still have a clear conscience.'

'I've no idea what you're talking about. I never have felt the need for such a thing. A superyacht, I mean.'

'That's because you're not really wealthy. Not in the established sense. More here today, gone tomorrow... and then here again.'

'Thanks for clarifying that. By the way, I didn't even know you owned a superyacht.'

'To tell you the truth, nor did I. In fact, technically I don't. It's owned by a company in the Caymans or somewhere.'

'How could you not know you owned it?'

'It's easy to ask that. The fact is, when you're head of an international foundation whose sole aim and purpose is the preservation of the planet—'

'Not that you're bragging.'

'Alright, alright.' Layne gave a grin. 'I was actually quoting from *Forbes* about someone else.' He paused for a stiff little laugh. 'The point I was coming to, before you so rudely interrupted, is that my lawyers bought it and didn't tell me about it.'

'Hard to believe.'

'For you, maybe. OK, so I've had the use of a superyacht and now it's for sale – so what?'

'OK.'

'And what is it about superyachts anyway? People are obsessed with them. Does everyone want one? Of course not. They just don't want people like me to have what they wouldn't want anyway. Imagine if everyone had a yacht. The whole of the south of England out on the Channel every weekend, all in their own little boats. It's absurd. Lots of people have boats; it's just that some are bigger than others. Well, so damned what?

If I decide I need a so-called superyacht to entertain people who support my charities and climate work, then so be it.'

'Not everyone involved with charities and so on needs a superyacht, though. Only the entitled few.'

'Entitled? If people think I have a sense of entitlement, my answer is, damned right I do! What with all I do for humanity with my money and time, saving the world.'

'It's a results-based business, though, Layne,' said Frank facetiously.

'How dare you! And who are you to judge me? What have you ever done? No, don't tell me. I don't want to know. You'll hit me with so much Californian twaddle I won't know what I'm hearing – and I certainly won't believe it.'

'Actually, I did know you had a superyacht. Wasn't there an incident in the hot tub on it once? Didn't someone get injured? Aren't they suing? Isn't that the real reason you're distancing yourself from the boat?'

'Who put you up to this?'

'Eh? No one. I read it in—'

'You read it in some rag. You read it in the *National Enquirer* or some such trash. So we're clear: I do not own a superyacht, my company does. There was no incident in the hot tub, as you put it in your insinuating way. Anything else, name your lawyer and I'll see you in court!'

'Keep your hair on, old man. You have to admit – and you've just proved it – you keep your attorneys busy.'

'There's only one case I know of. Nothing to do with yachts. Some kid that fell in the pond on the estate.'

'A visitor?'

'Yes, some little kid, and the mother was on her phone, not paying any attention, and—'

'You know this?'

'Yes, I know it. It's obvious. So the stupid kid goes waddling into the pond, falls over, gets a gobful of gunk and suddenly he's on life support – allegedly.'

'Gobful of gunk? What was in there?'

'It's a pond, for Heaven's sake. It has ducks and coots and I don't know what else. And it's summer and the water's down so it's kind of – I won't say dirty, on principle – not as pristine as it normally is. So this kid, whose mum obviously has attention deficit issues, is supposedly dying from toxic whatever, and the next thing you know he's at home giving an interview on TV. I mean, what the bloody hell! They wanted fifty thousand.'

'And what did they get?'

'Five hundred pounds and don't ever come back. There, you've had your entertainment now. Time for my dinner, then a nap.'

'I thought you already had your nap.'

'I am allowed more than one. And I still get more done than most. So put that in your *National Enquirer*.'

8

Gloria's team the Hummingbirds found their dream of a championship-winning season dented when their first three wins were followed by a 2-0 loss. She knew from the previous season that after any defeat the coach would be severe. As she left the pitch, she felt a sense of dread at the telling off she and the rest of the team were about to get. She was disappointed with her own performance, feeling she lacked the spark that normally inspired her. She'd been off the pace and had given the ball away several times. No coach could be more critical of her than she was herself but she still had to listen to him. Barti Caprato, a tall former goalkeeper, was an ambitious, passionate man in his late thirties, determined that success at this job would propel him to a higher league. He took defeat personally, and in the dressing room he shuffled impatiently as he waited for them to sit down. In the end, he could wait no longer. The words tumbled out:

'OK, listen. Today we were terrible. Not one of you can feel proud of their performance. Not a single one. The goals we conceded were... I've seen better defending in my kids' playpen. Three of you marking one player means two of theirs are free. I take it some of you did arithmetic at school.' He paused to look at them, gratified that they appeared insulted. He cared about them as though they were his children, but sometimes it was necessary to upset them. 'They were lining up for the crosses today. Every week we work on this. Every week!' He cast his gaze around the room. Most of the eyes were now staring hard at the floor. 'But it's not just the defence. Other teams play from the back but we can't do that, so we rely on the counterattack. And where was that today? Nowhere. Gloria, where was your speed? Jamie, you're my workhorse, but you weren't competing today. And as for you, Annalisa, you were non-existent. You might as well have been at home with your feet up. Some of you have ambitions. Some of you think you're too good for this team. But based on this performance, not one of you is good enough, even at this level. Some of you are just too complacent. You think you can't be replaced.' He slapped his thigh for effect. 'Be assured that I will replace the entire team if I have to. From now on, you fight for your places or you're out. I say to each and every one of you: when you get home, look yourself in the mirror, and apologise for your performance today.'

Gloria felt depressed and wanted to go straight home but she'd promised Annalisa they would go to a new coffee bar in Anaheim afterwards.

Annalisa, despite her aptitude for scoring goals, had a reputation for laziness. She never helped out in defence and, unlike Jamie, the other member of the strike force, she never scrapped for the ball. Annalisa was seen as a prima donna because the pass to her had to be inch-perfect as she made so little effort to meet it. Today Gloria's passes had been wayward, and, as soon as they'd sat down on the black faux leather chairs, Annalisa let her know about it. Gloria replied, 'Well, the coach said you were non-existent.'

'That's because there was no service. I can't score if no one gives me the ball.'

'Well, you could try harder to get it.'

Annalisa, miffed, reminded her of her career goalscoring record, which was an average of over a goal a game.

'So what?' said Gloria.

They looked hard into each other's eyes like cats about to fight. But there was a deep affection there. Neither of them wanted a row.

'What's the matter?' Annalisa asked gently, seeing her friend on the brink of tears.

'I'm sorry.' Gloria turned away. 'Everything in my life just feels so weird right now.'

'That's because you're dealing with it on your own. I know you have Lily but she's far away and married. And if you don't mind me saying so, it might help if you had someone here. A proper boyfriend.'

'Oh, not this again. How come you know so much about what I need?'

'When did you last have sex, babe?'

Gloria was taken aback. She looked round to see if anyone might be listening. If they were, they were subtle about it. She lowered her voice. 'I don't know. Months ago. Am I supposed to keep records or something? What of it?'

'You need it.'

'There you go again,' said Gloria. She imagined her friend had sex like she played soccer – minimal effort until the exact right moment, then an instant trip to ecstasy for lucky Jimmy, her beau for the last nine months. She had never been without a boyfriend all the time Gloria had known her. They could never get enough of her. But Gloria was defiant: 'Just because you get so much of it, there's no need to gloat. I have never found it very satisfying anyway.'

Annalisa was unsparing: 'It's not just the sex you're missing; it's the holding tight, it's the caressing, the kissing, the reassuring, the someone to tell your troubles to, the sweet words from the person who cares for you. You need it, Glo. We all do.' But seeing her friend was suffering, she stopped talking, grabbed Gloria's hand for a moment, and asked her to open up about all that was bothering her, though only if she wanted to. Gloria was reluctant at first but then started talking about her worries over her restless father's remoteness, her mother's depression, and her suspicions about Dr Mencius.

Annalisa listened intently and then gushed, 'Oh, babe, I'm so sorry! I shouldn't have said what I did.' She now took both of Gloria's hands in hers. 'And you know what else? Fuck the match. It doesn't matter. We'll come back from it. Fuck the coach too. If he organised the defence better, we'd never lose.'

'Yeah, fuck it all,' said Gloria with an attempt at cheerfulness. They clinked their coffee mugs. A look of mischief then appeared in Annalisa's face. She then said in an attempt at a male voice, 'So Gloria, where was your speed today?'

Gloria responded in kind, 'Well, Annalisa, you could have been at home with your feet up.'

Annalisa roared at this. 'And you think you can't be replaced. Be assured, you can.'

'Be very assured. Defending like my kids' playpen. Did you even do arithmetic at school? Every week we work on this. Every week!'

'Oh Glo, stop it. Every week!' Annalisa had tears in her eyes. 'How come I never knew you were so fucking funny!?'

'And don't forget to apologise to your mirror.'

'Oh God!'

On the drive home Gloria sang along to Smashing Pumpkins songs, feeling a mixture of exhilaration and disappointment. When waiting at a stop sign she looked in the mirror and apologised in a perfunctory way. It wasn't exactly what Barti had meant but she was annoyed with him over his speech which had knocked her confidence.

At the next stop sign she noticed smoke in the distance and wondered whether it was a brush fire. It was dry, but at least there was no wind.

Next morning, she read the coach's comments in the press: 'They're not the best footballing side but they always give us a tough game. It could have gone either way, but they had all the luck with the decisions. The result hardly reflected the balance of play.' Gloria was amazed. Asked if he was contemplating changes for the next match, the coach replied, 'We have a strong side and we don't give up easily. We'll be back.' She forwarded it to Annalisa, 'Can you believe this? Were we in a different game?'

Annalisa replied, 'Are you seriously surprised? My dad says I should definitely find another team.'

9

Following up on Jack Quick's recommendation, Frank went to see plaintiff lawyer Ed Shills in Chicago.

In his office inside a large imposing building, Frank found a large imposing man in a dark suit. Shills was not especially friendly. He was hard-faced and mean-looking, not a bit like the genial 'I'm your guy' character his TV advertisement portrayed: straight-talking and down-to-earth, happy to go however many 'extra miles' it took, but always 'no fee, no pay' to fix your problem for you, or at least make you feel as satisfied as if he had.

Frank's host in name only made it clear he wasn't keen to make visitors feel welcome, especially ones he'd represented clients against. He had a large Bible on his desk which he tapped as he said, 'Come to repent, Frank? It's about time. You know, I was trying to get to talk to you for years and your lawyers always blocked it. Now you show up wanting to talk to me? How ironic.'

Whenever Frank tried to look away from Shills' big, balding head, his attention was seized by the animals mounted on the wall behind the heavy, unsmiling man: the long-horned antelope to the left, the yawning male lion on the right.

'Life's full of surprises, Frank. So you want to work for me, is that right?'

'Well, I thought—'

'Are you serious? It's the funniest thing I've heard since the excuses your lawyers used to pull out. Remember, I've seen it all before. You're just the big man who thinks he's indispensable. Surely someone can't do without your precious expertise. Well, actually, I bet no one wants your expertise, Frank, if that's what you can even call it. I'm sorry to prick the bubble of your own self-importance.'

Frank, reciting a prepared speech, attempted in a lighthearted way to persuade Shills that he was a reformed character and that no one understood the ways of the corporate world better than he did. He'd always been keen to talk to him in his previous role, 'but you know what lawyers are like.'

'Indeed I do, Frank, and if I'd had the horse turd of a case they had I'd have been like them, trying every magic trick known to man to keep my client out of the deposition room. As told by your lawyer, you had so much illness it's amazing that you're here alive and well today.'

'It's not been the easiest time,' said Frank, shrinking within himself.

'And especially not for your former employees or creditors. And now you tell people how to run their businesses? That takes some neck.'

'I educate them on my mistakes,' said Frank in an attempt at humility.

'That alone would take a decade. But I'd far rather you'd educated the court on them when there was cash at stake. I'm sorry, Frank, I can't be fooling with this. We're done here.' With that he opened the heavy Bible and, in a great show of sanctity, began reading from the page.

'Your loss,' was all the disappointed visitor could think to say before leaving.

Meanwhile, at home his daughter was taking a call from the fundraising manager of a children's charity she'd supported for the last two years. The woman was ringing around to various donors to see how much they could commit for the coming campaign. 'Nothing this year, I'm afraid, Sherri,' Gloria said starkly.

'We have this exciting new adventure playground concept and lots of other projects we plan to do. It would mean so much to the kids. I will send you details. We were wondering, say... two hundred grand?'

'No, I'm really sorry,' said Gloria, 'but use wisely what I already gave you. Make the changes I suggested before, and I know it's hard, and in a year's time maybe we can talk again.' She felt bad for Sherri whom she knew was sincere and hardworking. It wasn't her fault.

'But think of the poor children.'

'Yeah, I do, believe me. But you're not the only charity working for them. And others do it better. I'm sorry, Sherri, really I am, but I did warn you before.' She gently ended the call.

She was surprised at her own coldness. She hated such conversations but they were unavoidable. All the charity's officers involved knew each other from previous jobs and protected each other's backs, even outsourced work to family members wherever possible. Staff claimed bullying and harassment, and there were NDAs to silence them. Then when a whistleblower claimed there was corruption and embezzlement by officers she was hounded by the charity. That was enough for Gloria.

She could seem overly tough, but when she saw reports of charity bosses raiding staff pension funds and giving themselves huge salaries and pointless luxury travel, she thought of the generous poor, seduced by witless celebrities into donating more than they could possibly afford and it made her mad.

Feeling guilty, however, after the call Gloria immediately phoned another children's charity, one she believed did their work better.

10

The Hummingbirds' disappointing defeat was followed by a string of emphatic wins. Gloria's pairing with Annalisa was working brilliantly, and the other forward Jamie was also amongst the goals. After the third of these wins: 3-0 with Gloria scoring from a free kick, a few of the team went out shopping together and later called in at an upscale coffee bar. Gloria soon felt a little uncomfortable because she became aware that a handsome young man there kept looking at her and pointing her out to a friend. This made her quieter than usual. When the couple were passing her table on the way out, he said to her in a loud voice, 'Hi, Vanessa, how are you?' but didn't wait for a reply.

After the couple had gone, one of her teammates said, 'He's hot. Do you know him?'

'Of course I don't,' she replied, embarrassed.

Ignoring her pleas for them to stop, the others then began speculating on which 'Vanessa' in the public eye the guy had mistaken her for. 'She's that singer,' said one. 'No, she's a soap actress.'

'What was she in, then?'

'No, she's on CNN. That's right.'

After several minutes enjoying her discomfort while they debated, they concluded that the 'hot' young man probably believed she was Vanessa Dereseau, a half-Mexican, half-French actress featured in a new film. 'She's beautiful,' said Annalisa as they walked out, 'just like my girl.'

When she was back home, Gloria noticed there was another message from her mysterious female Facebook fan: 'Another great win. You're such a brilliant player!' She had become used to these missives, but receiving one immediately after some random guy in the coffee shop called her Vanessa disconcerted her.

She could hear her father on his Skype call with Layne and found it oddly reassuring in the circumstances. Frank, still recovering from his buffeting at the hands of Ed Shills and wondering about his next step, was glad to hear from Layne. Although the old man sounded like he was struggling to breathe, he appeared uncharacteristically upbeat. After some initial chat about a conference in Milan on carbon offsetting he'd been invited to, Layne said he'd 'reached a major decision.'

'Don't laugh, but I've decided to look for a new girlfriend,' he said. This was followed by a big wheeze. 'I'm getting lonely, Frank. I don't miss my ex but I miss having a woman in my life. I just don't know how to find one.'

'I thought you had one. That one from Italy.'

'She never turned up.'

'Didn't you tell me you paid her?'

'She said she was financially embarrassed, so I paid her travel.'

'And she didn't turn up?'

'No. Her loss. But, if truth be told, I prefer them with a bit more meat on them, not some spindly-legged creature like her. I met her at one of my charity dos for something or other, I can't remember what. There's so many of these damned events, I get confused. Of course, I have assistants to help me, telling me where I'm meant to be, where I am at any given moment because I forget, but it's difficult to remember things like who I met and where.'

'What about online dating, Layne?'

'I was thinking about a Thai bride, actually.'

'Really?'

'I'm joking. But of course if a Thai bride met the requirements...'

'Huh. Requirements, eh?' He looked up and caught sight of his daughter walking past his half-open door. He blushed slightly. 'I guess I don't need to ask what they are.'

'Indeed. Use your imagination, then multiply it by ten.'

'Ambitious, Layne.'

'It's the only way to be, Frank. In truth, I'll just brush off the old charm – what's left of it. A bit of the faded grandeur chic.' He looked wide-eyed around him. 'A bit like this draughty old place.' He coughed theatrically. 'I'll play the bored aristocrat with infinite time and money. She won't have much to do beyond lie on her back.'

'Cooking?'

'No need. All provided. That's what staff are for. You have a chef, don't you?'

'We have someone, Suzie, that helps out.'

'There you are then.'

'Well, good luck, Layne.' He was keen to end the call in case his friend became too coarse and his daughter heard him.

In her room, Gloria had decided it was the right time to write back to Lily, even though it might be a mistake because the suspicious attentions of her mystery soccer fan in particular were beginning to make her paranoid, and this might creep into her correspondence:

'Do you just like to tease me? Or is it bragging because you've found the love of your life? I deserve better from you after all these years. Sometimes I think you secretly want to finish with me as your platonic friend, now you don't need me anymore. I was always there for you when you had it tough. But now you just want me to go away without doing the decent thing of telling me, is that it? Please don't tease me, Lily. I am vulnerable at the moment. I have to be strong for my father and mother, but I need someone to be strong for me. Please don't misunderstand. What I want with you is no threat to your relationship with Mack. It is something outside whatever other relationships we might have. That's what we both always said, remember? For me that means something deep, but for you? I don't know anymore. Perhaps you're not capable of understanding what I mean.'

She knew that last sentence in particular would hurt but decided to keep it in. She then changed the subject, writing about soccer and catfish, ending, 'Yours always'. Dissatisfied with what she'd written, however, she did not send it. She was unhappy at the harsh tone of it. She was jealous of the married couple and had made a shameful display of it. In its stead, she merely wrote, 'Stay as you are. I love you, Lily,' and sent that. Afterwards, she regretted sending anything. Really all she wanted was to be held tight by Lily and be reassured that everything was alright between them and always would be. After that she felt pathetic.

11

Early the following Saturday, Gloria checked the local *Patch* online newsletter as usual. She was hoping to find something on Dr Mencius, for she'd decided that today her campaign to unmask him would begin in earnest. Perhaps she'd find an advert; even better would be a story about a fake doctor preying on vulnerable women, robbing them of their savings while they were under sedation. Instead, *Patch* proved to be the usual odd mixture of facts, requests, complaints, and offers. There'd been a couple of brushfires at a local ranch but they'd been quickly snubbed out. Police were seeking information on a Chevy Camaro found in flames on Route 55 the previous night. A resident living by the local reservoir was asking if anyone else had heard fireworks at 2 a.m., and one of the replies was that this was the third night running it had happened. Gloria concluded her family's house was too far away to hear them, not that she wanted to be woken at that time of night. Someone was complaining about a helicopter flying over their house every midday. She had certainly heard that. One of the replies was, 'They're probably looking for you, jerk. You got a guilty conscience? Maybe you should have.' There was also a request for a 'forever home' for a litter of spangled cats. She imagined her father saying, 'Don't even ask.'

Over breakfast, Frank announced, 'I've decided to follow your suggestion.'

'Oh yes?'

'About teaming up with a consumer group. I thought you'd be pleased.'

'I am, I guess.'

'I wanted you to know that I listen to you, Gloria. We don't always agree but I like to hear what you have to say, and if it makes sense I'll follow it.'

'OK,' she replied, bemused.

'Now, have you thought any more about how we can use the charity money?'

She stopped eating her toast. 'What?' she said, and she folded her arms.

'The foundation money, of course.'

'No, Dad.'

'Then think about it.'

'No, I won't.'

'Gloria, are you defying me?'

'We discussed this subject before. The answer's no.'

'OK,' he said, and he stood up, 'I'm going out.'

He was hurt. She had hurt him. He was trying to make her feel guilty and he'd succeeded. As she cleared away the breakfast things, she heard

35

the front door close. She felt a pang in her chest. 'Fuck,' she said. She liked being tough-minded but hated conflict, especially with someone she loved, even when that other person was completely in the wrong.

She returned to her room feeling down. Her mood revived, however, on noticing a couple of her students had responded to her request for examples of the fundamental attribution error and how it affected a person's perception of others.

Marie wrote that she had a friend who was very obese and everyone else seemed to associate it with sloth and greed on her part. But when she went to her friend's house for tea she saw how the girl's mother kept piling the food on her plate over her objection, and making her feel guilty if there were any leftovers. Thus, the error was in basing a judgement about her on her perceived character traits, rather than being open to the possibility of external factors such as the mother pressuring her to eat more.

It made her think about Annalisa. Gloria herself and others thought her lazy and a diva. But suppose the 'external factor' with her was her father convincing her that, because she was a natural goalscorer, which she undoubtedly was, it was all she needed to do and so it was for others to make it possible for her to score. Gloria pondered over this, happy to graze on it like a horse finding fresh grass, but then she declared out loud, 'Nah, she's just lazy. I do love her, though.'

She next began initial research on Dr Mencius. She could not find anything, however; not even a website. Why? It made no sense. Was her mother his only patient? It was so frustrating – and weird. Her mother did not even have his cell number on her phone. Gloria looked up his surname, then in turn: local medical clinics, quack doctors, holistic medicine, Orange County, nearby towns, convicted fraudsters, court records, actors seeking work, and more.

She noticed she had received a new message from Trey:

'Gloria my darling, I have something I feel I must share with you. A dear friend of mine in the music industry has set up a surefire investment scheme backing movers and shakers in new technologies, such as batteries for solar power plants, and hydrogen cars. Only a handful of his private circle including me know about this. He's an expert on such investments, and this is a guaranteed winner. We're only allowed to invite one person each to join, so I've chosen you. If you're interested in this fantastic opportunity, all it will cost you is a minimum deposit of five thousand dollars and I'll set up everything for you. I get many investment tips from my many well-informed contacts, but I know you're hard-nosed and so I only tell you about something really sound like this. Others might want the more risky, even flaky, investments, but this one is conservative and so ideal for you.'

So this was what he was really about: inducing 'friends' into investment scams?

'Thank you,' she said out loud, 'I feel so gratified you chose me,' and she closed down the page without sending Trey a response.

From her room she could hear Layne on Skype talking excitedly about his rewilding programme.

'The beavers have arrived,' he declared.

'Why?' said Frank.

'That's a good question. Beavers help create wetlands, so my estate manager says.'

'You want to create wetlands?'

'Not really.'

'Not enough room on all your acres?'

'Actually, I don't want bloody wetlands. What would I do with them? But the estate manager says it's good for my image as a green campaigner. He wants me to bring wolves in too. I said, what next: lions and tigers? I'd do it, though, if it put people off.'

'It won't put people off. It will attract them.'

'Not if the tigers eat a few of them. And what about your problems? I read about the coyotes on the rampage. You got them running about in your back garden yet?'

'No.'

'No, he says. What you mean is: not that you know of, because you never go out there, do you? Would you even recognise a coyote if you saw one? I will say, though, I'm sceptical about this rewilding business. Rewild the garden and everything lets rip. You end up with all weeds, or pioneer plants, or whatever the term is now. Leave nature to itself and you end up with a briar patch. And eventually, if you're lucky, trees. I think we need a culling of cracked ideas, quite frankly. But the estate manager suggested it, so I thought, why not? Do you have rewilding over there?'

'We have everything in California, Layne.'

'Oh, of course. I forgot.'

'Every type of critter, every type of weather. We're prepared for everything.'

'Bats?'

'Everywhere has bats, Layne.'

'But not rabid ones. I saw the news report.'

'Oh, trust you to harsh my mellow.'

'What's up: did one of them fly in your window today?'

'No. Look, I've got to go and do something more useful, like save a business.'

'Not yours, I hope. Goodbye, Frank.'

That day's game was a late kickoff because the opposition the Ospreys had a long journey. It proved to be a remarkable match. Playing in brilliant sun the Hummingbirds dominated from the start. Gloria was at her best, constantly feeding the insatiable Annalisa the diamond-accurate passes she so depended on. With twenty minutes left, the Hummingbirds were 3-0 up when, after a corner there was a melée in front of the Ospreys' goal, Gloria mishit her shot, then Annalisa did the same, a defender tried to clear but failed, and finally after a further scramble the ball hit Gloria's knee and rolled into the goal: 4-0.

On the walk back to the centre spot she felt a kick on the back of her right leg and then heard 'Lucky bitch!' It was the Ospreys' blonde number 7, who'd been bugging her all game. Gloria instinctively raised her arm and caught her in the face, at which the player dropped to the ground. The ref must have seen the raised arm and the fall because she called Gloria over. 'She fouled me,' Gloria protested. 'She kicked me on the back of the leg!'

'I saw you deliberately strike her. I've sent off players for less.'

'Go ahead, then. Let's get it over with.'

'Don't get surly with me or I will.'

Gloria bit her lip and then said, 'Sorry, ref.'

Out came the yellow card. Its recipient walked away disconsolately. Cards were becoming a too frequent feature of her game. She turned to see her infuriated teammates surrounding the ref, complaining it was the

Ospreys' number 7 who should have been booked. The ref wouldn't listen and told them to get on with the game.

'Unlucky... bitch.' It was her nemesis again. Gloria did not respond.

Five minutes later, the blonde was writhing around on the ground once more. Micaela, one of the Hummingbirds' less experienced defenders, also blonde, had deliberately tripped her and then kicked her as well. She was immediately sent off. Before she left the field she grinned at Gloria and stuck her thumb up. Gloria grinned back.

Barti was forced to reorganise the team, and he pointed at Gloria to indicate he was replacing her. A rookie defender was jumping up and down on the touchline in anticipation of running onto the pitch. Head down, Gloria slouched off whilst, unbeknownst to her, Annalisa was remonstrating at the coach. Wide-eyed, Ant tapped her head furiously to indicate she thought him crazy.

As she approached Barti, Gloria mouthed the word 'Why?'

'Temperament,' he said.

'What?' she replied. He had never questioned her temperament before.

'That number 7 was determined to get you sent off. We can't hold the lead with nine players. Micaela was stupid, but she's inexperienced and did it to please you and the rest. Foolish. But you should know better.'

'She kicked me, my arm immediately went up, I barely touched her, she falls down and rolls around.'

'I know. She was kicking you all game. But it's the ref that matters. Besides, I could tell you were tiring.'

She stopped herself from replying and merely shook her head and sat down on the bench next to Micaela who seemed almost proud at being sent off. Although disappointed at being subbed, Gloria did not sulk. She and Micaela shared jokes as they watched the rest of the game. And what a game it was. The opposition brought on a slow but effective striker and also a midfielder, and without Gloria's pressure pinning them back, the Ospreys began to dominate the game, keeping the ball in the Hummingbirds' half. Annalisa was marooned, standing morosely just past the hallway line, merely observing proceedings. The opposition were able to score three goals before the final whistle saved the Hummingbirds the embarrassment of a draw.

The bizarre match was followed by a row in the dressing room. Barti lambasted the team: 'You all but threw the game away. We didn't deserve to win. Two of our goals were offside.'

'No, they weren't,' protested Annalisa who'd scored them.

'You might as well forget about being champions. You don't deserve it.'

One of the defenders Barti often singled out for criticism exclaimed, 'We won, for Heaven's sake!'

For her part, Gloria remained quiet in the corner next to Annalisa. 'It was all my fault,' said Micaela cheerfully, as though bemused by the negative vibe in the room. 'I shouldn't have got myself sent off. I'm sorry.'

'No it wasn't,' said Annalisa. 'It was a mistake taking Gloria off.' Gloria put her hand to her friend's forearm as though to calm her, but Annalisa was in the mood for confrontation. She glared at Barti and said, 'You will never admit to a mistake, will you?'

He was unfazed: 'I've told you before: all of you are replaceable. Don't get too big for your boots just because you score a few goals. Anyone can do that.'

'As a goalie, you would know, of course,' Ant replied acidly. 'Especially when they were shooting at you.'

Gloria intervened, 'Leave it, Ant.' But instead, Annalisa stood up. Standing barefoot in her shorts in front of the tall coach she looked diminutive and vulnerable. 'We'd be better off without a coach,' she said defiantly. 'You said once we weren't too big for this team. Well, nor are you. The difference is, you need to win the championship this year to get a better job. We don't care.'

'Please, Ant.' Gloria got up and grabbed her forearm, and this time Annalisa relented and slowly returned to her seat. The coach visibly relaxed, but then others joined in the attack on Barti's decision-making. In the end, he left the room defeated. Gloria remained silent while some of the others cheered like mutineers.

After a quick shower she left the ground as quickly as possible. Although she'd been quiet since being substituted, her mind had not been. She was upset by the row, seeing no good could come of it. Yes, Barti had erred, but so did everyone at times. Someone had to make the tough decisions, and sometimes they would get them wrong. You had to have a coach. You couldn't work it all out for yourselves, with all the jealousies and rivalries within the group hidden just below the surface and suddenly rearing up. Above all, she wanted to avoid talking to Ant about it.

Now on the road, she tried to forget the whole thing, although this had the effect of making her drive faster, more recklessly, until she almost rear-ended a Honda Civic when leaving the freeway. Shaking, she pulled to the side of the road at the first opportunity. She calmed herself down with a simple Vedic mantra she sometimes used and then continued her journey more sedately.

Once in the comfort of her own room with a hot chocolate drink, she found there was another message from the woman who was her fan: 'A great match. You deserved the win. Well played!'

Who was this woman, always writing? And why? Was she even at the goddamn game?

Next morning, she read the press interview with the coach. He said the team 'played with great heart and passion' and the result was 'never in doubt'. Asked about the dodgy decisions in the Hummingbirds' favour, he said he hadn't seen the incidents and had 'every faith' in the referee. Asked why he'd substituted Gloria he said, 'Unfortunately, she picked up a knock, so we had no choice.'

She stared at the piece in disbelief. A knock!? The interview was so ridiculous she laughed out loud. She wondered how she could take seriously someone who so blatantly lied.

12

On the following Monday morning, Frank was apprehensive. He had a meeting that was important to him but he was feeling underprepared. It was with a consumer group he was interested in. He anticipated breakfast with Gloria would be awkward. It would be obvious he was going out, she would want to know where, and an argument about using money from her charitable foundation would inevitably follow.

In fact, he found her subdued. She was unsettled about the match, her substitution, the dressing room rebellion, the weird woman writing to compliment her, and, above all, Barti's lies. None of it made any sense. It was moments like this when Lily was so important to her. Non-judgemental Lily. Lily whose love for her was unconditional, unencumbered by the tedium of day-to-day 'trivial disputes', unencumbered by the need for good sex, or indeed any sex. She was tempted to phone her but an uncertainty had come into their relationship lately and she had no desire to be seen as needy.

'Is everything alright, my dear?' her father asked. 'You seem very quiet.'

'I'm fine, dad.' she said.

'You won well on Saturday, didn't you?'

'Yeah.'

'I saw what the coach had to say. I like him. He says it like it is, doesn't he? I bet you all like him, don't you?'

'Yes, dad. There's one or two—'

'Of course there is, love. There's always one or two who like to have a moan. I had 'em at work, don't forget.'

'Speaking of work, what do you think I should do? With my life, I mean?'

'Well, there's a question. I thought you liked your psychology. I thought you would develop that further. No?'

'I wanted to study psychology so I could better understand people. But now I feel I understand less about people than I did when I started.'

'Don't worry,' he said. 'If it's any consolation, even at my age it doesn't get easier.'

She looked up, grinning. 'I'm afraid, Dad, that's the very opposite of consolation. It means my lack of understanding could last for ever. And get worse.'

They smiled at each other. There'd been rows in the past, there'd no doubt be rows to come, but for now they could enjoy each other's company.

Frank found the consumer advocacy group's HQ, which was based in a small, untidy office in a dirty, rundown street in Anaheim. It was the kind of scruffy little premises he'd been unfamiliar with, except perhaps in the early days of his first business when he was scratching around for financial backers, some of whom were not exactly main street.

The serious-looking young man and woman he met were not expecting him and did not convey the impression that he was welcome. In fact, they gave him no impression at all. They looked like two dazed college students who'd spent all day out of the sun in lecture halls and just wanted to rest their eyes and not have to pay attention to anyone. Just like Gloria at her most studious and earnest. Eventually they emerged from their desks - she with her large round glasses, mess of straw hair, and dilapidated yellow sweater, he with his librarian spectacles, blood marks from careless shaving, and brown corduroy Goodwill jacket. They greeted him effortlessly. He explained, with the patience reminiscent of a new geography teacher who'd once taught him, that he'd contacted their boss Mr Grish who'd said he would be welcome to visit with a view to possibly working with them in some capacity. Straw Hair said flatly, 'Naylor's out. He didn't mention anything about a visitor.'

'Do you know when he'll be back?'

'No.'

'Would it be worth waiting?'

'It might.' Some vague warmth at last.

He looked at his watch. 'Actually I'm kinda busy. Could I possibly talk to you about my proposals instead?'

'Proposals? I guess.'

'Excellent,' said Frank, clapping his hands, but lightly so as not to appear triumphant.

They took him into a conference room that was drab and untidy, the walls bearing portraits of Ralph Nader, Mahatma Gandhi, and, less congruously, singer Ethel Merman. With a tiny plastic cup of water on the desk before him, he proceeded to give them his carefully prepared speech, point by point. He soon began to think his audience were determined not to give him the notion that they'd been affected by it in any way. He pointed at the posters surrounding them, each one representing a campaign they had underway: 'I look at your campaign targets and my first thought is, I know these people. I know the CEOs. I know the big players. I know what makes these people tick. I can get into their end zone. I can get into their heads. I could seriously help you guys. I would love to be given the chance to do so.'

This was met by silence. He was like a standup comedian whose jokes are not connecting or a magician whose tricks, however sophisticated, are met by indifference. He continued, 'And I could also bring money in. When they see me involved, others, the big beasts in the philanthropy world, will want to join in, want to be at the party, believe me.'

The mention of money generated a flicker of interest in the faces of the hosts. Scarface scratched an imaginary beard, Straw Hair adjusted her glasses. Then Scarface spoke at last, softly as a verger politely asking an aged churchgoer to shuffle along. He said, 'This is interesting. But how do you get over the public perception of your corporate legacy?'

'I'm sorry?' Frank played dumb, but he knew the situation all too well. His name was known to them, and not for a good reason. His companies had been too flip with consumer laws in the past, and this self-serving laxity had consequences. People had suffered from it. These two knew that. No answer to his question was necessary, or forthcoming.

Frank had no ready response. Instead, he mustered an impromptu speech, seeking to touch this coldhearted pair with homilies. 'America loves a comeback,' he stressed. 'Everyone can be forgiven who has a contrite heart. As a Christian I feel that keenly. I want to atone for my failings. Businesses that fail destroy lives. I see that. The man before you is a humble and much changed person. The same zeal I took into business I would apply to your work. I just need the chance.' They stared at him, bemused. He tried harder: 'I understand your hesitation. I would likewise be hesitant if I were you. But believe me, I'm appalled at the suffering of people because of big corporations. I've seen that bright light. And I'm sure with my experience and corporate knowledge, I can make a real difference for you guys in your vital work.'

The couple still looked unimpressed. It was the same old hooey, as far as they were concerned. They'd seen his opportunistic kind before. He'd been a corporate boss once and now wanted to boss them around. He was the once big star helping out the little leaguers, the celebrity has-been donating his time at the Goodwill store. And who was to say his change of heart was genuine? After all, he was probably still working for the same corporation in some capacity.

Undaunted, he hoped that perhaps they would be impressed by his sincerity and keen desire to help. But then he thought: where would he physically work? Not in this poky little place, surely. Apparently reading his mind, Straw Hair said, 'I'm afraid you wouldn't have the kind of upscale office you're used to.' Frank replied that it was immaterial to him; all he cared about was the work. Then Scarface said, 'You'd probably want to work from home, wouldn't you?' He merely replied that it was a possibility. Straw Hair said they'd have a chat with Grish about it. As they all stood up, he was left with the feeling that they didn't really want him, perhaps seeing him as potentially toxic. But, on the other hand, surely they realised that his genuine enthusiasm and the possibility of new funding could not be easily dismissed.

It was then that their boss, Naylor Grish, came bounding in. He was a large, broad-grinning, energetic, flash-suited man with a self-important air, the big ego they already had in the team; was there room for another? He'd just been to a meeting with a sponsor and, for all his undimmed optimism, it was clear from his response to the other two's brief questions that it had been difficult. Frank surmised the sponsor had asked too many questions at a time when, now more than ever, they needed to find cash. Grish understood the importance of money, or the lack of it, more than the two youngsters. When they'd left the room, Grish sat down opposite Frank, with a flinch of recognition that Frank noticed.

Frank gave him a similar speech to that he'd given the others, although when Grish made a face like he'd just bitten into a mouldy peach on hearing the word 'contrite', he dropped the religious trimmings. Grish was more interested in money and pressed him for details, but Frank was forced to be vague though positive, still intending to break down Gloria's resistance regarding the charitable foundation, but also wondering whether he could cultivate Layne into coughing up for the cause. After all, the old coot was always bragging about his good works. Put an environmental spin on it and he was as good as theirs.

The meeting with Grish was going well from both perspectives until Frank's cell phone rang, much to Grish's noticeable irritation, as he felt close to obtaining a commitment to bring in significant cash following the disappointment he'd suffered earlier in the day.

It was Gloria ringing. There was anguish in her voice. She said Maria had fallen and hurt herself. 'Has an ambulance been called?' Frank asked.

'No. Dr Mencius is here. He's dealing with it. Mama told me not to do anything.'

'How is she?'

'A bit shaken. She missed her step and lost her footing. She hurt her back.'

'On the stairs? Oh my God. OK, Dr Mencius will know what to do. Listen to what he says carefully. I'll be home straightaway.'

He apologised to Grish who made an attempt at being gracious about the interruption but was clearly disappointed. The momentum of the meeting was gone. It was left that Grish would get back to Frank.

As he drove home, the thought occurred to him that having an 'invalided' wife might make the group more sympathetic towards him than otherwise. He felt good about the meeting.

At the time of her mother's accident, Gloria had been watching a video about Social Identity Theory, which discussed the concept of in-groups and out-groups and how people related to them. She started to think of examples from her own life and was jotting a few down when she heard her mother shout.

Her immediate thought was that Mencius had tried to take advantage of her but hadn't sedated her sufficiently, and she'd rejected him. Gloria rushed out of her room and into her mother's, finding the light on and the curtains closed. Maria was lying motionless on her back on the floor. Gloria assisted Dr Mencius, who was wearing a sickly sweet cologne that made her feel nauseous, gently easing Maria into a seated position supported by pillows taken from her bed. In that situation the patient became unusually talkative, making Gloria think she must have knocked her head, but then her mother suddenly stopped gabbling. Resisting offers of assistance, she lifted herself awkwardly to a standing position. 'I'm perfectly fine,' she said, before toppling sideways to end with the upper half of her body on the bed. Mencius and Gloria then helped her manoeuvre herself until she was completely on the bed and lying on her side so that the doctor could examine her back. As he did so, to Gloria he was like an actor with a stethoscope playing at being a doctor. He spoke softly to Maria in a tone Gloria found as odious as his cologne.

It was at this moment Gloria left the room to phone her father. When he mentioned the stairs, she deliberately did not correct him. Besides, he should have remembered that his wife never ventured downstairs before the evening meal, and often not even then.

Gloria returned to her studies despite her concentration and nerves being frayed. She gradually became absorbed and was startled on hearing a tap on her open bedroom door. It was Dr Mencius who now had his hat on, indicating he was leaving. He entered her room, something he'd only ever done once before and which felt like a violation. 'I thought I'd update you before I left,' he said obsequiously.

'Thank you,' she said, unable to hide her contempt.

'She's asleep now. She had a bit of a fright, that's all. Just a little soreness, but it's the psychological—'

'Of course it is.' She said this with the air of someone who had expert knowledge in this field even though she had none. 'It's a good thing she's got you.' She was appalled at how hollow her own words sounded.

'I see the pastoral aspects as just as important.'

'Bedside manner,' she said hastily.

'Quite. And how are you? Not too stressed from... everything? If you want, I can give you something that will help you with it, you know.' He stepped forward, led by his cologne, and made as if to place his hand on her arm, then withdrew, suddenly realising what he was doing.

'What do you mean?' she said nervously.

'I have everything at hand that can ease stress. Even for one as young as yourself.'

Gloria was tempted to switch to Spanish. She would give him such a telling off, complete with every swear word her mother had ever taught her, but instead she stuck to English in order to continue this ornate dance. 'I'm fine, thank you... Doctor.' She had tried but failed to disguise the fact she thought him fake. Her mind was dominated by the thought: wait till I tell my dad about this! But she knew he wouldn't believe her, and for that reason she wouldn't tell him.

But in the end she did tell her father when he arrived home and came to see her in her room, having found Maria asleep. She was right, however, in that he refused to believe the doctor had acted in any way inappropriately. He emphasised, as he consistently did, that her mother always seemed so much better after the old man's visits.

She pondered her response, leaving unsaid for the moment her belief that it suited him not to accept her allegations because he was afraid to contemplate the possibility they might be true. 'He's an old devil,' she asserted at last. 'And if he could, he'd seduce me too. He wants to. Perhaps I should let him try. Attempted sexual assault; that would get his license revoked. That's if he's even a doctor in the first place, which I sincerely doubt. In fact, that's it: he's an actor from her old movie days. Of course he is!' She felt enlivened at this realisation.

'Stop it.'

'They're playing you for a fool. How does it feel to be cuckolded, Papa, and by a randy old goat?'

'Gloria, you've got too vivid an imagination. I do not wish to hear any more of this.' And that was exactly the problem: he did not wish to know. Fortunately, he then left, removing the need for her to respond.

To her, all he cared about was his precious business interests. It had been the same when he'd been running the big corporation. His obsession with it had extended to the smallest detail. There were no breaks from it. He even stopped playing golf with potential clients, claiming 'lack of time', and became so fixated about 'business enemies' that he convinced himself his family were at risk of kidnap. In her teens, whenever Gloria asked if she could spend the weekend at a friend's house the answer was always a flat no. After a while, Maria had intervened, saying Gloria was spending too much time exploring the internet, had stopped going out, and was caring less about her appearance.

As well as Maria, she had Annalisa to thank for ending this phase. It was she who suggested Gloria sign up for soccer training, and that gave her a new passion and a better social life.

13

Frustrated at his inability to persuade his daughter to 'see sense' about Dr Mencius, Frank phoned his wealthy English friend, believing Layne's woes would make him feel better about his own.

'How goes it, Layne?'

'Disastrous. I've just flown back from a seminar in Venice and I'm not in a good mood just now. You can ring off if you don't want to listen to it.'

'It's alright. I'll hear you out. I know how you like to vent.'

'And with good reason.'

'Of course. Have at it, then. Someone's obviously got on your case.'

It transpired that Layne had come home from the three-day event feeling right with the world and then been upset by something he saw in the British press. 'It's all these troublemakers in the media saying people like me should give all our wealth away,' he thundered. 'But why should we? I'm called filthy rich like I'm some miser hoarding my money and not caring about anyone else.'

'So unkind.'

'Well, to be honest, I *don't* care about anyone else, but I damned well pay my taxes, or some of them. I sometimes wonder why I should pay any.' He carried on in this vein, but after scant response from Frank, who was happy to listen, he suddenly said, 'Anyway, I'm more interested in looking to the future. There's been a lot of talk lately amongst the set – and this came up in Venice – about emigrating to a private island to avoid the coming apocalypse.'

'That sounds a pretty weird set.'

'I'll ignore that. If everyone else in the world is out on the sea on their must-have yachts and superyachts, it might be the time to be on dry land. But not just any old dry land. The wealthy are not wanted here in Britain except to give up what they have. The country's become a nation of sneering whingers and moaners queuing up for handouts – nothing for the aspiring entrepreneur or the self-made man.'

'Or the readymade like you.'

'If you insist.'

'I can understand you wanting to get away, Layne, but sometimes a big change like that only leads to more problems.'

'You're right. You've obviously thought about it yourself.'

'Well—'

'The problem with getting away to a private island, as someone said in Venice, is that you still need staff to run everything. And how do you protect yourself from them?'

'That's right.'

'And are all their families going to be living there with you? And what if they decide to mutiny – where will that leave you? The bloke who doffs his cap every five seconds now, once settled over there could stick a screwdriver through your neck with no fear of retribution, and no police or courts to protect the innocent.'

'So much that you poor super-rich have to worry about. Who would want the burden?'

'Exactly. For a Yank you're pretty astute. And what if there's factions battling it out? When you take the "mutual" out of "mutual self interest" your life is hell and you need to escape it.'

'You do.'

'It's the same with robots. They might start out benign and simpering, but the first hint of malfunction and they'll be beating the devil out of each other while you're sitting there helpless, fearful they'll turn on you next.'

'You're frightening yourself to death, Layne.'

'And if climate change, despite my tireless efforts, goes full tilt, the bloody private island would be washed away anyway! Increasingly, I think I'm better off staying on this seething angry termites' nest called Britain and just shutting my ears to all the noise. I'll take my chances in the Scottish hills in an underground bunker with an AI buddy for company, watching old Test match videos while waiting for the hordes to show up. I'll be ready for them.'

'But what about Iceland or New Zealand or somewhere like that? I read they'll be good places to be.'

'Don't worry, I'm going to have passports for those countries too. And thirty others. But what about you, Frank?'

'I just let the future look after itself.'

'No plans? No underground bunker? No survivalist workshops?'

'No.'

'That's negligent, Frank. You know you owe it to your family.'

'No, I don't believe I do.'

'Well, think about it. Anyway, right now I need to be going, unfortunately. Flying to Paris, first thing.'

'Another climate meeting, Layne?'

'No, just lunch with an expat. He wants to sell me his Bentley.'

'Flying for that? Isn't it a little excessive for an environmental campaigner?'

'Excessive? Hardly, when *he's* flying in from Athens. But I don't know if I need another Bentley. I've already got three.'

'How many cars have you got altogether, then?'

'About twenty. Mostly in storage. You see, the more you've got stored away, the more they can't be polluting, so it helps the environment. It's the same principle as land. The more you own, the more you can keep sustainable for the planet. Get it? Anyway, I'll see you later.'

After Layne had gone, Frank was left scratching his head at his friend's reasoning.

14

For her students, Gloria had done further work on in-groups and out-groups, Henri Tajfel's Social Identity Theory. She would ask them to identify which groups they were in, explaining this would likely be more than they initially imagined.

The essence of the theory, as she understood it, was that individuals were typically in many groups simultaneously and sought to promote their own groups' interests to the detriment of others, consciously or not. The obvious example was her soccer team the Hummingbirds. That was the in-group. Other teams were out-groups. But within the team, her in-group were the forwards, the out-group defence. She, Annalisa, and another team member had, at least in part, Hispanic heritage, so that could be a group.

Other players had different ethnic backgrounds and were therefore in other groups. But beyond the team were yet more groups she was in: people who lived in California, people who lived in the south of the state, who lived in Orange County, in Mission Viejo, and in her part of town, and in her street. Each was an in-group and outside it was the out-group. It didn't make it a good or bad thing, but it was sometimes a way to understand behaviour.

She thought about Lily and her groups: young women in their early twenties, women in same sex marriages, young businesswomen, anyone who worked in investment, and in the City of London, anyone who never knew their parents, girls who'd learned to box, girls who lost their virginity to the local stud, girls who drank underage, girls who went to court for beating up another girl who tormented her, girls who were bullied at school, girls who self-harmed. Some of these groups she might not wish to identify with, or perhaps only with the passage of time, but they were part of her.

In fact, Gloria had chosen two children's charities to support specifically because of Lily's tough teenage years. She paused to look at a photograph of her as a blonde-haired teenager. 'Oh, Lily!' she sighed. 'How you turned your life around! How I can never lose you from mine!'

15

Early one morning, Frank received a call from Naylor Grish. 'We liked you a lot, Frank. We really did. We all sure enjoyed meeting you,' he enthused.

'Oh, thank you. I enjoyed meeting you, too. It was refreshing to meet people who think along the same lines, people who care about the consumer as much as I do. This is very reassuring and I know we can work well together.' Frank was almost purring. He was on the cusp of his new life.

'And that's what I'm phoning about, Frank.'

'That's great.'

'As I say, we really liked you and felt you have a lot to offer, but, unfortunately, not for us at this particular time.'

'OK. I get it. So what you're saying, if I understand you correctly, is that you have nothing for me at the moment but, dare I say it, you may have soon?'

'I couldn't say "soon", Frank.'

'No, of course, but maybe—'

'I couldn't say "ever", Frank.'

'I see. So should I approach you again in, say, six—'

'No. There's no opening, and there won't be one.'

'I see. Dare I say why?'

Grish's voice now took on a mechanical tone. 'After full and careful consideration, we decided we could not invite you to work with us because we don't feel your profile fits our core values. I'm sorry.'

'But—'

'It's the history, Frank. Too much baggage. I'm sure you can understand.' He now became more strident. 'Your corporation wasn't exactly consumer-friendly. In fact, we worked with people pursuing claims against you. It wouldn't sit well with some of our sponsors. Like I say, I'm sorry.'

Frank could not argue. It was final. Grish ended the call.

It took a few minutes for the news to sink in, and then the rejection hit him hard. The nerve of the man! Small-minded Grish obviously saw it as some kind of revenge, trying to make Frank feel guilty for his corporate career. Well, Grish had failed because he was proud of it. He had worked hard to achieve what he had. It wasn't his fault it had fallen apart. If others had made the same effort as him, it wouldn't have happened. They lacked his energy – the same energy he could devote to working for consumers. For him it would be completing the cycle. The aim of every good company was a happy customer. He'd always believed that. Only narrow-minded people like Grish couldn't see it. It was petty 'payback time'. That's what Grish could have said instead of 'Your profile, unfortunately, doesn't exactly fit with our values,' or some such hokum.

Never mind. Frank would use the same fervour he once employed in building a huge corporation to create his own consumer group. Bigger and more powerful than other groups. Grish's operation would be a cockroach in comparison. Grish would be seeking him out and he would reject him saying his profile 'unfortunately' did not fit the group's ethos. It would be 'payback time' for him.

But suddenly this trail of thought evaporated. He took a deep breath. No, he couldn't be like that. He literally hadn't the heart for it; it would merely be piling pettiness upon pettiness. It wasn't him. He'd learnt from his mistakes and moved on. Grish, cockroach or not, could do his thing undisturbed by him.

After the disappointment of the call, Frank decided to go for a drive. He wanted to be out of the house. He wasn't in the mood for a conversation with Gloria. But although the weather was sunny and he took out the convertible, it wasn't pleasant. He saw the aftermath of a serious accident on the freeway. A once fancy car, a Lexus, had its front smashed in. They would have had to cut the driver out. A life ended, or at least ruined. Someone like him or, statistically more likely, younger. Maybe someone with a family. No, everyone in the county who had a car had a family somewhere.

He went to a restaurant near the country club he used to go to. The place had seen better days. The décor was tired, the tables too close together, the chairs cheap-looking and uncomfortable for his back. The staff were as brusque as under pressure prison warders. He had ham and eggs and it was overcooked. No one returned his smile, not even the pretty waitress who flirted with the younger male patrons.

He drove home in a funk and with exaggerated care. Despite seeing the aftermath of the car crash, he still could not avoid feeling sorry for himself.

At home, tired and feeling down, Frank turned on the TV in the lounge and for a while sat watching a soap. It felt like a privilege to be able to waste time. Once, every moment was precious and put to work. These days, the metaphorical piano strings no longer needed to be taut, and languor had became his norm. As a consequence, he often felt deflated and even depressed, particularly when, as now, the thought arose that his legacy had cast a malevolent shadow across his future, and that shadow could not be erased.

He switched to a business channel, as if to remind himself of what he was missing. He quickly found himself becoming intrigued by an interview with a young female stock market investor known as a 'short seller'. It wasn't merely that she was attractive with her dark looks and appealing eyes, but that she clearly had a sense of purpose in her work beyond making money. He felt inspired as she explained how she saw short selling as a moral force to weed out bad companies. This impressed him; finding poorly run and fraudulent businesses with an artificially high share price and short selling on them to bring them down sounded a great idea. He thought about contacting her, but was momentarily concerned that this might merely present another opportunity for rejection. He was becoming used to it. But no, he insisted: he would not be so easily put off, certainly not by his own self-criticism.

16

A few days later, Layne phoned Frank, sounding upbeat. He said he hadn't bought the Bentley after all, but instead was having three other luxury cars shipped in from Malaga. He added, 'Believe it or not, I've got a new girlfriend.'

'Brilliant. That's quick, though. What's her name?'

'Tatiana or something like that.'

'Russian?'

'Of course she's not Russian. You Yanks are so... obsessed with Russians.'

'I think I'd know her name by now, even if I were as old as you, sitting there in your dotage and your dressing gown and slippers.'

'Alright, leave it out. But there are just so many of these women putting themselves forward. So many contenders, Frank. Fortunately, my estate manager was on hand to help me choose the right one. I like to think it's my looks, my charm, but that's vanity. I suspect money has more than a little to do with it.'

'You're kidding me now.'

'It's hard to believe, I know.'

'What's the age gap this time? Thirty years?'

'As if it mattered.'

'Of course, I should have realised: if you don't know her name, you're not likely to know her age.'

'Name? Of course I know her name. I told you, it's Tanya or something like that. You're feisty today, by the way. Something in your Wheaties? She's got long legs, I know that. Since you're so interested, I reckon she's about twenty-five.'

'So about forty years' difference.'

'Give or take. So what? Have you never heard of May to September relationships?'

'I have indeed. But this is more like January to November the thirtieth.'

'Tush! I can still satisfy them, whatever their age.'

'What is she, a good actor? She would need to be. Blonde or dark?'

'Brunette. Works in films. But it doesn't matter what she is. If she knows what's good for her, she'll do what I say.'

'Waste of a good woman, some would say.'

'Waste? Charming! Waste of a good woman would be if she turned lesbian.'

'She still might after you. Where did you meet her?'

'Online.'

'Was that wise?'

'Wise? What, you think I don't know what it's all about? Look, I know that any self-respecting young beauty is only after my money. Fair enough. So I may as well find the best-looking one I can.'

'But you've met her, right? In the flesh, I mean?'

'Not yet, obviously. I have to test her out first with a few questions, make sure she's not some bloke pretending to be her. Or some chatbot, or whatever it is.'

'Who's helping you with that?'

'Help? Are you crazy? I don't need help. I can do everything myself. I know how to use a computer, thank you. Because I'm older than you, you think you can patronise me about the internet and stuff – and everything else. "Was that wise?" indeed! When you've got as much money as me, Frank, you can patronise me all you like.'

'Security's everything these days, Layne. You know that.'

'No, it's not, actually. It's about fun. Something you don't seem to know much about. Or care even less. I live for fun now. Everything's taken care of. Nothing to worry about. I can relax and enjoy myself. And Titania if she plays her cards right—'

'Titania? I thought you said... Oh well, if you ever need help checking anyone out, my daughter Gloria's an expert.'

'I won't. But thanks.'

Gloria overheard this conversation and, when it ended, she went into her father's office to confront him. 'Why did you mention me?' she said.

'Did I?'

'You know you did, You called me an expert.'

'Well, you are. I'm very proud of you.'

'You have no right.'

'Listen, young lady, I have every right. It was just a gesture to a friend. He didn't accept it anyway.'

'So we're clear: I have no interest in checking out that man's girlfriend who's probably a scammer anyway. You can waste your time with his nonsense if you must, but please don't embroil me in it.'

He was not in the mood for this. 'Stop being rude. Layne is my friend, and part of that means helping him when he needs it. You might think about that when you have friends.'

'What?'

'You have no friends, Gloria. No real friends, admit it.'

'Yes, I do. How dare you!' She burst into tears, left the room, and slammed her door behind her. She put her desk chair against it. It wouldn't stop him coming in, but it would make clear he wasn't welcome.

She took refuge in her Facebook page. There was nothing new from Trey, thank goodness. Gone were the days when he would send umpteen messages a day. She almost missed them. It was a way to exercise her cruel streak, even if it disappointed her that she had one. Instead of him there was a new friend request from another handsome young man. So handsome that it was deeply suspicious; he might as well have had 'scammer' written across his forehead. His name was Dwayne and he was supposedly a surfer living on the coast north of L.A. He was Gloria's age and, like her, fresh out of college. He was working in a lawyer's office. She was sceptical but decided to accept the friend request, if only for a laugh, especially as the conversation with her father was still eating at her.

17

Gloria removed the chair obstructing the door and went to see her father. He was looking at a video presentation for a company that wanted his advice on marketing and he was chuckling. He looked up at her from his seat. He was careworn, his brow noticeably furrowed. Nothing was going right for him.

'I've come to say that I'm sorry, Dad. I shouldn't have said what I did.'

'And I shouldn't have...' He sighed. 'I shouldn't have tried to impose on you the way I did. Forget I said it.'

'I'll do what he wants.'

'I won't mention it again to him. And I won't commit you to anything.' She went to him for a hug. They were both reassured by it. He smelt of sweat but also of the subtle cologne she always associated with him. In her ear she imagined Annalisa saying, 'The only man who ever holds you, Gloria, is your dad.' She withdrew.

'Have you looked in on your mother today?' he asked.

'I have. And she was asleep.'

'I worry that she's not getting any exercise. I must talk to Dr Mencius about that.' This comment could have triggered another row between them, but Gloria allowed it to pass like a weary policeman letting off a harmless drunk. 'OK,' she said as she left his room, keen for the fragile harmony not to be disturbed. It was at that moment Frank's phone pinged.

It was a message from Layne saying he needed another chat and so was going to phone him, which he now did. 'Twice today, Layne? What's up?' he said in a sympathetic tone.

The older man gave a heavy sigh. 'It's my son.'

'Roane?' said Frank redundantly. He knew Layne had only the one male child, although it would not have surprised him unduly to learn that another had unexpectedly made himself known, given Layne's ostentatious wealth.

'He's been at it again. Three-day parties in a London mews. Neighbours unhappy. Drugs. Prostitutes. Drunks wandering about. Every kind of riffraff. They're claiming—'

'Who's claiming?'

'Neighbours. They're saying it's caused the value of their properties to plummet. How do I know if that's true? One of them wants to sue me as the owner. I didn't even know I did own it until I checked. It was my estate manager suggested investing in short-term lets. Supposedly a prestigious address in a quiet area. High-class. Now the only thing high-class is the hookers, and that's debatable. The neighbour complains he can't sit in his lounge or sleep in his bedroom because of the noise. He claims his house has become a fortress. He even had the cheek to phone me up. I felt like saying: "Fortress? Then you'll know what it's like for me living in one".' Layne was suddenly out of breath.

'How awful for you,' said Frank.

Layne paused before replying, 'I know. How could I know my son was living there? He's such a nightmare. He'll end up living in his car, the way he's going. It's all driving me to distraction. They say it's usually the third generation takes the family's wealth to ruin, and he's doing his best to prove that correct.'

Frank let the old man ramble on, repeating himself constantly until he was spent. As though suddenly awoken from a reverie, the Englishman then said, 'Oh well, I must get back to work. I can't spend all day listening to you. Good day to you, Frank.'

18

The Hummingbirds' next game, away to fellow title contenders the Traders, was an ill-tempered affair with bad fouls by both sides and players squaring up to each other. Gloria was at her best, weaving through the defenders' desperate attempted tackles, but when she was blatantly tripped just outside the penalty area, she was so incensed she wanted to punch the guilty party. She even ran after her. Fortunately, her team-mates grabbed her in time and dragged her away. She escaped with only the referee's wagging finger, while the opponent was booked. She took the free kick herself and hit the ball so hard the goalie had no chance; indeed, it could have almost broken the net. It was a happy day, winning 4-2 and Gloria scoring twice.

When she was home again, she visited her mother and found her awake and sitting up in bed. She merely smiled as Gloria told her about the match, emphasising the brilliance of her goals. Back in her own room she found on Facebook a new message from the mysterious woman, 'Fantastic today! Go, Gloria!'

She also noticed a message from Trey:

'Dearest darling Gloria,

I must apologise from the bottom of my heart for not being in touch earlier and the worry this must have caused you. Unfortunately, I have had some terrible luck. When driving to a studio for a recording of my music I was in a car accident that almost killed me. Believe me, I am not exaggerating. I wanted you to come to my bedside at the hospital, as I knew you would, but I was unable to even pick up a phone. I'm sorry about that. Now I am home again and can type. My injuries were severe (see the pictures below), and the medical bills were very expensive. I have had to get a loan from a shark just to pay them. I can't pay it back. I thought I had auto insurance but the broker was crooked and just kept the premiums. The documents he gave me were fake. My Ferrari which I need for work was destroyed in the crash, and it turns out I didn't even own it. The person who sold it to me had stolen it. The good news is that the third party who caused the accident will pay my damages, so all I need from you, my darling, is a quick loan, no more than fifty thousand dollars, so I can pay off the shark. I will pay you interest at the commercial rate.

I know you are kind, and have a little hard-earned money, and support charities, so I am confident you will see me as a good cause. Once I am well I will come and see you, so we can continue our relationship and get to know each other better and look back on these difficulties and laugh about them.

Your ever-loving Trey.'

She had a quick look at the pictures he'd sent of him in hospital, all staged in such a way that the person could not be identified from them. She sighed, 'Trey, I give you nine out of ten for imagination and zero for honesty. Nice try.' He and his ridiculous stories were history; surfer boy Dwayne was her new fake boyfriend.

The next thing she saw was a letter from Lily attached to an email:

'Dear Gloria,

How are you? I think of you a lot, especially now. I'm sorry to say that I am very much in need of your emotional support once more. I have done a foolish thing. A bad thing. I have been unfaithful to Mack multiple times. I have confessed to her...'

Gloria could not believe it. Was not Mack's love supposed to be "all-consuming", as Lily had once described it?

'...She told me she had also been unfaithful, which I knew already. I offered her a divorce but she said she didn't want one. The fundamental problem is that she is gay and I am not. People said it would never work. We wanted to believe it would because we loved each other so much - which we still do. I want us to be faithful to each other. And happy. All I can think to do is to get help for sex addiction for that is what I have. I seem unable to say no to temptation. If I did not have Mack it would be worse. I have always been promiscuous or completely disinterested, one or the other. In a marriage I can't be either. It is at times like these that the deep affection that you and I share becomes so important to me...'

Gloria shook her head. She had once believed their platonic relationship was the most important thing in both their lives, but since Lily's wedding she'd had to accept that was no longer the case. Now, it seemed, Lily's marriage didn't matter to her either. She wrote, 'I still love you but you're a slut,' in response – partially a joke – which she did not send. Later, feeling frustrated at the whole subject of relationships, she got herself tipsy on a large glass of Merlot, read the letter again, felt sympathy for Lily, then for Mack, then anger at Lily, then sent the reply to her.

19

One morning, Frank decided to contact the beautiful investment manager he'd seen on TV, whose name was Saskia. He had difficulty getting through to her on the phone and so left his name and a message with an assistant. The following day, Saskia rang him back. She had a cool voice, reminding him of wooded groves and streams, softer than in her TV interview, although her manner was not especially warm either.

Frank was uncharacteristically nervous: 'I saw you on TV. It must have been—'

'The Business Channel?'

'I guess. I was just—'

'What can I do for you?'

'I wanted to say that I was very impressed.'

'Thank you. What can I help you with?'

'You know, it's not very often—'

'Yes?'

'I would welcome the opportunity to do business with you.'

'Really?' She sounded amused.

'I think I could help your business in a meaningful way.'

'Thanks. I'm not really in need of help right now.'

'Well, it's difficult to explain over the phone. I—'

'So you want to meet, is that it?' Clearly this was a routine situation for her. Not that her physical attractiveness had anything to do with it, of course.

'Well, I—'

'I'll be in touch.' She rang off.

Overall, a partial success, he thought. But no more than that.

Early that afternoon, Frank, feeling subdued after the call with Saskia, heard from Layne again. Frank liked to think he never felt down for long, and by the time his English friend called his mood was on the upswing.

'What's up, Layne? This is kinda late for you. Is it your new girlfriend?'

'It might be.' This was said with the air of 'Of course it is; can't you hear how proud I am?'

'You obviously want to tell me all about her. You said before that she works in films. Is she an actor?'

'A model, actually.'

'What sort of model?'

'Beautiful. High-class. Nothing... distasteful.'

'Have you met her yet?'

'No, but any day now. She's just so busy with her work.'

'How do you know she's a model?'

'Look at her face.'

Layne immediately sent her photograph through. Frank studied it carefully. He recognised her.

'Her picture belongs to a real model,' he said.

'That's because she is a real model.'

'No, Layne, it's a famous model. I've seen that face before. On a perfume ad or something. Probably some influencer Gloria would know about. Your girlfriend's used her photo.' It was harsh but true. Layne was an old fool tricked again, abetted by his own vanity.

'No. You're just jealous.'

'Have you even talked to her?'

'Not yet.'

'Not on the phone? Not even seen her on Skype? Layne, this is ridiculous.'

'She's shy about showing her face on video, that's all.'

'That's not very encouraging. And surely a bit odd for a model.'

This narked Layne: 'Like you would know anything about it, eh? You're so full of yourself, you think you know everything. You can't let me have my bit of joy, can you, you bastard?'

After a pause to catch his breath, Frank again asked him if he would like Gloria to check out the girlfriend, owing to her ability to expose scammers online. But then he remembered he'd promised her he would not raise the subject again.

'Why?' said Layne, affronted. 'Why do I need her or anyone else to check out my beautiful girlfriend? How dare you! How mean-spirited!'

'Well, I—'

'Do you think I'm not capable of working out who's genuine and who's not?'

'No, I didn't say that.'

'Well, you sure as hell meant it. Anyway, the answer's no... but thank you. Oh, got to go now. Someone's phoning about next week's conference in Dubai on... something or other.'

After the call, seeing Gloria was in her room he decided to broach the subject of Saskia's short selling operation. He explained to her about his unsuccessful foray into consumer advocacy, and his fear that Naylor Grish's rejection would be mirrored by others jaundiced against him because of his 'legacy'. Saskia's short selling enterprise would not have such scruples.

'That's because it's immoral,' Gloria said.

'Immoral? No more so than predators in the natural world.'

'Bringing down companies impacts people's lives.'

'So does everything. Like weak and slow creatures being eaten by lions and tigers, but that's called ecology, just Nature's way of cleaning up.'

'Short sellers sound more like hyenas than lions,' she said.

'So what? Hyenas have their role to perform too. Nature isn't all pandas and daffodils, you know.'

He rambled on a bit and then said, 'Of course, it would be good if I could tell her that I could get her some financial backing.'

'If you mean, from the foundation, that would be a lie because it's not happening. We discussed that already.'

'I know you're worried about it, but I was thinking we could get a lawyer to help us unravel it all.'

'Really? Are you serious? I think you must have a crush on this woman. If you hire a lawyer, I'll hire my own lawyer who'll say why it can't be done. Besides, are you seriously saying you have no investments of your own you could use? You must have some squirrelled away.'

He felt like a tired boxer surprised by an opponent's tenacity. 'Yes I do have investments, but they're for the family's future including emergencies.' She was unmoved, and he decided to settle for a draw and retreat.

20

The Hummingbirds continued their successful season, building on their fine start. They found themselves up against another championship rival, the Bluebirds. It proved another fractious game. Gloria had sustained kicks all up her legs and towards the end her patience was running out. As she cut inside from the left wing, about to pass to Annalisa, she found herself dumped on the ground by a wild tackle at knee height. Rather than stay down she struggled to her feet and shoved the offender in the shoulder causing her to fall over. A brawl involving ten players immediately ensued in a sudden release of pent up anger and aggression. Four players were booked including Gloria and the player who'd fouled her. She felt subdued for the rest of the game, but fortunately Annalisa had already scored twice from her assists, and the Hummingbirds won 3-2. After the game Barti praised them for the win but criticised their 'lack of discipline'. Later, the teams encountered each other in the car park, and there was a standoff and shouting match between them. Gloria, determined not to be caught up in it, walked straight to her car and drove away.

On arriving home, Gloria found on her laptop that her new admirer Dwayne had written to her again. There were pictures of himself on a jet ski, and surfing, and on a yacht. He wrote to her that she had 'beauty beyond compare. I cannot envisage life without the opportunity to spend time with you. Such a life would not be worth living.' He then asked her if she liked to surf. She replied that she did, not revealing it was something she'd only tried a couple of times.

She was highly suspicious of him. Why had he chosen her to write to? She noticed he had very few Facebook friends, which was a 'red flag'. She looked at them and found they also had very few friends. Indeed, all seemed to be part of his local surfing community, whether that be real or invented.

He responded immediately to her reply, 'I would love to take you surfing. You're so much fun. It's gonna be great!' Had she believed in his persona, she would have declined to go with him, worried lest she make a fool of herself and he be disappointed. But since she didn't believe it, she saw no danger. She replied, 'I can't wait!'

The pair were testing each other out, but from her perspective there was only one possible outcome: she would prove he was a fraud.

21

Frank did not hear from Saskia and so he rang her. Perhaps sensing he was the type who was not easily put off, she suggested they go to dinner, now that she was spending more time at her new office in Los Angeles. She was free the following evening. Frank couldn't believe his good fortune and told no-one about the dinner date, lest he jinx it. He merely told Gloria and Suzie he was going to a business dinner with a client.

Accordingly, he met Saskia at an upscale Spanish restaurant she had chosen: Gabi James in Redondo Beach. She said she'd been there before and it had become one of her favourites. They agreed on her suggestion of the small plates menu with Albariño wine.

He found her beguiling, reminding him of his wife in her younger days, except Saskia was more petite, quiet and contained within herself. She spoke calmly and directly. By comparison, he was unable to relax, as though his emotions were puppies straining on the leash to race off in multiple directions.

'So what is it you want to talk to me about exactly?' she asked. 'You said you wanted to see me about my business. You were rather insistent about it.'

'I'm sorry,' he said, accepting the clear reproach. 'I find it fascinating what you do. I would like to help you in some way with your work.'

Smiling, she waved the notion aside: 'Thank you, but I work alone supported by my hand-picked team of assistants. It's the only way. I make my own decisions, answerable to no one.'

'I thought perhaps my corporate knowledge—'

'I have all the corporate knowledge I need. I have my assistants to get me that. But again, thank you.' She appeared to thaw slightly. 'I should feel flattered, I suppose.'

He talked a little about his experience in business. She appeared interested, although he was sure she must have known about his past already. Perhaps she was good at pretending. He didn't mind. The serenity he saw in her he found compelling. She was making serious money and that was compelling too.

The meal was enjoyable but low-key. Frank found the conversation stilted and the room was becoming noisier. The evening ended abruptly, for as soon as they'd finished dessert she requested the bill, paid it, and was gone. He was left wondering what the point of the dinner had been. She was not interested in his tentative proposal, although it was only tentative because of her dismissive attitude. On the other hand, she had said that she did not need anything, which was fair enough. He admired her candour.

Feeling overall a little disappointed and humbled as he drove back to Mission Viejo, gradually he began to mellow, as though some unwanted confusion had been lifted from his mind.

Frank slept poorly and wasn't in the mood for another call from Layne the next morning, but he felt a sense of duty to listen to his friend. As Layne talked, Frank couldn't help thinking he reminded him of an impotent old bull:

'I just can't win,' said Layne.

'What is it now?' Frank couldn't hide his tetchiness.

'A luxury hotel some fraudster persuaded me to buy is mixed up in a dispute over money laundering, if you can believe that.'

'With you, I can.'

'I don't even know whether I own the damned place or not. All the staff in it have left and it's gone downhill. And now all I see is competitors shedding alligator tears over it. And the bloke who put me up to it was last seen sipping rare Chablis in some French count's vineyard!'

Frank did not reply. Instead, he let Layne wind down. Then the old man said quietly, 'One good piece of news, sort of: some bright spark has suggested I do this thing on the telly where you swap lives with someone else.'

'That sounds great.'

'But who would want my life, Frank?'

'Someone with rather less money than you?'

'I told them it would have to be somewhere I could fly to and where my courier could bring my Beluga caviar and champagne.'

'I bet they thought you were joking.'

'Of course I was joking: the caviar doesn't have to be Beluga. I don't know what they'd be like about expenses, though, but I expect my team could thrash out a deal.'

'Right.'

'For myself and my chef. But then I thought about it: suppose the person I swapped with got a taste for my life.'

'Hah! I can see the problem.'

'There I'd be, stuck in some hellhole of a sink estate, terrified that any moment I'll get attacked by a meth-fuelled nutter with an axe—'

'Indeed.'

'—and when I decide to call it a day, thank you, and go home, I'm told the undeserving oik I swapped with has decided he wants to stay there. I phone him up and he says, "Sorry chum, I'm in charge now," and I turn up at the estate to find he's taken over the bloody place. And my staff – my own staff – chase me off the property with my own dogs!'

'I can't think of anything more awful.'

'So I said, sod that, thank you.'

'Quite right.'

'But then they suggested being a homeless person for a day like politicians and celebrities do.'

'That's interesting.'

'But I said I wouldn't have time. A day's too long. I thought maybe half an hour. And what does one wear for it?'

'All these things you have to worry about, Layne.'

'Indeed I do. I'm glad you recognise how trying it all is for someone at the forefront of... of... whatever it is.'

22

Gloria made a point of going out more with her friends, especially at weekends to local events of all kinds. Because of her mother's condition she had tended to want to stay at home as much as possible, but lately she'd come to think that was a mistake. She would never find someone to date by staying indoors, and her friends such as Annalisa liked her company. Moreover, because she didn't drink much, she was a popular choice as designated driver.

One of their mutual friends was hosting a party at a new bar in Irvine so Gloria went to it, picking up Annalisa and another friend on the way. They had a fun time. Several of the Hummingbirds were there. One of the younger players, Micaela, said to Gloria, 'So are we gonna be champions?' Before she could answer, the goalie Raffie broke in and said in a deep voice, 'You can forget about being champions. You don't deserve it!' They all laughed and Ant said, 'That sounds just like him!'

There were also some interesting guys there, guys Gloria hardly knew and some not at all. There was one called Tommy, tall, lean, and athletic, who particularly had his eye on Gloria and she, likewise, was attracted to him. No words passed between them, but he smiled at her and she smiled back. 'Tommy fancies you,' said Annalisa.

'How can you tell?'

'It ain't difficult,' she said. 'Nor that you fancy him.'

'No!'

But Tommy and a couple of the other guys were suddenly leaving. Seeing her interest, Ant said, 'They'll be going to Spoons in Santa Ana, His brother works there. Wanna go?'

'I'm a little tired,' said Gloria.

'Me too. Let's split... unless you don't want to, of course.' The other girl they'd brought was going on to another bar, so they picked up their coats.

As they were leaving, a couple of guys who had not been part of their group called out, 'Hey Vanessa!' It was clear they meant Gloria, but she ignored them. One persisted, 'Vanessa, don't be rude.'

'What?' she said, keen not to have a pleasant evening spoilt. 'I'm not Vanessa.'

'Yeah, you are,' said one.

'Yeah,' the other added.

'You're mistaken,' she said. 'That's not my name.'

'What is your name then?'

She was about to tell them to mind their own business when Annalisa grabbed her arm and said, 'C'mon.' When they were outside the bar, walking to the car, Ant said, 'What was that about?'

'I don't know. Some guys mixing me up with someone else. Annoying really.'

'Maybe they think you're that film star. The one with the French name. It's kind of a compliment.'

'I don't think so,' she said in a tone intended to close down the discussion. 'A good crowd there tonight,' she commented, hoping to manoeuvre the conversation around to Tommy.

But instead, on the drive home Annalisa had a revelation to make. 'It was fun, wasn't it? Except for those guys at the end. Vanessa, eh? You must have a doppelgänger. I'm really going to miss you, Glo.'

'Miss me? Why, what do you think's going to happen?' She became nervous and so concentrated harder on the road.

'My dad has put in for a transfer. To Santa Barbara, no less. If that happens I may go with them. He wants me to.'

'Santa Barbara sounds cool. But don't you want to be independent?'

'Says *she*.'

'Alright.'

'But, yeah, I do. It's difficult. I don't know if Jimmy's the one, but if he is, well, I know he wouldn't want to go up there.'

'Have you talked to him about it, then?'

'No, but I know from things he's said that he wouldn't. He's OC through and through.'

'I think I am, too. Or I may as well be because I can't see me leaving. Especially not the way my mom is.'

'Is she no better?'

'It's hard to tell. She's just not like she used to be. The odd flicker maybe. I tell her about the match and it's like talking to one of them stone sculptures at Heisler Park.'

'That's near where I work.'

'I know.'

Annalisa started giggling. 'I'm sorry, it's not funny but—'

'No, it is. She has some weird doctor who calls round. Creepy as hell.

Seventy, if he's a day. Really sketches me out. He massaged my leg with ointment once after a game.'

'What?'

'But I learnt my lesson. So I was ready for him the next time when he came into my room and was going to touch me up.'

'Touch you up!?'

Annalisa who'd had several drinks was finding it hard to resist bursting into laughter.

'Then he stopped. He obviously realised what he was doing.'

'His wandering hands.'

'Right. Then there's my dad who's got some new crush.'

'Yeah?'

'Saw her on TV. Some investment lady.'

Annalisa could contain herself no longer. 'Oh, Glo, you've cheered me up no end!'

'Always keen to be of service.' Then she herself joined in the laughter. She pulled the car over and the pair of them let it all out. Then they hugged and continued the last few miles to Ant's house.

The fact she might be losing Annalisa made Gloria more concerned not to lose Lily from her life. Annalisa was not the writing kind. The odd text or Facebook message would be the most she could expect from her. By contrast, Lily's messages, although sporadic, were thoughtful and affectionate. But Gloria now recalled that she had, in a rare moment of lost self-control, sent Lily a rude message. It was too late to correct the situation; the sting the message would have left in Lily's sensitive skin from calling her a 'slut', a word she rarely used even in jest, would have already done its work. Gloria's dilemma, repeated over and over in her head, was whether to apologise or not. She decided not to. She decided to pretend she hadn't sent it. If Lily reacted to it, she would deny all knowledge, maintaining that someone had hacked into her computer and sent out all sorts of things, invariably rude, fraudulently and cruelly in her name. In other words, she would lie to her. But that made her uncomfortable. No, she decided: lying to such a dear friend was unacceptable. She would have to accept responsibility.

23

Eventually Lily wrote back. She was unhappy: 'I still want you in my life unless you think I'm too much of a slut and don't deserve it. I'm used to being called that. Mack used to call me that all the time, and she was right. But she behaved worse than me. And she acknowledged that. I don't mind you thinking bad of me over it, but I wish you'd said before that you were so censorious of my morals. I thought you still adored me like an imperious goddess, the way I adore you, even though I'm obviously a fallen one. Do you think I feel proud of myself? Do you think I need to be told? You used to make me feel so good about myself when I felt low. I feel low now. In fact, I feel like the dirt on your shoe. I wish you were here to slap me round the face because it's what I deserve.'

Distracted by Lily's message, Gloria received a call from Annalisa. She said the brother of a friend of hers wanted to meet Vanessa, and by that he meant her.

'It's a mix-up,' said Gloria. 'You know it is.'

'No, they definitely meant you. Why are you using an alias, all of a sudden?'

'I assure you, I'm not. I must have a double, like you said in the car.'

'Or a secret twin. You look like an actress he's seen. You'd like that, wouldn't you?'

'No, I wouldn't.'

'My friend told him your real name, but he didn't believe it.'

Gloria wondered whether it was one of the guys at the party or someone she'd heard say it in the coffee bar on the previous occasion. No, she didn't care to know. 'Whatever,' she said. 'I have no interest in meeting him. No doubt he'll show up in some bar when I'm there and start calling me Vanessa. It's putting me off going out.'

'He is kinda cute, though. A real snack.'

'I don't care. I'm not interested.'

'Oh, that's right: it's Tommy you fancy. Well, good luck with that. He ain't exactly the reliable kind.'

Gloria drafted a response to Lily, 'I still love you, slut or not. I didn't mean it anyway. It's just a word. I never meant to send it. It sounds like you need to sort out your love life. I don't know what it is you want from me anymore but whatever it is, you have it. I'll support you, whatever you do in your life. One thousand per cent. Always. Always. Always.'

She later deleted the sentence about Lily needing to sort out her love life and sent the rest of the message.

24

Frank was looking online for companies that might be ripe for short selling when he noticed from the morning's market updates that one company's share price had dropped from 450 down to 10 in two days. He recognised the name. They had asked him to help with their marketing strategy and he'd declined the opportunity. They were selling a plastics substitute but he wasn't convinced they had a legitimate product. It was his suspicion that the 'substitute' was probably just another form of plastic. He had no way of physically testing it, but he did not believe the company's claims plausible.

The latest story behind the share collapse was that they had claimed huge commitments from potential industrial buyers when they had none. That story he could believe. He wondered whether Saskia had picked up this one for short selling. Clearly someone had. He chuckled at the thought that she could short sell every single one of his actual and potential clients with their grandiose claims and, leaving aside the handful of legitimate ones, make a serious fortune.

He was about to send an email to Saskia about this when Layne phoned. He sounded excited, having just returned from a conference on 'whatever it was, I can't remember'. Frank thought about taking the opportunity to talk to him about short selling, hiding Saskia under the subject of 'little known investment opportunities', but the old man was bubbling with his latest news:

'It looks like I may be moving into the wedding business now.'

'It seems a bit early for that, but congratulations!'

'Not me, you fool, the estate. You do like your little jokes. No, it's to raise some cash. The manager suggested it.'

'The same manager who suggested the sand lizards?'

'Don't make fun of the sand lizards. You know I can't abide mockery. Especially from someone in California. Believe it or not, it's not just re-wilding he knows about. He's perfectly capable of managing the business side of things.'

'I'm sure he is.'

'He's trying to convince me I need to get into the wedding event business to make the place viable. But I'm not entirely relaxed about it. I don't like to think of my precious Vermeers getting wine chucked on them even if they are fakes, and having ne'er-do-wells throwing up on the carpet and urinating in the garden. And although I couldn't care less about the bloody neighbours' wellbeing, I can do without them moaning and groaning about the noise. They're already wound up over my environmentally friendly and entirely sustainable development plans—'

'Oh dear.'

'—like my state-of-the-art solar power farm which got stopped because of newts and badgers, so I don't want any more trouble. And I already pay lawyers more than I can live with – and that's without pursuing my ex for libel.'

'But wedding events sounds a good idea.'

'I suppose so. In theory, at least. Twenty grand a time, my manager reckons. And people will love it. Beautiful grounds, lovely lake with fish in it. Sixteenth century. That's history for you; none of your pipsqueak Yankee stuff.'

'I hear you, not that we care.'

'Romantic, too. I reckon that'll seal the deal with the lovely Dania. Our wedding can be the first one here.'

'I thought her name was Tatiana.'

'Oh, could be. She's proving a little elusive lately.'

'Are you worried about that?'

'Not really. She's a model, so she has assignments all over the world. Mind you, with those legs it's hardly surprising. Just wish they were wrapped around me instead of inside a fur coat or something.'

'Isn't anticipation part of the joy, Layne?'

'What are you, a philosopher now? To hell with the anticipation. I can't wait to get hold of her.'

'What does she say about it?'

'She says she loves older men because they're mature. She loves English gentlemen in particular, and is fascinated by aristocracy. She says she believes she could help me manage my property.'

'And your money.'

'You're such a cynic. But since you're so damned interested, she has a brother who's an investment banker and she has broached the subject of my putting some money aside for our future together. But being a prudent man as I am—'

'Of course.'

'No sarcasm, if you please — I've decided not to pursue it at this point.'

'Want me to look into it?' Frank now saw the opening to talk about Saskia: 'By the way, I know someone—'

'Believe it or not, I have people here who do all that. You think everything is done better over there when more than half of it is, as you call it, a crock.'

'Harsh, Layne. But I was thinking—'

'It's true. I watch *American Greed*, you know. Anyway, I'd better go. Someone wants to convert the old pig sheds into a somatic healing centre or something. No idea what that's about. I just sign the papers.'

Rather than emailing Saskia about the latest company flop, he decided to ring her. He needed to hear more of that voice, even if it was only her recorded message. To his surprise, however, she answered him straight away. She sounded upbeat. 'Frank! How goes it?'

'First of all, thank you for the dinner. It was—'

'It was my pleasure. So lovely to meet you.'

He mentioned the company that had dropped from 450 to 10 and asked her if it was one she'd picked up. 'Yeah, we did,' she said.

'When did you learn about them?'

'Oh, about three weeks ago. We got a tip-off and then did the research.'

'I knew three months ago.'

'Really?'

'Yeah. They came to see to help them with their marketing. I could tell there was something fishy with them.'

'Wow. That's really interesting. So sometimes these dodgy companies come your way.'

'Yes. So you see I could—'

'Like I said at our meeting, I already have my team. We don't pick up everything. Got to leave some for others.' She gave a little laugh. 'But nine times out of ten we do. Anyway, Frank, so good to hear from you. I'll bear what you said in mind.' She was gone.

After the call, he could not stop thinking about her. That voice was at times like aromatic smoke, sometimes a cool gentle breeze and subtly scented. He was becoming mesmerised by her and he knew it but could not prevent it. The most irksome thing was that she probably had no idea of the effect she was having on him, although perhaps that was a good thing. Nor did he think she would change in that regard. Most importantly, she would go on ignoring the huge benefit he could bring to her organisation. In frustration, he thought about setting up his own short selling operation, a rival to challenge hers. That would get her attention. But this notion was immediately stymied by the simple fact that he had no available capital.

Gloria noticed, as she always could, that her father was in an odd mood. He was listless. She went to tell him about what Annalisa had told her - the Garcias possibly moving - and he barely seemed to be listening. All morning and afternoon he spent moping about, preoccupied, which was so unusual for him. He was a doer. Feelings were not usually of great significance to him. You did things, regardless of how you felt; that had been the secret of his success in life, though perhaps also the source of his failure in not listening to his emotions on occasion. She was aware he'd been talking to Saskia and surmised it was connected with that. She had already looked her up online and could not avoid the suspicion that the woman's physical attractiveness was a strong factor in her father's interest. This made her deeply uncomfortable.

She was diverted from thinking about this by a message from surfer boy Dwayne. The person she really wanted to hear from was Tommy whom she'd exchanged smiles with at the party, but he was the real world and, in Gloria's current frame of mind, this made him problematic. Even though she knew all too well that it was virtual people who were the biggest risk, she found herself drawn into that world.

Dwayne was asking her about soccer: 'I'd like to come and watch you play, then go for a coffee and chat. How does that sound?'

She was not naive. She knew he would either not turn up or, if he did, that he would likely be a man in his forties or older. The whole thing would be humiliating. If he did watch her, just the knowledge of it would distract her so much she would be unable to feed Annalisa the passes her friend's insatiable appetite for easily scored goals required.

She wrote back, 'That sounds great, but I do not like family and friends watching me play as it puts me off.' She decided against suggesting an alternative arrangement for meeting. The fact was, she did not believe this young god with a zest for the outdoor life was a real person. Nor would it be a great attraction for her if he was the athletic surfer dude, since she preferred the indoor life. But she enjoyed what to her was the 'game' of pretending to be naive and interested and then ensnaring the catfish. And if Dwayne surprisingly did turn out to be who he claimed, and sweet of heart, she would make the effort to engage with those things that interested him. She did after all love the ocean.

At this point, she cast her mind back to her childhood days, when her father was more relaxed and her mother was well, and they took Gloria and her two brothers to the beach at every opportunity.

She was distracted from these pleasant thoughts by her phone ringing. It was Lily. Was she in the US? The two rarely spoke on the phone, partly because of the nine-hour time difference. Lily had a finance business and, because it often involved entertaining clients, she had a long day.

Lily sounded stressed. She got straight to the point. 'I wanted to be sure you were OK with me.'

Gloria felt apprehensive. Lily was clearly on some kind of mission. 'For sure, why do you ask?'

'I wasn't sure how you felt.'

'That hasn't changed. Why would it?'

'You called me a slut. That really hurt.'

'Sorry.'

'It doesn't matter. I just wanted to be sure that underneath it you weren't really upset with me.'

'No, I'm not. I hope you realise I didn't mean it. I just wrote it. I didn't mean to send it—'

'Yeah, well, mistakes show what people really think. I suddenly felt you thought me contemptible.'

'No, no, not at all. It was just a bit of a shock what you wrote. And I was a little drunk.'

'You, drunk? That must be a first. Anyway, I'm sorry for what I said that upset you.'

'It's fine, Lily.' Since her friend had been so direct Gloria decided to air something that had been bothering her. 'I guess, since you got married I haven't been sure what my role is in your life.'

'Your role?' Lily was taken aback. 'You saved my fucking life once. How much of a role is that? Yes, I love Mack. I love her to bits. If I lost her I would want to die. But if I lost you I *would die*. Do you understand that?'

'How did I save your life?'

'By being there for me when everything was darkness. You know that. I never will forget it. But since my marriage, quite honestly, you have seemed a little cold towards me. I understand it, I think. I just don't want to lose you from my life. Please.'

'You won't. I promise, you won't. It's just... I don't need to know when you've been unfaithful to Mack.'

There was a slight pause. 'OK, I understand. By the way, thank you. You've made me see things more clearly.'

'I have? When?'

'Right now. If I'm unfaithful to Mack it's like I'm unfaithful to you. I realise that now. I'm determined not to stray again, believe me, even if she does. I'm getting help with my sex addiction because that's what it is... or was.'

'OK.'

'But enough about me. Tell me what's new in your life.'

'Not much.'

She told her about Tommy, but mainly about Dwayne since he'd been so much on her mind that morning. Lily said that if she needed it, Mack could help her find out about him. Gloria declined the offer but thanked her. They ended the call, both a little subdued but happy.

25

One morning, Frank was startled to receive a call from Saskia. The further surprise was that she had a question for him. She asked whether he knew anything about a particular company called Smith Thursday. His heart skipped a beat on being asked. He said the name back to her. 'What do you need to know?' he said.

'Whatever you can tell me.'

'I wouldn't know where to start. There's so much.' In truth, there wasn't. He knew nothing about the company. He'd never heard of it. It was solid cast bullshit he was talking, just like in his old corporate boss days. He was momentarily annoyed at this reminder of his former self. Smith Thursday? It could be an actor or a pop singer, but a company? He said he would put something in writing about it. In reality, he would ask Gloria to find out what she could. But then the thought occurred to him: what if it was a trap Saskia had set for him? Maybe she'd sussed him out and was seeking to trick him by giving him a fake company to research. He was sure she could be deceitful. He had to guard against such guile.

'Oh, did you say Smith Thursday?' he said. 'I thought you said something else.'

'So do you know them or not?'

He ought to be truthful and say no, but instead he said, 'I believe so. I'll have a good think.'

She laughed. 'OK, you do that. That would be great.'

Soon after Frank's call with Saskia, Layne phoned. Buoyant from talking to the captivating investment manager, Frank was pleased to hear from him.

Layne said he'd just flown in from a three-day conference in Berlin which he couldn't remember much about except that it was a waste of time. He then said he had 'important news'. He revealed that the chosen one was not a model after all. He'd found out she wasn't who she claimed to be.

Frank stopped himself from saying that it was hardly a surprise. 'How do you know, Layne? Did you hire a PI or something?'

'PI? I don't need a bloody PI! I had one of my lackeys investigate and he gave me a report. That was enough. I told myself, I know how Henry the Eighth felt waiting to meet Anne of Cleves. Oh, I forgot, you probably have no idea what that's about.'

'You forget my father was English.'

'Of course. Impressive, Frank. But I'm actually glad she's not a model. The trouble with models is that they think it's going to be one big party. A party in their honour. Caligula's nothing compared to the ambitions of some of them. But the reality's too old and tired for them. They soon get bored with the day-to-day, once there's nothing to put on Instagram. Nothing to convince their brainless friends why dating someone older than their father can somehow be vaguely fun. Believe me, the average street prostitute's got more class than some of those that come on to you... er, I expect. But at last I've found a real gem. This one's different.'

'Brilliant,' said Frank, glad for him but sceptical.

'You see, although she's not a model, she looks like one. And she's actually a nurse, which is ideal. I told her I had cancer.'

'Oh Layne, I'm so sorry.'

'No, of course I haven't got cancer! It was to get her sympathy.'

'And I can see your early mortality might be an attraction.'

'You're so cynical. Later I'll tell her it was a false alarm. The important thing is that she wants to marry me, and for that to happen she knows she has to please me.'

'It sounds like an evil plan, Layne.'

'Oh excuse me, you think she's so innocent? Why do you think people like her go on dating sites to pick up older men – Help the Aged?'

Layne then said he had to go and get ready for an 'Earth-friendly din-ner' in London, although he was dismissive of its value: 'Probably just a load of merchant bankers preening themselves about their "journey to carbon neutrality" or some such piffle, but at least I can expect a decent steak.' He was happy and Frank was happy for him.

26

Gloria continued corresponding with Dwayne via Facebook messages until he wrote, 'I have information on the Vanessa issue,' which was weird because she could not recall mentioning it to him. He added: 'Someone's used one of your pictures. They made multiple Facebook pages using it, all with different names including Vanessa. That seems to be the only active one.'

'I don't believe you,' she replied, though in her heart she feared it.

'Probably someone you went to college with set it up.'

'No!'

'You should be flattered.'

'I'm not.'

'Some guy online is infatuated with you. Thinks he's in a relationship. He'll be mad finding out he's not in love with the real you.'

'It's not my problem.'

'It is. He's in love with Vanessa. And Vanessa is you.'

'No, I don't believe you.'

'It's your life.'

'Get lost!'

She wondered whether she'd been harsh on Dwayne. After all, if what he wrote was true, whoever he was had done her a favour in warning her. He would expect her to be grateful. Perhaps, however, it was he who was the real problem. Maybe he'd done all of it, set up the whole 'Vanessa' business so that he could then pretend to fix the problem as a way to earn favour with her. She tried not to think about it because it could drive her crazy. Her own research into catfish and scammers had led her to believe no one. But clearly some people thought she truly was Vanessa.

Frank was able to obtain information on Smith Thursday without seeking Gloria's help. His fear that it was a joke on Saskia's part, or a trap, proved unfounded. This is what he learned when his old lawyer friend Jack Quick rang him about it. Jack had felt bad at not accepting his proposal to work with him and was keen to assist with Frank's enquiry. 'I checked with everyone I know and one of them came back with all the bad stuff. And there's plenty.'

'It's not a well-known company,' said Frank.

'No, it's that sweet combination of secretive and profitable. It's not only that it has a shady business as a sideline, but that it has no legitimate business at all. In other words, it's a scam. Not something your friends want to get their pinkies dirty on.'

But a fraudulent company with an inflated share price was *exactly* what Saskia wanted to become involved with so that she could expose it and bring the price down. When Frank presented to her what Jack had told him she was delighted. 'I knew you'd come up with something,' she said. 'I'm grateful for what you've done. But was it easy to uncover?'

'It took a bit of digging, but it's what I routinely do. Detailed research. Extensive contacts. It's just work.' He did not mention Jack.

'Impressive. I'm wondering: would you like to be kind of an "ad hoc consultant" for us? I have my team in place, but now and then—'

'Of course,' he said.

He could scarcely believe it. He felt gratified and yet, as he pondered afterwards, it wasn't enough. He wanted to help her business more than he wanted to make money for himself. He told himself this was out of a kind of corporate altruism, but in reality what he wanted more than anything was a relationship, even a fantasy relationship, with the exotic beauty. He resisted this urge and yet it drove him on.

27

Layne was 'fresh from the airport' when he next phoned Frank. He had to report that his girlfriend was moving into the mansion imminently. 'I think she'll settle in well, although I detect a bit of a sense of entitlement about her. I think she's expecting to have a gold carriage to go about in, or something.'

'She thinks she's associating with royalty, Layne.'

'I'm sure she does. Well, we'll soon get her cleaning out the new pig pens. That'll give her the rude education she clearly needs.' He laughed.

'I'm a bit shaken up, actually. We had a close one today. Old Woody sent someone sprawling.'

'Who's Woody, your dog?'

'No, my driver. Almost killed a pedestrian. Stupid woman shouldn't have been there.'

'Was she jaywalking?'

'No idea where she was, but she wasn't paying attention. But when Woody's driving, watch out. I checked the car's alright, though.'

'And the pedestrian?'

'If she's hurt, no doubt we'll hear about it.'

'By the way, Layne, why don't you drive yourself these days, with all your cars?"

'I did until the police got me on some trumped-up charge.'

'What was that for?'

'Mobile phone, red light, over the limit.'

'All three at once?'

'Why do things by halves? Or thirds?'

'How'd it happen?'

'I was in a hurry for an important climate change meeting.'

'Of course you were. And the phone?'

'I was expecting a call from the American ambassador.'

'Naturally.'

'No, on reflection, it was my dry cleaning, but even so—'

'And the drink?'

'I'd been at a reception for a newly appointed president of somewhere or other. It's vital I make new connections for my work.'

'Layne, you're so funny I sometimes think you could write copy for God.'

'Thanks. Of course I should have got off because of what I do for the planet and climate change, but the judge was biased. I made a strong case for exceptional hardship which he ignored.'

'I guess it's not easy for a multi-millionaire claiming exceptional hardship. You should have got a better lawyer.'

'You people and your lawyers! Even your pets have lawyers. I got banned for nine months and decided to call it a day. Besides, old Woody's been driving the family for sixty years and is probably legally blind, but being his passenger is the closest I get to excitement these days. But the whole system's rigged against the wealthy. What is it about the rich that gets other people so riled up? It's not my fault I'm not poor. By the way, I was meaning to ask: how's the fires over there, Frank? Licking around your door yet?'

'There's no fires anywhere near here, Layne.'

'For all the crooks and creeps here, I wouldn't live in California for all the dollars in the world.'

'You couldn't anyway unless you married an American.'

'I'm sure with the right education and training one could make an acceptable wife. But no doubt a legitimate-looking US passport is obtainable from somewhere.'

'You wouldn't survive anyway.'

'I know what you mean: every scammer north of the Mexican border would be round me like the mosquitoes you're plagued with there.'

'There's no plague, Layne. And even if there was, we're resilient over here.'

'Hah! You should be in politics with all your patter.'

'Believe me, I'm not subtle or clever enough.'

'In other words, you're a sweetheart, Frank. I've always thought that. I may take the rise out of you, put the digs in, but you know I appreciate your friendship. No one could ask for a better pal. They just don't show up too often in life.'

'Take it easy, Layne. Don't overstretch the blanket there.'

'Take it easy, you say? You think I'm larding it on? Well, maybe I am, Frank, but you're more important than ever to me now. But teach me how to be better, to be a gentler me. Tell me more about your life.'

'When, now?'

'No, I know you're a busy man. Over the next weeks or months, whenever we talk.'

'Well, Layne, I don't know what to say. I'm not sure I can make you better, as you put it.'

'Then say nothing. I have to go now - Tania's calling me on another line. Bye.'

28

When Gloria came home from soccer – another tough game but a 4-3 victory with her assisting with the winning goal – it was to find more from Dwayne. He wrote, 'I know who's behind Vanessa. It's the ex-girlfriend of someone called Tommy who's interested in you.'

This made no sense. 'Vanessa' had shown up prior to her even seeing Tommy for the first time in the bar, assuming it was the same one. The only possibility was that Tommy had expressed an interest in her before then - maybe he'd seen her at a match - and that had got back to his ex. But how did Dwayne even know about Tommy?

Gloria wrote back, 'I don't believe it.'

'She's going to troll you,' he wrote.

'Why? I have done nothing to her.'

'She has pictures of you.'

'What do you mean?'

'Private photographs.'

'No.'

Up came a picture of Gloria in a bikini. Such a photograph had never been taken. It was fake.

'That's not me,' she wrote.

'Yes it is.'

It was indeed her face but it was obvious her head had been placed on someone else's body. She did not even own a bikini that colour.

'Never. How did you get it anyway if she had it? How many more are there?'

She knew the answer to her own question. He could bring out any number of such pictures, as many as he wanted. Then he tightened the squeeze: 'She has these pictures. I can stop her sending them out but I want something in return.'

'What?' She knew the answer. He then confirmed she was right, 'I want intimate pictures of you. Naked. If the ones she has are fake, I want the real thing. It's no more than I deserve.'

'I thought you were trying to help me. Clearly you were merely pretending. So it's blackmail then.' She stopped typing. A moment later, she could barely see the keys for the tears in her eyes. In her mind she suddenly saw her life spiralling out of control because of deepfakes. She had seen it happen to others before. Younger women, not as strong as her, who'd been broken by it. Cast out of their group of friends, at odds with their family, frantic, unable to sleep, unable to stop the abuse online, self-harming, suicidal, at the bottom with nowhere to look but further down. That was not her. It could never be, could it?

She did not read what he wrote back. She left Facebook for the day. She thought about abandoning it forever, to simply ignore whatever happened, plead ignorance to anyone who asked her or confronted her about it. Denial without expressing the words. The difficulty was that she could never give up social media for long.

She went to see her mother. She would tell her everything. To her surprise, she found her sitting up reading an Agatha Christie novel in Spanish. 'How are you, Mama?'

'Fine, my dear.'

'Can I talk to you?'

'Of course, my darling. You don't need to ask.'

'Well—'

'I understand. Go on.'

Gloria proceeded to tell her everything she knew about 'Vanessa' and Dwayne. Maria said nothing but was clearly listening. When Gloria had finished she looked at her mother for a reaction. Maria reached for her hand and squeezed it gently. 'It will be fine,' she said. 'I know it's tough but it will work to the good. I pray for you and your brothers every night. They are just fine and you will be, too. Just have faith.'

'And what about you, Mama, will you be fine?'

Her mother smiled. 'Of course, my dear. But pray for me, just in case.'

Gloria felt glad she had told her mother. Next she decided she would phone Lily. She would seek Mack's help. She didn't need it, of course, because she could do the research herself, but it was too painful for her. Moreover, casting her problem at Lily's feet was a way of showing her vulnerability, to erase any vestiges of the hurt she'd inadvertently caused her.

Initially, she did not find Lily welcoming, however. 'A bit late,' she chided.

'Sorry,' said Gloria.

'I am still quite newly married, you know. And it is past eleven. My wife is asleep.'

'I'm sorry.'

'I know you think I have no morals but—'

'I don't think that. Please.'

'OK.' Now Lily had got her punishment out of the way, Gloria thought, she would do whatever she could to help. 'You sound stressed,' said Lily. 'Let me get up and go into the lounge in case we wake Mack.' A few moments later: 'Right then, I'm all ears.'

When Gloria had told her all about Dwayne and the latest, Lily said, 'Bloody hell, that's a lot to deal with!'

'I know.'

'I'm really glad you phoned me. But you said before, you don't want Mack's help, is that right?' Lily clearly wasn't yet done with hurting her a little.

Gloria almost broke into tears and it showed in her voice. 'I do want her help, if she'd be prepared to give it.'

Lily was now warm. 'She will,' she said. 'Of course she would be glad to. She'll get it sorted for you. That's what she does. She's brilliant.'

29

On his next Skype call with Layne, Frank found his English friend in high dudgeon and with a hubbub in the background.

'What's up, Layne?'

'It's all hell since I replaced that damned estate manager.'

'Why did you do that?'

'Tania insisted on it as soon as she moved in.'

'But why?'

'She found him creepy. She didn't like the way he looked at her. He always struck me as a bit weird anyway. I agreed with her we needed new blood. It's not turning out the way I expected, though.'

'Nothing ever does. So how are you right now?'

'I'm in a state of panic, can't you tell? Protesters at the gates. It's anarchy. They're burning effigies of me out there. I'm going to blast the buggers with a dose of Puccini in a minute.'

'I can hear chanting. What's happening? A revolution?'

'You'd like that, wouldn't you, you bastard? Always trying to do old Blighty down.'

'No, Layne, but where's the new gentler you?'

'Bugger that. This is a time to fight. The bloody police won't do anything. They'd arrest me for a trumped-up charge on a hate crime or something, any chance they got.'

'What does Tania make of it all?'

'She loves it. She thinks they must be making a movie and she's starring in it. She gets all dressed up and leans out of an upstairs window shouting abuse at them. She thought the protesters were extras and wanted to play Lady Bountiful and give the buggers coffee. Oh, just a minute—' Layne left his chair and Frank could no longer see him, though he could hear him shouting angrily. A few minutes later, he returned, red in the face and breathing heavily. 'That's better,' he said. 'I hired a private security firm and they've just arrived. They'll break a few heads if they have to.'

'Do you want me to get off the phone?'

'No, it's fine. Tania is dealing with it. She's a good practical sort.'

'Why are these people protesting?'

'They claim I and my sacred ancestors got rich from fossil fuels, as if there's something wrong with that. They say I should pay reparations. To whom? To them? These people have no idea of industrial history. What would they have us do – uninvent the combustion engine and go around in stagecoaches? Without fossil fuels, where would this country be? And they have the nerve to accuse me of greed. *Me!*'

'But is greed that bad? It never goes away so you might as well make the most of it.'

'All I know is that everyone's throwing cow manure at the windows of people like us, who've been careful and prudent all our lives. It's not my fault Tania and I need separate private planes because our dogs don't get along.'

'Dogs?'

'When we're flying around in the UK, I mean.'

'Always so considerate, Layne. But don't you get flak for your private planes anyway, when you're on your international jaunts?'

'Only from idiots. Do they expect me to travel economy to do my crucial work?'

'There is such a thing as business class.'

'Not for my business.'

'So do your entourage travel with you in your plane?'

'No. Do you think I want to have to listen to their inane chatter? It's bad enough being pestered in the hotel when I'm trying to listen to my precious Wagner.'

'How do your people travel, then? Your assistants?'

'I don't know. If they want the job, they get there.'

'Harsh.'

'Oh, don't get me started. Look, I'm in the family business which is philanthropy. Someone suggested I be more selfish and set up in the south of France and give up the acreage here for the casinos down there. But it would be impossible; I can never stop selflessly giving away my money and time, so I said no. Besides, down there I'd be a kidnap risk. Do you ever worry about such things, Frank?'

'Not anymore. I used to worry about Gloria in that regard, but now I worry that she'll get some kind of religion and seek to give away what's left of the family wealth to a bunch of schmucks.'

'I don't know about religion, but that damned estate manager had a reverse Midas touch alright. It turns out that everything he got me to do has turned to guano. Nightclubs, shops, green energy businesses – all going bust. All the bad business decisions he made me make. Buying fifteen residences, a castle, an Italian coastal villa, a Buddhist temple for Heaven's sake. Now I'm hounded by the tax people because of all his crackpot ideas. The latest thing is a fake ethical tree planting scheme in Malaysia he had the nerve to put my name to. Then there's the overpriced additions to my classic car collection. And ridiculous lawsuits he wanted me to back. And I find he even set up thirty scam banks in my name – just websites selling fake finance products on Facebook, if you can believe that.'

'Incredible.' Frank didn't find it so, but he was wilting at Layne's barrage of complaints.

'You would think.' At this point, the background noise returned loud and clear. Layne stood up and left the screen. Frank could hear him swearing. A door was slammed, then Layne returned even redder in the face. 'You're lucky you don't have my life.'

'We all have our trials. We all fall on evil days. I find it best just to ride on.'

'Ride on? We're not in some trashy Western, you know. In fact, it wouldn't surprise me if you'd sent this upon me somehow. That's it: you're behind it.'

'Why on Earth would I be?'

'You see me as some kind of rival.'

'Rival for what? Come off it, Layne.'

'Well, rest assured you could never get within a million miles of me as a rival. You're dust, Frank, in my eyes at least.'

'You're paranoid.'

'Paranoid? That's what they always say: the sneerers, the haters... Oh, Tania needs me. Bye, Frank. I didn't mean it. None of it.'

30

Lily arranged a Skype call with Gloria to introduce her to Mack. The pair sat next to each other on a new-looking black leather sofa, Lily as cool as ever in pale yellow box jacket, silver trousers, and black ankle boots, as though she were going out to a fashion show, and Mack chewing gum – long red hair, bedraggled, and bare-legged in a short dress. It felt weird to Gloria. It was a little humiliating to see the woman she adored sitting there with her wife who looked almost contemptuous, ostentatiously making no effort to impress at all. And she was the one who was supposedly going to help with her problem?

But Mack would know all about Gloria, perhaps seeing her as a rival and a potential danger, although not a serious one because she held the prize and someone thousands of miles away was never going to deprive her of it. Mack, if she was jealous, could afford to be magnanimous.

Lily, with a slight hauteur Gloria had detected in her voice recently, briefly introduced the subject of Dwayne, which was itself embarrassing to Gloria, and then Mack took over. What struck Gloria from the first word Mack uttered was the Scottish cadence of her voice. It was beautiful. This, coupled with a childlike quality she found in her, soon endeared Gloria towards her.

Mack explained that she worked with a private investigator called Paz Wheat based in Brighton on the English south coast. 'I mainly do the on-line searches. Paz is kinda "old school" and not up with it when it comes to the internet.'

'She's really hot on that stuff,' said Lily.

'She's hot stuff herself,' said Mack, looking at Lily and then straight into Gloria's eyes, grinning self-consciously. Gloria smiled weakly, hoping this kind of embarrassing talk wasn't going to feature in future conversations. But in the discussion that followed, Mack quickly showed she was conscientious and sincere, and Gloria liked her. She felt glad for Lily. The world was a dangerous place, and she liked to think that her friend, who always seemed slightly vulnerable and a bit of a dreamer, had someone so down to earth to protect her. Gloria's biggest fear for Lily had always been that amongst the men she dated she would stumble upon someone who was downright toxic. She gratified herself with the thought that, however much Lily strayed despite her new 'sex addiction' therapy, Mack would take her back, wrapping her arms around her both physically and emotionally.

Gloria told them about Dwayne's blackmail demand. She felt uncomfortable talking about it, as though she'd been stupid, but in the end she told them everything she knew, only pausing for a moment on realising she'd entrusted her worst secrets to a woman she'd never met before; she felt psychologically naked with all her defences down. Mack could destroy her spirit just by casually laughing at her problems, but instead she listened carefully with great attention, nodding now and then, posing a few questions, and at all times respectful. Only when Gloria laughed nervously at what she called her own folly did Mack smile at her revelations.

31

Frank began spending more time with Maria. Or rather, he tried to but found it difficult because she was sedated most of the time, and whenever Dr Mencius arrived she insisted she be alone with him. Frank acquiesced whilst wondering whether he was being made a fool of, as Gloria maintained. He realised he'd been neglectful of his wife. He was at risk of losing her by his indifference. And yet, what was he losing? She was no longer the same person. She had lost interest in seemingly everything and almost everyone. He spoke to Dr Mencius about it: 'Is she improving, doctor?' he asked him.

Mencius was a model of calm as he sat in Franks's office in his beige seersucker suit and pale floral tie. '"Improving" is very subjective,' he replied quietly. There was a long pause while Frank merely waited, determined to extract more from him. Reading the situation, Mencius finally added, 'But I remain confident. Some days, she surprises me in a positive way. Other days, she disappoints. It is a complex condition.'

'But you're confident, you say?'

'Yes. If I were not confident, I could not do my job.'

'Are you busy, Dr Mencius?'

'Always very busy, yes.'

'Many patients?'

'Yes. Many patients.'

'Others living around here?'

'I cannot discuss other patients, owing to confidentiality.'

'Of course. Do any of your other patients have a similar condition to my wife?'

'Again, I could not discuss that.'

'I understand.'

The doctor looked at his watch. 'And now I must be going. Thank you, Mr Salesman.'

As soon as the doctor was gone, Frank went into Maria's darkened room. She was lying on her back in bed with her eyes closed. 'Hello, my dear,' he said. 'How are you feeling today?'

She slowly opened her eyes. 'I'm fine,' she said with the minimum possible effort.

'Do you think you're getting better?'

'I don't know.'

'How do you think you will know?'

'When I feel motivated to do something, which I don't right now.'

'What does Dr Mencius do when he's here?' He went to the window and opened the curtains a few inches.

'Do?'

'Yes.'

'What a strange question. He talks to me, of course.'

'Does he sedate you when he's here?'

'No.'

'Why's he here so long?'

'Hypnotherapy. Why all these questions?'

'So he hypnotises you?'

'Yes. Why all these questions? You never asked me about all this before. Are you worried about something?'

'I was wondering about a second opinion.'

'From another doctor? No. I won't see another doctor. All they'll say is that it's clinical depression, same as he says.'

Frustrated, Frank left. He was quickly bored thinking and talking about her condition. He never got anywhere with her. It was just the same story. He'd rather think about money, specifically short selling opportunities.

He was keen to find cash to invest with Saskia and desperate to get involved with her business. The question he kept asking himself was whether his interest arose because he was committed to the idea of short selling, or was it really all about Saskia herself? He knew what Gloria would say. His brain rocked back and forth on the question, and he couldn't quieten it, until finally he accepted that he was gradually falling in love with the mysterious woman. There was no other way to describe it. He knew it was wrong but feared he lacked the strength to resist. He was aware his feelings for her were hopelessly unrequited but believed it was only a matter of time before they became otherwise. It was dangerous territory and part of him still cared about that, but increasingly he did not.

Out of compulsion he rang Layne to ask if he wanted to participate in an 'exciting new investment opportunity' since he supposedly had millions to spare. As far as Frank was concerned, Layne had a pretty cavalier approach when it came to money, perhaps because he had so much of it. But when he suggested the idea to him, Layne laughed. 'Invest through you?' he said. 'Why would I want to do that? By the way, I must apologise for the way I spoke to you in our last conversation. It was totally uncalled for. You're a good friend and I was in the wrong. It was rather a stressful day as you can imagine, with the protesters and all.'

'That's OK, Layne. No harm done. I thought I'd ask you about this investment because it sounded to me like something super-ethical that might appeal to you.'

'Super-ethical, eh? But are you really sure?'

'One hundred per cent. Otherwise, I wouldn't suggest it. So do you think you could see your way clear to supporting your friend whilst making a chunk of change at the same time?'

'You mean, do it for you?'

'And for yourself, of course.'

'You must be kidding. Frank. I like you, but not enough to give you money to invest. Besides, I have experts who make those decisions for me, although I can't say that's always been the greatest success. I know at least half of them will turn out to be defrauding me.'

'So you can't help? That's a little disappointing.'

'I'm supporting you in spirit, Frank. I just don't want to trust you with my money. Imagine if it went wrong. I wouldn't want you to be embarrassed. You know I can be very ruthless. But I have to be so careful after being let down by others that I trusted. Only today there was a case in point. I've got this highly tasteful eco-hotel development on the west coast, but it can't go through because of the sand lizards. Now the man who wanted me to put the bloody sand lizards there in the first place wants to buy the land off me at a knockdown price. That's a scam if ever there was one.'

'Do you mean the man who was your estate manager?'

'Yes. A conman is what he is and always was. He wanted the sand lizards there in order to devalue my property. I'm sore as I can be about it.'

'I can tell. OK, anyway, have a think about what I proposed.'

'I already have, Frank. But look, Tania tells me she's got an inheritance coming through soon, so maybe she might be interested in playing your funny money game. I'll ask her. Oh, my son Roane's here... Roane, come and say hello to my friend Frank. He's a Yank, but he's alright.'

'Thanks,' said Frank grinning. 'Hi there, Roane!'

'Hello, Frank.'

At that moment, he noticed his daughter walk by his door. 'Gloria, get in here!' She stepped inside. 'Come and say hello to Layne and his son Roane.'

'But, Dad, I'm in a tatty T-shirt and torn shorts.'

'Never mind that. Get over here.' He adjusted the screen slightly to be able to accommodate her.

She obediently stood beside him, tried not to look too closely at the old man filling most of the picture, and instead focused on the slight young man beside him. 'Hi there!' she exclaimed nervously.

'Hello, Gloria,' said Layne.

'Pleased to meet you,' said Roane smiling. She was immediately reminded of the easy arrogance and posh accent she associated with the English upper class from films like *Brideshead Revisited*. He was handsome but at the same time looked a little rough, a little undernourished. She felt embarrassed, but fortunately Roane's phone rang and he left the scene. Gloria did likewise.

'That was nice,' said Frank. 'Good to meet your son.'

'Don't get carried away. He's here for one reason only: money. He needs his old dad to bail him out. And like a mug, he knows I'll do it. He's out of control.'

'Could a good woman not sort him out?'

'Oh, I doubt it. He's met plenty. Well-heeled, too.'

'Really?'

'Oh yes. He's had more than his share of baronesses, duchesses, countesses, and heiresses.'

'Princesses?'

'No. Except for a couple of Scandinavian ones, but they don't count. Probably one of them on the phone right now.'

'What about a good homely girl with a tough exterior?'

'Oh, I don't think so, unfortunately. He'd soon ruin her. He'll go on the same way until he gets fed up with it. He's off the phone now. I'd better go and talk to him, find out how much he wants.'

32

On waking up on the following Saturday morning, Gloria found she'd received a message from Lily:

'Dear Gloria,

Mack apologises but she is fully occupied with work on a fraud case which has become urgent. However, she has looked briefly into Dwayne and found that what he is trying on with you he has tried with other people, using a variety of names. He is therefore a danger. She will revisit it when she can.

All my love,

Lily'

A couple of hours later came a message from the 'danger' Dwayne himself:

'Gloria,

There's no avoiding me. No escaping. You have not been cooperating like we agreed and so must be punished. Where are the pictures you agreed to send? I'm losing patience with you. Time is running out. By the way, I know where your team is playing next and will be there to watch. How will you feel about me following your every movement, willing you to fail? There's still time to save yourself, bitch.'

She felt sick, the energy draining from her. She could not face the game. She even rang the coach to tell him she was injured, but he did not answer his phone. She went to the bathroom and sat there for twenty minutes trying not to cry. Gradually she regained her composure. This turned into resolve. She would not be defeated by this evil person.

With renewed energy, she quickly prepared herself to leave, grabbed a sandwich from the kitchen, shouted goodbye to her father, and bundled her kit into the car. She tried using music to occupy her thoughts – Lana

Del Rey, Alicia Keys – but she kept returning to Dwayne and his threats. By the time she was in the changing room she felt ill again. It was a big game but she wanted to go home. Annalisa asked her if she was OK. In response, she merely nodded.

As she feared, she was not up to it. The Hummingbirds were continually on the attack, mainly on the left side where Gloria's speed did its usual job of terrorising the opposition's defence, but her passes were wayward. Two corners she took were equally wild. She was constantly looking into the crowd, searching for Dwayne, isolating a couple of faces that could be his, then finding others. At half-time she left the pitch dejected, and when the coach approached to speak to her privately, she merely said, 'I know!' She asked to be subbed.

'Are you ill?' he asked. She told him she'd had some upsetting news and it was affecting her game. She was struggling to concentrate. 'Play through it,' he said. 'They're not landing a glove on us, so just keep trying.'

In the dressing room, Annalisa was moaning about lack of service, but rather than agree with her the coach, annoyed, told her she didn't scrap enough. She wanted everything 'on a plate'. It was like the great unsaid now being uttered. Annalisa was furious and she stared hard at Gloria, blaming her with her eyes. Gloria felt it and looked down. As they walked back to the pitch Gloria said to her friend, 'I'm sorry.' Annalisa did not even acknowledge her. And when play started again the same pattern of play ensued with Gloria easily outrunning the defenders but her passes just as erratic as before. She could feel the malign presence amongst the small stadium crowd. Nothing inspired her, especially not Annalisa's admonishments, until she made a terrible mishit and glanced over at the coach who looked to the Heavens and then at his watch. Something clicked with her. She was aware of beginning to tire and was surely about to be subbed. She had the ball once more and, seeing Annalisa waiting expectantly, ignored the script and continued her run into the penalty area. Instead of passing to her, she instinctively tricked her way past three defenders, rounded the goalie and tapped the ball home. It was an incredible piece of play. The coach and staff and players went crazy. The game was effectively won, and to make certain the coach brought on a defender and subbed Annalisa. It was the first time she'd ever been replaced other than due to injury and she could not believe it. She refused to leave the pitch and was booked for time-wasting. When Gloria returned to the dressing room, she found the contents of her sports bag had been tipped out onto the floor. Annalisa had left.

Later that day, Ant posted on Gloria's Facebook: 'Congratulations on a brilliant goal!' Gloria responded with a phone text message, 'Thanks for what you wrote. You OK?' There was no reply.

Annalisa did not appear at training the following week. The coach told the group they would be bringing in a new striker, a twenty-three-year-old called Dessie who could also play in midfield. What he didn't say, because it was obvious, was that Annalisa had been dropped. Gloria called her but Ant did not pick up.

33

She heard nothing further from Dwayne straight away. That was the pattern with him. He would be silent until she thought he'd gone away, and then he'd pounce again. Had he even been at the game, she wondered? But although she'd triumphed in the end that day, she felt she'd lost. She'd been distracted, totally put off her game, and the casualty had been Annalisa and her friendship with her.

But then it came, several days later. One morning, there were pictures of her at the game. There was no doubting it was her or this particular match because she recognised the opposition's kit. Then there were the words:

'Gloria,

Just when you thought it was safe, I'm back to ruin your day and your life. How lucky were you! How were you not subbed at half-time? There's only one possible explanation, and everyone in the team knows what it is. I wonder if Barti's wife knows. Poor wife. Three kids and expecting again. I'm sure she would be delighted to know her husband's making out with a blatantly underperforming player – underperforming on the pitch, that is. You're an entitled little slut. You even threw your best friend under the bus. I'm still waiting for the pictures from you, by the way. Not a bad deal in return for silence about your disgusting behaviour.'

Gloria lay on her bed and tried to quieten her mind. After a while, she went to see her mother. She found her sitting up eating a yogurt with Suzie fussing round her. Maria patted the bedclothes to indicate she wanted Gloria next to her. She seemed remarkably positive. It was a complete change in her.

Suzie left the room and Gloria sat on the bed beside her mother. Maria then said, 'Tell me how it's going. How's soccer? And how's the psychology tuition?'

'Well, we won 1-0. I scored the goal'

'Well done, my dear!'

'I created it from nothing. But, honestly, it was the only decent thing I did.'

'Never mind. You did the one thing that mattered. And next week you'll play brilliantly and not score. That's life.'

'As for the psychology tuition, that's been quiet.'

'OK. So what do you like best in psychology? Put your head on my chest, darling. Like you used to. Only if you want to. Gently.'

Gloria complied with her request and once she was settled Maria began softly playing with her daughter's hair and caressing her neck. Gloria listened to her mother's heartbeat, felt her clammy warmth. 'OK,' said Gloria, 'in answer to your question, I'm especially interested in groups.'

'OK. Like?'

'Like my team is a group.'

'Of course.'

'But there are other less obvious groups. Like people in our street. Like—'

'How about daughters of actresses, is that a group?'

'I guess.'

'OK. And goddesses? You're in a group of lonely goddesses.'

'What?'

'Don't deny it.'

'Mama!'

'Yes, you are. Oh, I rather like this game. Yes, you're in a group of beautiful young women in need of a man.'

'No, I'm not.'

'When was the last time you had a kiss from a man?'

'A while ago. I don't know. So what?'

'You must frighten them, Gloria.'

'Eh? No, I don't.' She laughed. 'How could I?'

'It's true. They don't think they can match up to you. And it's more than that. It's fear of losing you. If they lose an ordinary girl, they say "Oh well, I'll find someone better." But if it's a girl as beautiful as you and they lose you they think, "I let that one slip through my fingers. I could have had her," and they're heartbroken.'

Gloria was tired of the conversation. She raised her head, looked over at Maria's medications on the bedside table and said, 'Do you know what drugs Dr Mencius gives you?'

'Just some old herbal remedies. That's all I know.'

Gloria manoeuvred herself off the bed to inspect the tablet containers. They were not elucidatory. She thought about stealing a few pills and taking them to a pharmacist who could maybe identify them. Perhaps they were merely harmless placebos, in which case she did not want to know, lest she unwittingly break her mother's mood.

With her mother the most upbeat she'd seen her in months, Gloria wondered whether she could be encouraged to take an interest in something – a book or embroidery or artwork. Maria once had a penchant for drawing little cartoons and caricatures. Maybe she could revisit that. Perhaps she could become interested in the world again, even if only that little portion of the world outside her bedroom door. For months her mother's TV had not been switched on, even for light comedies; *especially* for light comedies because they made her feel depressed, reminding her of her lost acting career.

Gloria's musings were interrupted by the sound of Dr Mencius' car on the drive. Maria suddenly withdrew within herself, as though assuming the acting role of the sick woman. Gloria wanted to stay with her for the doctor's visit, to be there for the whole performance, but she knew Mencius would object and now her mother was softly saying, 'You'd better go, my dear.' She was tempted to defy her, but her overriding desire was not to cause her mother distress because she was so fragile. If she wasn't fragile, why was she so submissive towards the doctor? It made Gloria even more sure he had an evil spell over her. Rather than make a fuss, however, she quietly left the room.

Gloria began studying documents on a mental health charity based in Orange County that she was interested in supporting. She'd met representatives and liked what they were doing. Moreover, since her father had become interested in her foundation she'd felt a desire to use more of its money. What was the point of a foundation if it wasn't put to its intended use? People were crying out for help while its assets remained locked away for safekeeping, mainly in gold. Accordingly, she was spending more of her time analysing charity-related documents to help her decide the best use for those assets.

She was disturbed from her deliberations by Dr Mencius. Having completed his regular consultation, he'd been about to leave but changed his mind on noticing Gloria's door open. Fortunately for her, today his cologne was less strong than the last time. He appeared to sense she was uncomfortable at his being there, probably assuming she was stressed. He might surmise that one of her fears would be that she might have a genetic disposition to her mother's mental frailties. He said, 'I thought you might like an update on your mother's condition.' Remaining sitting on her desk chair, she turned her head to face him. 'OK,' she said, curious to hear what he had to say, bearing in mind what she'd learnt on her own visit to Maria just before he arrived. 'Shall we go downstairs to the lounge?'

'Here is fine, thank you. It will only take a minute or two.'

'Is she better, doctor?'

'I would say, slightly better. Her main issue now is severe anxiety as well as her depression, and this is keeping her confined to bed. She is afraid to leave her room.'

Gloria was puzzled because her mother seemed almost normal at times, but then as soon as she heard his car arrive, she would become once more this shrivelled husk of a person. He was keeping her ill for his own selfish ends. 'Tell me, doctor, what is in those pills you give her?'

'They are a sedative for when she needs them, but not when I'm here.'

'Yes, but what's in them?'

'They are a traditional remedy.' Observing the blank look she was giving him, he added, 'Psychology is a vital component in her treatment.'

'That tells me they're worthless placebos.'

For once his usually placid face twitched with annoyance. 'You may call them what you like. You obviously fancy yourself as a doctor.'

She swivelled her chair to face him. Her long naked thighs unnerved him and he blushed. A small victory for her. He immediately rescued himself: 'Everyone fancies themselves as a doctor these days.' A slight condescending chuckle followed. 'But they are not, I assure you, worthless placebos. As I've stressed, psychology is key, and so I am encouraging your mother to gradually take on the outside world. She does not want to, and so it is not straightforward. I understand she goes downstairs for dinner, but infrequently.'

'That's correct.'

'So, you see, it is a gradual process requiring great empathy and sensitivity.' Gloria nodded, even though she thought he was like a tricky old guru, spouting clever-sounding nonsense to people who never challenged a word he uttered. She remained satisfied he was fake, but why did no one else think that?

Then he started on her. 'I'm aware you've had a difficult time of it,' he said in the same cloying tone she'd heard him use with her mother.

'Really? Who told you that?' The fact it was true was not about to become his business.

'Well, your mother said...' He paused, his face showing he was disconcerted by her attitude, a fact that pleased her: another victory and a more lasting one.

'I'm fine,' she said, determined not to give him any excuse to prolong his visit, especially as she suspected he was probably keen to leave to save face.

Mencius mumbled, 'Well, if you ever need anything...' and then shuffled out.

34

Frank was subdued, uncertain about what the future might hold for him, and he was ready to be inspired by his English friend when he next phoned:

'How's it going, Layne?'

'Challenging, I must say. It turns out Tania's a yoga expert so I'm getting in shape. All the twisting is not good for my back, though.' He talked about the aches and pains of old age, but Frank was not interested in hearing about that, and he asked, 'Did you speak to Tania about her inheritance, Layne?'

'Not yet. It will take a while to come through anyway. I don't want her to think I'm only after her money.' He chuckled at the obvious irony.

'Any news on the wedding event business?'

'It takes time, Frank. We take time here. Not like you over there. We have planning laws. Besides, Todd, the new estate manager Tania insisted I bring in, has a new money-making scheme for me to think about.'

'Yeah?'

'He wants to turn the place into a kids' fun palace. Bouncy castles, little trains running round the estate, people dressed in Victorian clothes. It's supposed to educate them and give them the "stately home experience to remember". I said, if they really want an experience to remember they can be here in the winter when it's freezing cold and the heating and plumbing's knackered. No, I'm not enthusiastic. I just think they'll wreck the place. They'll daub stuff on the tapestries, damage the woodwork, draw beards on the family portraits. Then one of the silly herberts will go and drown in the lake and that will be that. Lawsuits. Health and Safety. It doesn't bear thinking about.'

'Oh dear.'

'I tell you, I'd like to pre-empt it if I could. I'd like to fill the lake with every dangerous water creature known to man that will survive in there. With climate change it'll be warm enough for most of them. Piranhas and barracudas and water snakes. Maybe an electric eel. That'll give them some excitement. That'll give them a stately home experience to remember. I'm enjoying this, Frank.'

'I can tell.'

'Maybe a little zoo. But instead of a petting zoo, it'd be a refuge for all the worst behaved animals out there. The criminals.'

'Criminals?'

'You know: llamas spitting in handbags, monkeys stealing jewellery, the tiger that ate the neighbour's poodle. That kind of thing.'

'Cruel, Layne, you're getting vindictive.'

'It's my war on the indifference of humanity, Frank. I've got to get what's due to me.'

'Haven't you got all the riches you want?'

'Not riches, Frank. Respect. I have no respect from anyone – not even you – and that has to change. I want proper respect for all I do for mankind and the climate. I want an airport named after me like—'

'What!?'

'I'm kidding – almost. And I didn't mean it about you. You're the only one that does respect me. Sort of, in your way.'

'What about Tania? Doesn't she respect you?'

'I think she respects my money, but that's alright. I know where I stand.' With that, Layne ended the call, saying he had to prepare to fly to Dubai the next day for a three-hour meeting on 'pioneering green solutions'. Frank realised he could never envy his friend the life he had.

35

Gloria began to worry about Annalisa. She had not heard from her and felt guilty over the rift between them since Ant got upset at being subbed instead of her. This worry was heightened by her father saying, 'What is going on at the club?'

'What do you mean?'

'I heard from Mr Garcia, Annalisa's dad. He's pulling her out of the team. That coach Caprato has really got to him.'

'Surely it's up to her. She's not a child.'

'He's like her manager. You know how he is. He thinks Annalisa's a potential superstar.'

'She's not,' said Gloria in a tone she wished was less catty.

'He thinks that with her stats she could walk into any team. He's had a big row with the club, tried to get the coach removed.'

Gloria felt the need to correct herself: 'She is good, though.'

'It's caused trouble at junior school. Annalisa's sister and the Caprato girl got into a fight. Mrs Garcia has quit working at the Caprato family store. I think that's how Annalisa got in the team in the first place. I want you to keep out of it. Garcia's trying to get players to withdraw from the team.'

'Why would they do that?'

'Exactly. But he thinks he's some kind of big shot in the soccer world. I told him once he should coach his own team. I was joking, but he said, "Yeah, maybe I should," like I'd given him some kind of endorsement. He's a hothead alright. As we've always said, my dear, it's up to you about the team but if you want my advice – though I know you don't – stick with it. Don't let Annalisa dissuade you.'

What she did not reveal to him was that she did not expect to hear from her friend because she blamed Gloria for the latest rumpus. Indeed, Gloria blamed herself over it. The substitution of Annalisa had seemed bizarre at the time. And yet, the fact remained: the human goal machine was lazy. The coach wanted the attack to help out defence when they needed it which was often, and he was right. Nevertheless, she missed her friend, missed having coffee after the game, and missed her playful kicks from the other side of the table.

She also missed her in the next game which was a disaster. The Hummingbirds' defence crumbled and, despite Jamie being able to score twice, mediocre mid-table opposition crushed them 7-2. It was the worst performance of the season and the worst scoreline since anyone could remember. The coach was in tears. He blamed everyone for the loss except Jamie. There would be extra training because of it. Gloria had been ineffective. She was hacked down in the third minute, constantly kicked, and felt intimidated for most of the game. All the coach said to her afterwards was 'Gloria, get your head right before the next game.' Returning home, she drove recklessly, almost collided with a classic Corvette, and received a speeding ticket from an officer who apologised as he issued her with it.

Later that day there were two messages. One was from the mysterious fan: 'Don't worry, you'll be back. You're the greatest!' The other was from Dwayne: 'Ha! Ha! Ha! The coach can't save you now!'

A couple of days later, Gloria phoned Lily who said, 'This is a nice surprise.'

'I'm sorry, I just needed to talk.'

'What's the matter? I mean, I always love to hear from you, but you sound a little stressed.'

'I am. More than a little.'

'That's not like you.'

'I know. Miss Serenity. Well, I'm pretty strung out – for me.'

She told her about the latest with Dwayne and the last two matches and the fallout from them, and her mother and Mencius.

'I wish I could be there for you. Do you want me to come over?'

'Really? To California?' The idea was immediately tantalising to Gloria.

'Sure. I've been thinking about it.'

'No, I'll be alright, but thanks. Any news from Mack?'

'You mean, about Dwayne? Like I mentioned in my message, she's been called away. A drop-everything case.'

'Yeah?' Gloria wanted to believe her, but it sounded like a brush-off.

'Yeah, a murder. A fraud that turned out to be a murder.' OK, so not a brush-off. 'I'll ask her to call you. You don't mind, do you?'

'No, of course not.'

'I wish I could hold you in my arms.'

The thought of it excited her. 'Lily, what are you saying? You're married.'

'Of course, but I can still love you – and Mack in a different way. Sorry, you don't want to talk about this.'

'I do. But maybe not now.' She felt that for the sake of their marriage Lily and Mack needed to spend more time together. If Lily came to California, she could imagine driving to John Wayne Airport to pick her up and finding her with some guy she'd just met on the plane about to go to a hotel together. But that was unkind. She wanted to believe the sex addiction therapy would work for her friend.

'I'm being good,' said Lily as if reading her thoughts. 'For me and Mack... and you.'

Gloria, slightly unnerved, asked her about business. Lily gave her the usual slightly bored answer she was used to. Lily asked her about her charities. Gloria said she'd had to tell one that she couldn't support it anymore until it cleaned up its act, but she was exploring new ones. She then mentioned her dad's interest in the investment short seller. 'Although I'm not convinced it isn't the manager he's most interested in. He clearly has a crush on her. But I think it may end badly. When does it ever work out well?'

'You're right. It doesn't.'

'Unless they have a crush on you, right, Lily?'

'Don't. It's not the way I am, even if you think it is.'

Gloria regretted her comment. 'I know you're not,' she said. 'I don't think the short seller is either.'

'I feel I need to explain myself better,' said Lily. 'I know you don't want to talk about it, but sometimes I feel you don't understand me, even now. I do think we're in the same situation, in a way. I know I'm too easy, and I regret it. You're hard to get, and I sense you regret that. But none of that matters to me because my love for you endures regardless. You're like my guiding star. Well, not "guiding" in the sense I look to you for—'

'Thank God for that!'

'—but that you're always there in my life.'

'But what about Mack? You love her, don't you?'

'Totally. I will never leave her. I offered her a divorce because I... because I'd behaved so badly, but I didn't want her to go through with it. But when I wrote recently that you mean more to me than ever, I meant it. My love for Mack obviously has the physical side in the same way the person you marry one day will. But a love for someone, for you, who I can't even touch, free from the day-to-day superficial stuff - that is a different kind of bliss. And it's real and intense.'

'For me, too.'

'It's more real than anything else to me. There, Glowie, you've gone and opened me up; you've unzipped my heart like you would a favourite handbag or something.' She laughed. 'You see what you do to me? Anyway, I need to get back to Earth now. I'm interested in that investment person you mention.'

'She does seem ultra-professional. And she makes plenty of money from it.'

'Send me the link and I'll look her up. Sounds cool. I'm interested in how short selling can be used for ethical purposes. I guess it's a misunderstood aspect of financial life.'

'Being misunderstood and wealthy? We all have our cross, I guess.'

Lily sounded amused by this. Gloria was glad she'd rung her, reassured her love was reciprocated every bit as much as she'd always wanted to believe it was.

36

While Frank was frustrated with his current life, Layne's was moving incredibly quickly.

On his next Skype call he revealed that he had married his girlfriend Tania. Frank was amazed and concerned, but because his friend was so full of joy he merely said 'Congratulations!'

'Thanks. We thought we'd pop over to the Bahamas because it's so quick over there. Marriage licence the day we arrived. Easy to organise. It was Tania's idea. Of course I knew some narrow-minded creeps would have a gripe about the flights, so I went and bought some NFTs of Amazon rainforest to shut them up. Someone Tania met at the airport arranged it for us.'

'Really? So do you actually own a bit of the forest, then?'

'No. It's an NFT, whatever that is. It's all done online.'

'I see,' said Frank, not seeing at all.

'NFTs are the future, so Tania tells me. I've bought a bunch of modern artworks the same way, too. And a virtual house she wanted.'

'Are you kidding?'

'It's the green revolution – owning things online in the metaverse instead of in the real world. That's what the man we met at the airport said anyway.'

Layne then said he'd asked Tania about her inheritance. 'She's an heiress of a Lebanese business tycoon and it will take a while to sort out the estate.'

'Tycoon? Really?'

'I know what you mean but I'm prepared to believe it. Besides, I feel flattered by the idea that she might want to deceive me. It means she wants to impress me. She must see me as a good catch.'

Frank looked at the heavy, jowly old man before him, older indeed than his years, myopic, developing a slight tendency to drool, and said, 'Yes, I can see that.'

'I know how it works. I'm no fool. I know one day she'll want to put me in a home where everyone else is gaga. She'll have power of attorney and that will be goodbye to my wealth, but will I care? No. At least they'll be able to say "survived by his wife" at the end of my obituary, which will make everyone happy, except my son and daughter, of course.' He started laughing, then he roared. It was a lonely avalanche of laughter, so lonely that Frank felt he should join in. He was able to, although his heart was not in it. He wasn't convinced Layne had done the right thing in marrying this young woman, but his friend seemed so happy that he didn't want to spoil it for him.

Gloria heard the laughter. Mostly it was the awful old man, but she could also detect some of it coming from her father. That was a rarity. She could not recall the last time she'd heard him laugh out loud like that. Naturally, she was curious. When his Skype call was over, she went to see him to ask what the reason was.

'He's got married,' he said.

'Layne? Who would marry him?'

'A nurse who looks like a model.'

'Oh, yes of course. Well, good luck to her. I hope it's a short marriage and she inherits everything.'

'That's cruel, although it's the very thing he was laughing about. He knows it's all about his money but doesn't care.'

'It sounds like they deserve each other. Doesn't he have children to worry about? Won't they expect to inherit? I wouldn't like it if I was his child.'

'Gloria, I never knew you were so mercenary.'

'Mercenary? Is it mercenary to not want your father bamboozled by some gold-digger who's intent on taking all his money and depriving you of your inheritance? I don't think so.'

'By the way, have you spoken to Annalisa?'

'Why are you changing the subject?'

'No, this is important.'

'OK, go on.'

'Her dad's been fired.'

'Oh. Why?'

'I know she's your best friend but—'

'I'll be careful.'

'Embezzlement. Of course he denies it; I only know what the company says. I heard it last night.'

'OK. Of course Mr Garcia wouldn't phone you himself to tell you.'

'No. I'm not that close to him - you're right. He's always been a hot-head. I have nothing against him personally; he's just someone I wouldn't want to know well.'

'Especially now, right? Tarnish the image, what's left of it, is that it?'

'Gloria, please.'

She'd meant it as a joke but realised she'd hurt him. 'I'm sorry,' she said.

37

Gloria was now even more worried about Annalisa. They hadn't spoken since she was dropped, or indeed communicated in any other way apart from Ant's one Facebook post and her own text. Gloria phoned her. She had to reach out to her, make her feel that someone cared. That was arrogant, she recognised, because no doubt lots of people cared.

She did not receive a favourable response, however. Her first call went to voicemail. Her second attempt was answered only when it seemed to be about to go the same way.

'What do you want?' Annalisa said.

'I heard.'

'Heard what?'

'About your dad.'

'What about him?'

Gloria wondered whether her friend was being deliberately obtuse. Could it be that Annalisa didn't even know? 'So is everything alright?' she said.

'With my dad? Yeah. Why wouldn't it be?'

'I just wondered.'

'Yeah, well, don't. My dad's fine. He's being transferred, that's all.'

'OK.'

'Why, what have you heard?'

'Nothing.'

'Why are you even phoning, then? You've got some nerve.'

'I was worried about you.'

'Really? Well, don't be. I can't believe you phoned after what happened. It must be just to gloat.'

'No.'

'The coach was out of line. He phoned to tell me I was dropped. Everyone knows you should have been subbed that day.'

'I'm sorry.'

'Everyone knows there's something going on between you and him.'

'How can you even think that?'

'There can be no other reason.'

'Excuse me. I do work hard.'

'Yeah, to no effect. Your passing was all over the place. And where were you on Saturday? 7-2! What a bunch of losers – literally!'

'At least I try.'

'What's that supposed to mean?'

'I love you, Ant.'

'Don't say that. Don't call me that. My goalscoring record speaks for itself.'

'It doesn't, actually.'

'Why? What do you mean?'

'You know why. You've been told why. You don't scrap. You don't chase lost causes like Jamie and find them again. You don't just... work.'

'Fuck you, Glo. Look what happens when I'm not there. 7-2! I couldn't believe it. Who wasn't scrapping that day? Don't call me again. Calling me to gloat—'

'I wasn't.'

'—supposedly about my dad. Unbelievable, especially with your dad's reputation.'

'What do you mean?'

'He wrecked the company he was running, for his own ends.'

'No, he didn't.'

'It went out of business. Lots of people lost their jobs. And he's sitting pretty. You've got a nice house. Everything you could want. He trashes the company and ends up smelling sweet. Like father, like daughter.'

'Eh? That's horrible. You know what? You're right. I won't phone you again. You're not worth it. Surely you don't believe what you're saying. You can't.'

'Goodbye.'

Gloria's head was in a spin. Her best friend had walked out of her life and ostensibly for good. She now wished she had agreed with Lily about her coming over. She'd done it twice before, although once it had not been the main purpose of her trip. She wanted to phone her again, but with the time difference it was too late.

She went to visit Maria. She found her sleeping. She looked at the new pill bottle beside her and once again was tempted to steal a couple of the contents. There was a label but it was illegible. Part of her thought it best to leave her mother to her own devices, her own choices. But then there was the nagging fear that perhaps they were not her choices. Not informed choices, at least. She fretted over it but finally decided to do nothing for now.

That evening, she watched true crime dramas on TV before going to bed. One concerned a wife who was gradually poisoned over time by her husband using arsenic.

During the night Gloria woke up from a dream in which her mother was being poisoned by an evil nurse. She couldn't return to sleep from thinking about it. Apart from brief periods of lucidity, overall her mother had been getting more drowsy lately, hadn't she? But if Mencius was poisoning her, was it of his own volition or was it for her father? Perhaps he was having an affair and he wanted her out of the way. That would explain why he was soft on Mencius. But what an evil thought that was. She shouldn't have watched those true crime shows. She decided to get up. She would go to her mother's room and look for anything suspicious.

When she opened Maria's door, to her surprise she found her sitting up watching a TV drama in Spanish with the sound down. Maria appeared relaxed but fully alert, which was not what she nor her father had become used to. She did not want to startle her, but the instant she entered the room Maria looked up. 'Can't sleep?' she asked. 'What's up?'

She decided to come straight out with it: 'Are you sure Dr Mencius is doing you any good?'

'Why?'

'Because he seems so weird. Not like a normal doctor.'

'I think I agree with you.' Maria laughed gently. 'No, sometimes I think he's an old fraud.'

'What!? Then why?'

'Your father insists on it. I sometimes wonder if Mencius has something over him. I don't know what to think about it all, so I try not to. Slowly I feel better, but is it because of Mencius, or despite him? He's a good talker at least, and maybe that's the secret.'

Her father insists? Gloria revisited her earlier thoughts: that he had some evil intent with regard to her mother. No, that was incredible. She felt bad for even thinking it.

Gloria returned to her room completely confused. She wasn't able to think clearly, and with no way to work it out she instead imagined Lily already up and going about her day in England, even imagined herself as Lily in her office and on the phone, and eventually she was able to fall back to sleep.

38

The following morning, Annalisa phoned from work. She spoke quickly: 'I'm so sorry, Glo. I'm really sorry I said what I did. I didn't mean it. It was terrible. I was out of order. You're my best friend and you always will be. That's if you're not too angry with me. I had a long chat with the coach. I had to apologise to him because Dad chewed him out. I've got to work on my game. I thought because I was getting all those goals I was doing everything I could. But I wasn't. I'm too selfish. I'll never achieve my dream. But I'm so sorry, Glo. I can't believe what I said to you.'

Gloria was startled at the rush of words but was forbearing, happy to receive her friend's apology and be able to move on. 'It's alright, Ant. Don't worry, I knew it wasn't you; it was the stress of the situation. It's fine, no harm done, darling. So tell me: what is your dream you talk about?'

'I don't know. Play for a big club maybe.'

'Would you put it above your career?'

'I shouldn't, but I probably would. And then there's having a family one day, but I don't know. Anyway, it would be really cool to hang out like we used to. That's if you forgive me.'

Gloria took a quick breath. 'Of course I do.'

They made arrangements to meet up. They rarely went to each other's houses. Gloria found it awkward having friends over because of her mother's isolation and having to explain it, and Annalisa felt the same level of disquiet because her parents were always rowing with each other, and her father was always rowing with other people over the phone and that caused an atmosphere. So they met for breakfast in a small family-run coffee shop overlooking the ocean at Laguna Beach, near where Ant had her temporary job.

'Congratulations on that goal, by the way,' said Annalisa brightly. She looked relaxed in her blue denim jacket and jeans. 'It was a real peach.'

'Thanks. I guess I was proud of it. It seems so long ago now because of the last game – the one you... missed.'

'No. I was dropped,' said Ant firmly, shuffling in her seat as though uncomfortable at having to remind her of the truth.

Gloria did not wish to talk about why she'd been playing poorly before the goal and about Dwayne supposedly being in the crowd, but she could tell Ant was expecting an explanation. And since she'd made the gesture of phoning and apologising it felt mean not to share. 'I'm sorry my passes were off,' she said.

'It's OK. I mean, it was so unlike you.'

'I know. I was distracted. Things on my mind. And I know I shouldn't let it but—'

'Was it a guy? Was it Tommy?'

'No. It was some creep called Dwayne.'

'I know a Dwayne. He was in the crowd at the game. Must be a different one.'

'You're kidding me!'

'Sure he was. My friend Saffron dated him. Surfer boy. He's a lot of fun. So are you dating him now? You're the sly one.'

'No, he's threatening me.'

'No, not Dwayne. He's a darling. He wouldn't do that.'

'Well, the person who's been threatening me was in the crowd and he says his name is Dwayne. Oh, I don't know. Believe me, Ant, I don't want to sound like I'm making excuses, but I'm totally weirded out by this Dwayne.' She held back from mentioning his demand for intimate pictures.

'It's got to be a mistake,' said Annalisa. 'Show me him on Facebook.' Gloria flashed up the photograph on her phone. 'Yeah, that's him,' said Ant. She took a small bite of her scrambled eggs and nopalitos.

'What!? But I didn't see him at the game.'

'You wouldn't because he doesn't look like that now. That's an old picture. How many followers does he have?'

Gloria checked. 'Twelve.'

'You're joking. There's no way that's him. He'd have hundreds. Someone's using his picture.'

'I'm just too confused,' said Gloria. 'Let's talk about something else.'

39

At the next training session, the coach introduced the new player Dessie to the team. She was of Caribbean heritage and had a slight accent which Gloria learned from another team member was Trinidadian. The coach said the new addition would give more depth to the squad. He said they were too much of a counterattacking side. Dessie could play as a forward but was more of a central midfield player. It seemed strange: why was the coach changing the system at this time of the season, when they were still on course to possibly become champions, assuming they recovered from the shock of the last game?

Training was initially chaotic. Dessie had clearly been told the rest of the team would play around her, but others had their own ideas. Gloria realised she was lost without Annalisa, but the coach told her he wanted her to run into the penalty area rather than send passes across from the wing. The new player Dessie was slow compared to herself but, unlike Ant, her hold-up play was brilliant. In a match it was likely she would score less than Ant used to, but make more for others.

Despite the initial confusion, Gloria soon found she could work well with Dessie. They began playing one-twos between them, something Annalisa never did. But Gloria was becoming so paranoid about Dwayne that her mind began wandering, and she started to think her nemesis might even be watching her at training. She told herself there was no one present that could possibly be this mysterious person, and yet how could she be sure? Every time this thought arose, she made an error. That was obviously the purpose of it. Dwayne didn't even need to be there. All he needed to do was be the threat. The thought could arise anytime. When she was driving home on the freeway, for example. So she had to clear her mind for her own safety.

She was awoken from her reverie by the shout of her name. A chance had been missed. She wasn't switched on; she was going through the ritual of playing.

During the break the coach spoke to her privately: 'Do you want me to rest you for Saturday?'

'Why?'

'You're not focused. You got stuff going on?'

'Online stuff,' she said.

'Deal with it, Gloria. I want to rely on you but I can't if you're distracted. I need a big performance from you.'

'I'll be fine.'

'Any doubt, I want you to tell me.'

'Is Annalisa out for good?'

He paused before answering. 'I had a long conversation with her. Look, I know she's your friend, but she has too many issues right now.'

'Issues?'

'I want you to make it work with Dessie. I like what I see, but you've got to give it a hundred per cent.'

She understood what he meant. Annalisa had not given a hundred per cent. Gloria noticed that whenever Ant was mentioned by others it was in the past tense.

Soon after Gloria arrived back from training, Frank was phoned by an excited Layne. He'd woken early and was unable to return to sleep:

'Roane has only gone and won a quarter of a million in Monte Carlo! Is that boy lucky or what?'

'Of course he is: he's got you as a father.'

'Oh, don't give me that old toffee. He's caused me headaches aplenty, as you know. Now he's living in a caravan off-grid. And even a quarter of a million won't pay off his creditors, not that he'd pay them. You've got sons, haven't you?'

'Two. They're away. Independent. But of course I have a daughter to keep me on track.'

'The wonderful Gloria. How is she?'

'She's as lovely as ever. And as earnest. Up since six just like every other day. In the gym room at six fifteen. But I'd rather she got out more to enjoy herself.'

'You liar. I bet you're secretly glad of it. You don't want her head turned yet. A beauty like her; God knows, any real man would be attracted to her.'

'I guess.'

'So is there a handsome young man in her life already?'

'No, and that's what bothers me.'

'So what does Gloria do? Is she running her own business yet, like her dear old papa?'

'She does a bit of private tutoring. Psychology. But mainly she runs her foundation. And she's tough. She can be ruthless if the charities are not run properly. She wants to do good in the world.'

'Oh dear, at such a young age too. Twenty-two, isn't she?'

'That's right. Like I said, earnest. And kind. She's always been like it. If it wasn't food baskets for the poor, it was selling "gently used" clothes. Beach cleanups or Goodwill dump days – you name it.'

'So she's making up for her dad, I take it, eh? Bit of a tall order. Takes more than a few pairs of "gently used" knickers to make up for a corporate collapse like that.'

'Woo, Layne, take it easy.' He had not expected the old man to touch on such an awkward subject as his company's failure, and it made him instinctively defensive. 'I've always had good intent, though, as you know. The business grew too quickly, but by the same token we saved a ton of little companies from going under. Until it all fell apart, of course. I'll say that before you do. But I like to think that overall I was a benign influence on the business world.'

'I can hear the violins playing already, Frankie boy. You'll get your sainthood. I'll put in a word, don't worry.'

'I had a can-do approach. Nothing wrong with that.'

'Indeed.'

'You have to make things happen. That's the American way. You British always have a hundred reasons why something can't be done.'

'That may be true. But sometimes those reasons are right, Frank... Oh, I think I hear Tania stirring. Speak to you later.'

40

One of the Hummingbirds' team members had a birthday and Gloria was invited to the party which was just a few streets from her house. She was disappointed Annalisa was not there. It felt like she was history as regards the team. It was as though the dispute between her father and the coach had been decided by everyone else as being the Garcias' fault. Indeed, Ant was suddenly a threat to the cohesion of the squad and now firmly an outsider. There was an air of 'I never liked her anyway' whenever her name was mentioned and it upset Gloria. Her efforts to defend Ant sounded hollow and she knew it. She gave up trying and concentrated on having a good time. This was made easier by the surprise arrival of Tommy at the party. She'd wondered if he would show but it was late so she'd assumed he wouldn't. Everyone knew they had a crush on each other.

She was standing slightly apart from the rest of her group at that moment, and Tommy, after saying hello to everyone, came over to join her. 'Can I get you another drink?' he asked.They went into the kitchen and he got himself a beer while she had a spritzer. 'I really like that dress, by the way. It's beautiful.'

'Why, thank you.' It was a long white plunge dress with little red flowers embroidered on the neckline and down the middle to the hem.

'It's kinda Mexican. Did you buy it down there?'

'My mom got it me for my birthday. You look pretty cool yourself, by the way.' He was in a pale green jacket with a white polo shirt and grey Levi's.

'Thanks.'

'What do you do?' she said. 'For a living, I mean?'

'I sell cars. Classic cars to high rollers in L.A.' She asked him about what types of cars and who the buyers typically were and was amused by his answers. After a bit, he said, 'Someone told me you teach psychology, is that right? If so, I guess I'd better watch out.'

She laughed. 'You don't need to worry. It's social psychology I tutor. It's all about theories not facts. It's not all "this means x and that means y" but "it might be this or it might be that". But there are certain things that really strike me as true.'

'Like?'

'Oh, no, not now,' she said firmly. 'I can be very boring about my favourite theories.'

'Let's go outside,' he said. He'd finished his beer and she'd had enough of her spritzer. 'It's a little warm in here, and it's lovely and cool out there.'

They slipped out, though not unnoticed. The scents of the garden flowers and the breeze relaxed her. He held her hand and they walked for a few minutes, stopping to listen to a barn owl, then he put his arm to her back, swung her towards him and gently kissed her on the mouth. 'You're a little tense,' he said, although she didn't feel tense.

'I'm sorry. It's not because of you.'

He now held her tight and kissed her hard on the lips. She was caught by surprise and it seemed in that moment that all her worries, all her inhibitions had gone. 'You're not tense anymore,' he observed.

'Let's go in,' she said after several moments of silence. It was a long time since she'd been kissed, and it felt good, although she suspected it didn't mean anything to him and pretended to herself it meant nothing to her either. She reminded herself that Tommy was unreliable; he had a reputation for playing around; he had already been out with several in the loose group surrounding the team, and it had been only a matter of time before he would try it on with her. And after her it would be someone else, maybe even that very night.

She held his hand as they walked back into the house, but then they split to be with their respective friends. No one said anything to her about going outside with Tommy or hinted at anything. It was as though it was the most natural of things. And it was.

She left the party early. She was not one for staying out late. Besides, her time with Tommy had been so perfect she wanted to draw the evening to a close in order to keep it that way. She knew that stories would emerge of him having sex in the back of his car with one or more of the other girls there, but that didn't bother her. She was going to win his heart. He would take her to the beach one night where they would make love and he would confirm what she knew already: that she was the special one he'd been waiting for all along. On the other hand, she tried to assure herself, she didn't really care.

41

A couple of days later, in her father's office, Gloria learned that he had his own ideas for her immediate future – and they did not include Tommy.

'How would you like to go to England? I'll pay for your trip, of course.'

She was suspicious. 'What's this about, suddenly?'

'Just an idea, a holiday for you.'

'Hmm. It would be nice to see Lily again and meet her friend Mack.'

'Lily? Oh, don't mention her.'

'You know you've always had a sneaky admiration for her.'

'She only ruined my company. Nothing serious.'

'No, she didn't. She merely asked for an apology because of something in her smoothie—'

'I assure you, I do not need reminding.'

'Your company was too dumb to give it. Then everyone else piled in, and it all got out of control. Public relations disaster.'

'You're right, my dear. It's just too painful to think about.'

It was obvious that it wasn't Lily that Frank had in mind for her to visit. She said, 'Is this about Layne, by any chance?'

'Well—'

'I might have guessed.'

'You've met his son, Roane. A very good son—'

'Dad! Are you serious?'

'Why not? He's a bit of a firebrand but... he's got spirit, that's all. Layne thinks that he needs calming down. Maybe someone like you could settle him.'

'Did Layne actually say that?'

'No.'

'That's a relief at least. If he had, I'd be pretty sure he was joking. He is very weird, though, so I don't know. But I see what this is about. You want Layne's money so you can invest it with your floozie.'

'My what? How dare you! All I'm suggesting is that you go to England on an initial visit to meet them. It would broaden your horizons. You could promote your charities. You never know, Layne might want to support them.'

'Initial visit? Meet the son? No way! I would like to go to England but not for that reason. What you're suggesting is so medieval. What next – an arranged marriage?'

'I think you're grossly overreacting.'

She walked out.

An angry Gloria immediately went to her room to try to find Roane online but had barely begun when Tommy showed up at the house. Seeing his car arrive, her mood quickly became frantic excitement which she immediately needed to somehow replace with calm. She stopped at the top of the stairs to take a few deep breaths, a pause with the added benefit of forcing him to ring a second time.

Standing at the front door, he looked so handsome, so full of confidence and with the promise of the outdoors. He said he'd called round to take her out for a drive. She felt silly, like a young girl with her first crush. It wasn't just his rugged looks and bright blue eyes, it was his gentle, considerate manner that made him, as she saw it, the guy all the girls wanted. He was trouble, too, and that was part of the excitement.

He didn't come inside the house. They left straight away.

They decided to try out a new ice cream shop at Capistrano Beach, where they talked about not very much, except Tommy said it was a spot where he liked to go surfing. Gloria was still nervous, and he sensed it and tried to calm her. 'Your soccer team's quite a wild crowd,' he said. She might have a crush but she wasn't naive. She wondered who he'd ended up making out with at the party. At least no rumours about it had reached her.

'Shame you had to leave so early,' he said.

'I was a bit tired. It's been hectic. It maybe makes me a bit boring but I—'

'Not at all.' He meant it. He wasn't going to have her in the back of his car, and he knew it. And that made her more of a prize.

He started a conversation about their favourite cars which she enjoyed, then he asked her about her work running the charitable foundation. He seemed genuinely interested. He was a good listener which, in her experience, was rare in a young man. Of course he had to be a salesman – it could be luxury cars, it could be luxury houses; but above all, it was himself. Everything about him exuded the air of someone happy in himself, ready for any challenge, be it breaking down the hesitation of a man who can't afford the Lamborghini he wants, or the girl who says no to him but is tempted. He was a danger to wealth and mental health, and Gloria was thrilled.

But after they'd had their ice creams and walked on the beach for a while and gone to a bar for a drink, he said he needed to get back to work. He brought her straight home and said he'd call round again soon.

If there was anything wrong his leaving kiss didn't reveal it, but she wondered whether he was disappointed in her, that perhaps she wasn't easy enough for him. Even though in her heart she wanted him, maybe he detected a resistance that he was reluctant to break down just yet. She decided it was going well, though. She was keeping something back and he would have to work to get it and they'd both want him to succeed.

In the house she found panic. Frank told her in an admonishing tone, as though she were not allowed to come and go when she wanted, that her mother had passed out and hurt herself. A doctor had been called. It wasn't Mencius, thank goodness. It was, Gloria felt reassured, a real doctor. Perhaps at last the despicable charlatan would be exposed. Despite feeling nervous when she'd left the house, her mere presence now seemed to calm everything and everyone.

She went to her mother's room full of hope, but although she'd seen the arrival of a 'real' doctor as a positive, this did not make him likeable. In fact, she found him distant and arrogant. Tall and unhealthily pale in his late forties, though probably younger than he looked, with a thin moustache and a distinct smell reminiscent of stale milk about him, he was the opposite of the energetic, debonair, tanned skin hero she'd hoped for and even expected. Her mother, who appeared uninjured, was lying on her back on the bed. The doctor, who looked ready to leave, acknowledged Gloria without a word. He was standing on one side of the bed, and she took up position on the other side of it, directly opposite him. She picked up her mother's hand which felt hot. Maria did not react. Gloria immediately felt the doctor resented her presence; he'd finished his consultation with her mother and saw Gloria as an obstacle in the way of his departure. He said little in his hurried response to her questions. All she got from the conversation was that he dismissed Mencius' pills as 'junk' and that low blood pressure had led to Maria's fall. She gained the impression that he thought her mother a time-waster, and he clearly wanted to extricate himself from the scene as quickly as possible. His own relief at leaving was more than matched by that felt by both women.

42

One morning, Gloria received a call she hadn't anticipated.

'Is that Gloria?' It was a British accent.

'Yeah. Who is this?' As she said it, she realised she recognised the voice.

'It's Mack.'

Gloria felt unnerved by this direct approach. It seemed illicit.

'I'm in Berlin. Is it OK to talk?'

'Sure. Is everything alright?' Gloria meant about Lily. 'Or do you have news for me?' She couldn't help feeling uncomfortable but wondered whether this was Mack's intention.

'I'm reporting back on Dwayne.' The way she said the name indicated she thought him fake.

'Oh, good.'

'It hasn't been easy.'

'I'm not surprised.'

'I am. Usually I can find things out pretty easily. Not this time. And I'm sorry about the delay. And I'm sorry you had to ring Lily. Not that I mind, of course.'

'Right.'

'Just so busy on a case.'

'Yeah.'

'So, anyway, do you know a woman called Carmina Rodriguez?'

'No. Is she somehow connected with Dwayne?'

'Sure is.'

'Then, how?'

'She is Dwayne.'

'You're telling me Dwayne is a woman? The surfer boy?'

'It happens. I see everything doing this work.'

'Of course. I know you do. Any clues?'

'Clues?'

'Yeah, you know, connections. I mean, how is this person connected to me? Why are they harassing me?'

'I've no idea. You asked me to find out who Dwayne is and I've told you.'

'To me it's just a name. I have no idea who this Carmina is.'

'Want me to find out?'

'I thought... Yes, please.'

'You thought I would anyway? Well, I have a job to do for which I get paid.' Mack was clearly a little annoyed and Gloria felt it was her fault.

'I'm sorry. I'll pay you.'

'I don't want your money, Gloria.'

'Help me, Mack, please.' She was taken aback by her own sudden desperation.

'Of course I will. By the way, what's with Vanessa?'

'What do you mean?'

'Do you go by the name Vanessa?'

'No, of course not. Why would I do that?'

'Because you have another persona called Vanessa. I take it she isn't your twin.'

'No.'

'Well, Vanessa is more active on social media than you are.'

'You're kidding.'

'I'm surprised you didn't know.'

'You're right, but I guess I didn't want to know. I didn't want to think about it. No, actually, I didn't believe it. I thought it was just some mistake. A mean joke.'

'It might be a mean joke, but it's also more than that. You could be in danger.' That she was so matter of fact saying this made it worse, though Gloria wondered if this was for effect. Mack appeared to realise this and softened: 'There's a guy in Texas who's fallen in love with you – or rather, Vanessa.'

'Oh no. I guess it's not always good to have someone fall in love with you.'

'You're not wrong. He thinks he's been deceived. Someone's told him his Vanessa's not real, that Vanessa is really someone else, someone in Orange County, California.'

'Thank God.'

'No, not thank God. He's very angry. Vanessa has been leading him on, telling him he's the one for her. He isn't. He's a loner who's into militaria. You know, old weapons and stuff.'

'Fuck!'

'You said it. "Fuck" is indeed the best word for it.'

'How do you know he's angry?'

'People have been making fun of him on Facebook, and he clearly doesn't like it.'

Gloria couldn't believe this latest nightmare had descended upon her. Why were the Fates so cruel? 'Is Vanessa the same as Dwayne?'

'I don't know.'

'Mack, please help me. Please do what you can.'

There was a pause. 'You know I will. Any friend of Lily is a friend of mine. At least, that's what I like to think.' A slight chuckle. 'But you're more than a friend to her, I know. That's alright, I'm not jealous.'

Although disconcerting, this was also reassuring.

'By the way,' said Mack, 'I'm sorry I was short with you. You're a sweetheart. Well, anyway, I'd better go now.'

'Nothing you said is a problem. I'm sorry I reacted how I did.' Gloria wanted her to stay on the line. 'Is it a difficult case you're on?'

'Yeah, but it's nearly over. I'll have more time soon. The situation with that guy in Texas bothers me. I think you need someone over there to help you. To go visit this guy or something.'

'Hmm.'

'Tell you what: my boss Paz Wheat is going over there on a case. Maybe he can set something up.'

'OK.'

'Actually, it's more important you speak to the cops about it as soon as you can. They need to talk to the guy.'

'Thanks, Mack.'

'No worries. Just talk to the police as soon as you can.'

'I will.'

'And remember: anything you need, I'm here for you. Anything.'

After the call, Gloria lay on her bed, trying to make sense of everything. She spent time thinking it through, then changed the subject, then returned to her problems. She felt incredibly vulnerable, completely dependent on others. She did not like that feeling. She had someone called Carmina she'd never heard of saying poisonous things about her in the guise of Dwayne, and then she had some freak in Texas angry with her because he thought he was in love with her as Vanessa. She'd had a row with Annalisa which had been resolved, but their relationship was not as it was before and maybe never could be again. Then there was the whole issue of Dr Mencius, as well as the fact her new boyfriend Tommy seemed unsure about her. And on top of everything, her father wanted to send her to England to meet some dreadful aristocrat's son. What a mess it all was! On the other hand, if this Roane was even vaguely acceptable, being over there could protect her from Carmina and the whacko in Waco, or wherever else in Texas he was based.

She wished she'd had the chance to talk to Mack more, but it was clear she either didn't want to or couldn't afford the time. She would have liked to have found out more about her, to hear about the case she'd been working on, and above all to bathe in the luxuriance of her voice as she talked about Lily.

She went to see her father. He was on the phone in what sounded like a difficult conversation. He was trying to encourage someone to put up money to invest with Saskia, and it was not going well. He was so starry-eyed about the short seller that he could not understand others' reluctance to share his enthusiasm. The person he was talking to was clearly keen to get off the phone as quickly as possible. At least Frank was self-aware enough to realise he was getting nowhere. He was conceding defeat with good grace, seeing no reason to lose a friendship over it, although Gloria suspected that very thing had just happened. He put the phone down.

'Ah, Gloria, come to talk money? Had a rethink? What can you do for me?'

Her dad was obviously still in a haze. This was how it was: either she moved money from her foundation, which she would never do even if she could, or she gave herself up to his crazy plan of going to England as a mail-order girlfriend for a rich man's son. But at least the 'buyer' wouldn't be insisting she be a virgin, although if he did it would be easier to put him off.

'No, Dad, I haven't changed my mind. I have something more important to talk to you about. Someone is threatening—'

'Not now, my dear. As you know, I've got to make these calls. This is a major initiative that will help—'

'But I need—'

'OK. In a sentence tell me what you need.'

'If all I'm worth's a sentence, I won't bother.' She left his office.

'No, that's not what I mean. You know— Gloria, come back here!'

She ran to her room. She was determined not to cry.

43

She rang Tommy but he did not sound enthusiastic to talk to her. They had a non-committal, hesitant kind of conversation until finally he said, 'Are you really dating the team coach?'

'No! Why?'

'It's what I hear.'

'Where do you hear it?'

'All around. I don't date girls who two time.'

'I'm not like that. Believe me, I'm not.'

But what a hypocrite he was! He had quite a reputation himself for 'unreliability'. And why would he care anyway, if he liked her?

'Can I see you?' she asked.

'Sure.'

But when it came to making arrangements he was vague. She got the message: she was getting the brush-off. Or at least, she suspected that was what he wanted her to think. But she knew it wasn't as simple as that. Even if she really had been sleeping with the coach, she'd still be a good catch.

'It's OK,' she said. 'I didn't call for a date. I just wanted to talk to somebody I thought I could trust. Someone I could open up to. It doesn't matter.'

'Don't go.'

'It really doesn't matter.' She rang off.

The call did the trick. After lunch, Tommy's red Accura Integra appeared on the drive. Gloria saw it arrive but retreated from her window. She had to give the impression of surprise. It was just a shame a car that looked like Barti Caprato's wasn't already parked out there to make him jealous.

Naturally, she delayed going to the front door. She changed her mind and decided to appear not surprised. 'You made it, then,' she said. This appeared to take him aback a little. 'Let's go to my room.' Yet she wasn't entirely sure why he was visiting; maybe he'd decided to tell her in person that he didn't want to see her again.

Once they were in her room she made a point of leaving her door ajar. After the initial hug, he removed his vintage buckskin jacket that she thought looked a little odd on him although endearing. She offered him a drink but he declined. He sat on the bed while she sat on her desk chair facing him.

'What's been going on?' he said.

'What do you mean?'

'Are you my girl or not?' The way he said this amused her, though she tried to keep it from her face and did not reply. 'I mean, all these rumours. I have to know where I stand.' This was an odd turnabout, she thought. 'I don't want to waste my time,' he pressed.

'Sure you don't. What rumours exactly?'

'Like I said on the phone, about you going out with the team coach.'

'I haven't. I wouldn't. But what if I had? Would you not still want me?'

She stood up, and he slowly rose to his feet. They hugged, awkwardly at first, but he held her tight, and it felt good to be held by him. She slowly withdrew and they sat back down.

'It's all a malicious campaign,' she said.

'Who by?'

'I'll explain. I have a friend in England who has a friend called Mack who does internet searches and stuff for a PI. Mack is helping me. The other day, we had a call, and she told me what she'd discovered. Tommy, it's scary.'

'I see,' he said, a little confused but looking and sounding genuinely concerned.

She then told him the gist of the call she'd had with Mack and mentioned Carmina by name. 'Do you know her, by any chance?' she asked.

'No. And this guy in Texas – Gloria, how could it happen to you? I never wanted to believe... never seriously believed you were having an affair with the coach though it was what I was hearing. But this guy in Texas... It sounds so totally weird.' He shook his head and she wondered whether she'd told him too much.

'I'm a simple girl, really,' she said.

That didn't help. He frowned. 'You certainly don't sound like it.' But he knew he had to stand by her, even though he realised whatever he said to comfort her would probably sound wooden.

Next moment, her father entered the room. 'Oh sorry, I didn't realise,' he said. Of course he did; he was curious to know who her visitor was. She introduced them. Tommy stood up and clumsily took Frank's proffered hand. Tommy blushed which she found divine; she blushed too. Her father said, 'Er, when you've got a minute later, I need to show you something.'

'OK,' she replied nonchalantly.

After her father had gone they laughed, although quietly in case he heard. They both sensed these shared moments drawing them closer. Tommy would be protective; he would stick with her during this difficult time, even if their relationship faded after that.

'Have you talked to your father about this Vanessa business?' he asked.

'Haven't had the chance. He just brushed me aside. He's obsessed with this short seller investor he wants to support.'

He raised his eyebrows.

'I know,' she said, sighing. 'I'm too much of a mess, aren't I?'

'Not to me.'

'Well, that's something, I guess.'

'Seriously, Gloria, you need help. This guy in Texas... you've got to find him.'

'At least before he finds me.'

'So who is he?'

'I don't know.'

'Didn't you ask this Mack?'

'I was just so shocked.'

'If she was really helping you, she'd have told you by now. You could always get someone else to find this guy.'

'You're right.'

'You really need to do something.'

At that moment her phone rang. By coincidence, it was Mack.

'This is a lovely surprise,' said Gloria, who mouthed the caller's name for Tommy's benefit. He guessed this would not be a short interlude, so took the opportunity to visit the bathroom.

'I'm sending you the stuff on the man in love with Vanessa,' said Mack in a hurried tone, as though she were in a hotel lobby.

'What's his name?'

'Arnett... Tommy Arnett.'

'No, that can't be.'

'Why?'

'I can't say right now. You said Texas – are you absolutely sure about that?'

'I can make mistakes but—'

'What time is it there, by the way? In Germany, I mean?'

'About eleven.'

'Oh.'

'It doesn't matter. Sleep is hard so I'll be up for a while. Besides, Lily was adamant: I had to help you above everything. Even work, now that case is nearly over. When she's adamant I obey.' She laughed and Gloria tried to join in.

After the call, Gloria said, 'Well, that was weird.'

'Why?' Tommy said with a hint of nervousness.

'It was Mack phoning from Germany. She said the man in Texas in love with Vanessa is you.'

'Eh?'

'I assume you're not.'

'How could it be me? Who is this person Mack? She's messing with you.'

'No, she's not. She's the wife of my best friend.'

'She must be nutso.'

'No way. It's you who's messing with me.'

'You're crazy.'

'Do you know this Carmina woman?'

'What?'

'Look, this is all too much. I think you'd better go.' She hadn't meant to say that and immediately wished she hadn't.

'You're right there. You're out of your mind. Like mother, like daughter.'

'What!'

'Everyone knows your mother's a bit—'

'No, that's— You shouldn't—'

'Don't worry, I'm going.'

She sat down on the bed heavily as he grabbed his jacket. As he was rushing out, she asked, 'Will you call me?'

'I don't think so.'

She heard the front door close behind him and merely listened as he started the car and drove off. But then he stopped. Was he coming back? Had he had second thoughts? Was he going to apologise? She hurried to the window. A woman was standing on the drive shouting at him.

Gloria ran downstairs. As soon as she was out through the front door, Tommy's car pulled away. A short, middle-aged Hispanic woman in a beige coat and yellow dress was standing shaking her fist at the retreating car. But who was this person? Not someone she recognised.

'Can I help you?' said Gloria.

'That man nearly hit me. What's his name?'

'I'm not telling you. He didn't hit you anyway. Who are you and what do you want?'

'I've come to see Mr Salesman.'

'And what do you want with him? I'm his daughter.'

'Are you? I see. Well, it's not for your ears.'

'And who are you?'

'Never you mind.'

'Wait here,' Gloria insisted as they stood by the front door. She went inside and ran up to see Frank. He was not in his office. She looked in on her mother but she was alone, drowsing despite the ruckus. Gloria stood at the top of the stairs and called out to her father. No answer.

She glanced from the window. Yes, his car was still there. Finally, she found him in the lounge; he was lying on his back on the sofa with headphones to his ears. He was relaxing. He looked happy, beatific even. It pleased her to see him like this: at peace for once. His eyes were closed. Perhaps he was even asleep. She was not going to disturb him, certainly not for someone so rude.

She went back outside to the woman. Gloria told her Mr Salesman was asleep and could not be disturbed. Could she leave a message? The woman continued shouting: 'I've come all this way and I'm not going until I've seen him.'

'Is everything alright?' called a voice from above.

Gloria looked up. Her mother was at the window. Seeing her, the visitor launched into an abusive rant in Spanish. Gloria now realised who it was: señora Mencius. This revelation made her pause; she felt almost sympathy. The woman scuttled through the front door and was already heading for the stairs. Gloria, caught off guard, raced in pursuit. She grabbed the woman's coat, causing its wearer to turn abruptly, missing the step. She cursed, but Gloria would not release the coat and was trying to grab the woman's arms. Then the furious visitor lashed out with her heel in desperation. Gloria felt it sharp on her thigh, causing her to slip; she bashed her knee on the stair's edge and twisted her ankle.

'What's all this shouting!?' It was Maria at the top of the stairs in her dressing gown. The woman started bellowing, in English this time, but Gloria now had her arms around her legs, ignoring the woman's kicks and curses.

At this point she heard her father's voice, 'What the absolute fuck is going on!?' But he immediately understood the situation, or something like it at least. 'Please leave or I will call the police.'

'My marriage is broken and it's that woman's fault.' She pointed in Maria's direction. Before she could continue ranting, Frank ordered the woman to quieten down. The visitor was momentarily becalmed.

Gloria sighed as she contemplated the last few minutes. It was a bittersweet moment. She'd been proven right about Dr Mencius but lost her boyfriend; Tommy would surely never be back again.

After a few moments of silence, Maria announced she did not want the police called.

'Afraid of the publicity, bitch?' snarled the woman. Gloria was tempted to slap her face but stopped herself.

Señora Mencius revealed that what she was so angry about was her husband's theft of her potion for depression which he'd used to treat Maria. He was wrongly claiming it was his. To Gloria it seemed a lot of fuss about not very much. 'So what?' she said.

'It's not his,' she insisted. 'He stole it.'

Gloria thought the woman completely mad but did not interrupt her. It appeared she was estranged from Mencius and thought he was going to market her potion as his own once they'd divorced, thus depriving her of her business.

Gloria decided to assist the distressed woman, less from any real concern for her well-being than to find out more about her husband. Neither of her parents wanted to have anything to do with the unwelcome visitor, so Gloria said she would take care of her. The others retreated to their rooms. Although señora Mencius was deeply suspicious of her, Gloria, limping, managed to entice her into the lounge. Gloria made clear she merely wanted to hear her story. The woman's hostility gradually faded, thanks to coffee and painkillers.

'You're not your mother,' said señora Mencius.

'I'm my own person,' said Gloria.

The woman brightened a little. 'I can see that. Just like me.'

Gloria knew she was in a tricky game but understood how to play it. Although she despised Dr Mencius, if she criticised him too heavily his estranged wife would defend him. So, instead, she asked the woman about herself. Señora Mencius said she was a herbalist dedicated to 'health remedies'. She had her own shop and made her own tinctures and potions. She stressed this was not some passing fad as she'd always been interested in the subject. Gloria wondered why she'd never heard of her before and, as if reading her mind, the woman said, 'You probably won't know of my shop.' She explained that she used her maiden name Tiresata and then Gloria remembered she'd seen the shopfront. 'And was Dr Mencius once involved with the business?'

The woman seemed delighted by the question and she gave a hearty laugh. 'That lazy bastard never did jack shit!' she said triumphantly.

'Does he have many patients?'

'I don't know what he does. He was a salesman for the business and he got carried away with it. We've only been married four years. And separated two months. Then I learned he's been pretending that one of my potions was made by him.'

Gloria was still unconvinced this wasn't firmly within her 'So what?' category of human activities, but played along with it. Then the point arrived at which she suddenly decided she'd had enough of this self-pitying woman who didn't deserve her time, whilst her mother did.

'So what has this got to do with Mama?' she asked sharply.

'She put him up to it.' The woman looked at Gloria as though she were an ignorant child. 'The business, of course. He's set up his own business using my stuff. She encouraged him with it.'

'How do you know that?'

The woman became impatient. It was clear she now had the same intent as Gloria in getting through the conversation as quickly as possible so she could leave. 'Because she gave him money to help him do it.'

'What do you mean?'

'You heard what I said.'

'How much?'

'Ask her. She set him up in business. It would have cost him over a hundred thousand, I shouldn't wonder.'

'What!? But why didn't you just divorce him to be free to pursue your own business in competition?'

'He'd kill me if I did that.'

Was that a joke, Gloria wondered? She said, 'Will you tell this to my father?'

'Sure.'

'Wait while I get him.'

In pain, she struggled up the stairs. Frank was on the phone to someone he was trying to get money out of. 'Not now, Gloria.'

'Dad, please—'

'Give me five minutes.'

'This is important.'

'So is this.' Dejected, she left his room. She checked in on her mother. She was lying on her bed dozing. As Gloria left her room, she said out loud: 'Am I the only one who gives a damn about what just happened?' She hurried awkwardly downstairs. As she'd feared, the woman had slipped out. She went to the front door in case she'd just left. There was no sign.

On re-entering the house, she saw Suzie who looked flustered and confused. She said, 'I saw señora Mencius. She was leaving as I came in. What was she doing here?'

Gloria wasn't in the mood to talk about it. 'Just some misunderstanding,' she said.

'Misunderstanding? That would be right. That old witch: I wouldn't believe a word she says.' Clearly this was a favourite subject of hers: señora Mencius' lack of credibility. 'She lives in her own world, that one. I don't know why the doctor put up with her for so long.'

'Tell me, are they really separated?'

'She said so? Well, that much is true. But I wouldn't believe anything else she said.'

'She said she runs a herbal remedy shop. Is that true?'

'Yes, I believe so.'

'OK, so it's everything else I shouldn't believe? I'll bear that in mind.' Tired of what she saw as Suzie's nonsense, she made her careful way back upstairs. Her dad was still on the phone, her mother still dozing. She really was the only one who cared. She hated that feeling because it was followed by self-righteousness, something she despised so much in others but most particularly in herself.

Gloria was sure Tommy had gone from her life. He thought her unhinged, and who could blame him? Anyone else would think the same. But she was not giving up on him quite so easily. If only for her own mental wellbeing, she texted him: 'Sorry about earlier. Crazy day. Great to see you.'

She had thought more about the possibility of escaping to England as her father wished. She found herself growing increasingly relaxed about the idea for she needed respite from the madness that her life had become. Maybe she could stay with Lily. No, that wouldn't work. She was a married woman and Mack was unlikely to be relaxed about it. It would mean more problems, more feelings of isolation.

Who was this loser Roane anyway? She could not believe that Layne could have sired a son that was anything but a waster. But life and people could be full of surprises. She had learnt to be wary of making assumptions. She looked for him online. He didn't have much of a presence on social media. An old Facebook account he hadn't done anything on in years. There was a newspaper account of him being arrested on drug offences though never charged. It didn't make him sound a very attractive proposition. He was twenty-eight years old. She recalled meeting him for a few moments on Skype. He'd looked so confident and that voice so incredibly English upper class. In the photographs he looked bohemian, romantic even, and she could see how impressionable young women (unlike her, naturally) could become hooked on him, wilfully ignoring the obvious and thinking they saw someone they could change for the good. It was a fool's errand. She knew well enough that people like him were set in their ways. They could perhaps be encouraged to change but only if they were fully open to it. She stopped. Why was she even thinking like this? There was no possible way she was going to have anything to do with this man.

Later she was able to catch her father the moment he was putting his phone down. She was determined to have a conversation with him about señora Mencius. 'That woman's completely mad,' he said. 'No wonder they're estranged. Poor Dr Mencius having to live with that. I can't blame him for walking out.'

'I kinda feel sorry for her. Maybe I shouldn't.'

'Indeed, you certainly should not. God preserve us from such crazy people.'

'Doesn't it make you wonder about his professionalism?'

'I don't see why. Your mother is quite happy with him. And I see no evidence of anything untoward.'

'Doesn't it strike you as odd that he doesn't even have a website?'

He paused for a moment, puzzled by the question, then said, 'Not at all. Not everyone does. Why should he? He has no need for publicity. He has all the clients he needs and has no desire for more.'

'I see. So is my mother going to permanently be his patient? What sort of treatment is that? Obviously one that doesn't work so he has to keep coming back. And what about the money that señora Mencius claims Mama gave him?'

'Firstly, your mother wouldn't dream of doing that. Second, she'd have spoken to me first.'

Gloria was miffed: 'Don't they say there's none so blind—'

'Stop it. Not in this house, they don't. I know your views on the subject but there's nothing more to discuss. If you think there's something suspicious about him, give me the evidence and I will examine it.'

Gloria next wanted to express her concerns to her father about Roane, citing what she'd found online. But when she mentioned his name, Frank was dismissive. 'I don't know what you've found, and I don't want to know,' he said.

'Why?'

'Because people make up stuff on there. People distort things.'

'Do you think I don't know that?'

'I sometimes wonder. You spend too much time on social media. I'm pleased to say that many people including, I suspect, Roane, aren't preoccupied with all that.'

'Are you telling me not to go on Facebook?'

'No. But ask yourself if it makes you happy. I get the impression it doesn't. Not everyone wastes their time on it, thank God. And certainly not anyone successful in life.'

She ignored the jab of the last sentence. 'Dad, it's not the point. It's not Facebook talking about him. It's the news. He was arrested on drug offences.'

'And was he prosecuted? No, he wasn't.'

'Not yet.'

'OK, not yet. And it won't happen.'

'How do you know? Have you talked to Layne about it?'

'Not specifically. But I have every confidence. And what if Roane does have the odd rough edge?'

'Rough edge?'

'He may just be waiting for someone like you to sort him out.'

It all sounded incredibly hollow to her. Her father would not be told and, disappointed, she returned to her room. She closed the door firmly to shut out the madness. Psychologically she felt she was being hemmed in on all sides.

At that moment she would have loved to have gone for a drive in the countryside, but even if she hadn't sprained her ankle, the way her luck was going she'd have probably encountered some weirdo, harmless or otherwise, and regretted it, assuming she survived the encounter. She wanted to call Lily but it would be past midnight in England.

In the end, still restless, she hobbled downstairs and walked gingerly into the garden. Old Ray was out there, doing nothing much as usual, but doing it with at least the appearance of diligence and with a smile on his face. How he kept his job would be a mystery to most people but not to Gloria. It was the same reason Dr Mencius was able to call round to see her mother: her father's indolence in facing reality. Standing on the lawn, she peered up at her mother's bedroom. She expected to see her look out, as though her daughter gazing up could summon her from her bed. In the sunshine and the lightest of breezes, warm and rose-scented, and with the hum of bees, Gloria felt relaxed, momentarily freed from her troubles, as if they were held within the walls of the house and all that was necessary was to escape through the front door.

Ray shuffled towards her with what was, surely for him, remarkable agility. It meant he had a secret to tell. There was nothing that enlivened him more than a secret he could quietly share or hear for the first time. Gloria felt she should warn him, lest he strain himself and become injured.

'Take it easy, Ray,' she said. He seemed too excited for his own good.

'That woman is right,' he said.

'What do you mean?'

'Mrs Mencius. She's not as crazy as she looks.'

All the time old Ray had been working there, it had never occurred to Gloria that he might be acquainted with the Mencius family.

'My wife knows her,' he said. 'I figured she would show up here one day.'

Gloria immediately realised that the antagonism her mother felt for Ray was likely reciprocated. She now wondered if he might be in cahoots with señora Mencius. How did he even know what the woman had said in the house? Could he have heard her? Or had she told him beforehand? Was he some sort of spy for her?

These notions seemed wild, but she had always thought him a bit creepy, always watching. But despite her misgivings she decided to hear him out. 'What do you know?' she said.

This had the effect of making him pause. He had something to reveal but appeared to want something in return. Her instincts had been right. He was a creep. And a lazy one at that.

'I don't have time to play games,' she chided. He adopted a fawning demeanour which only made her more annoyed. 'Tell me,' she demanded, just able to restrain herself from adding 'you wretch'.

'Señora Mencius split up with her husband because of his relationship with your mother.'

'Yeah!?' She paused for breath. 'What relationship? There is no relationship. He's her doctor, that's all.'

'His wife knows otherwise.'

'What evidence does she have?' She found herself arguing against something she herself had long believed was probably true, which was bizarre.

'She gets things for him,' he said. She noticed how sharing this made him smile. Perhaps that was reward enough for him.

'What do you mean?' she said.

'All kinds of things.'

'Like what?'

'A car.'

'Are you saying my mother bought him a car?'

'No.'

'Then what?' Her patience was running out, just when it should have been in abundance.

'She doesn't buy him gifts; she gives him money – an allowance.'

'An allowance?' Instinctively she looked up at Maria's window. She was aware of her mother having just left it. 'My father obviously pays him for his care, if that's what it is.'

'She pays him too.'

'Why does she pay him?'

'I don't know.' He looked disappointed. Having run out of facts for her, he would have to start giving interpretations instead. Perhaps he meant blackmail was involved but couldn't bring himself to say it. 'Investment,' he said.

'Investment? Is he some sort of finance expert?'

'I don't know.'

'Does it occur to you that this is just malicious gossip?'

He shrugged. Then she remembered a key question she kept always in the back of her mind: 'Is she his only patient?'

'No.'

'Are you sure?'

'Yes.' This upset one of her theories: that he was not a doctor at all but a pure charlatan preying upon her mother. She had thought it was about sex – and that could still be part of it – but really it was about money.

She looked at Ray. He appeared happy, though still expectant. She gave him a grin and thanked him with a sincerity she convinced herself was genuine. She gripped his hand in a conspiratorial way. At that moment his face was beaming. It was almost as though he were in love. She perhaps reminded him of a girl he once fell for. Gloria even felt a slight temporary affection for him. He sensed it and was glad. She released his hand.

'I must get back to it,' he said, 'or your dad will fire me.' He chuckled and, although she felt she shouldn't, she joined in. Dad would never fire him. The fact Maria despised him made Ray all the more valuable to him.

On leaving him, she looked up again. Her mother had just returned to the window. She smiled at Gloria, then the window opened. 'When are you coming to see me?' she said. Clearly her mother had noticed her with Ray and wanted to know what was said.

'I'll be straight up,' Gloria replied.

In fact, she dawdled for a few minutes, enjoying the garden scents and colours to the full. Whether it was Ray or other members of the gardening crew, someone was doing a good job. The roses of different colours, the large white poppies, the red fuchsias and purple bougainvillea were a delight for the eye, and everywhere was tidy. Perhaps he was one of those mysterious people who achieved much whilst appearing to do little.

Twenty minutes later, she was in her mother's room but the occupant was fast asleep. She was relieved, feeling she'd avoided an inevitable confrontation, although one she felt perhaps she should have had.

She needed to rest her ankle but first wanted to talk to her father. However, he was on the phone to Layne. It was obvious they were talking about Roane. She did not want to listen, but to the extent she heard the conversation it did not ease her anxieties.

'That reminds me: your son's an eligible bachelor, isn't he?' said Frank.

'Only in the very narrowest sense of the word. Bachelor, yes. Eligible, I don't think so. His relationships never last. I don't think he is, as they say, boyfriend material. And certainly not husband material.'

'Is he a loner?'

'The very opposite. Too much the social butterfly, I'm afraid.'

'OK. So if I send Gloria over, maybe he could introduce her to some of his friends. A young lord or an earl. Just kidding.'

'"Just kidding" is right. I fear it would be a nightmare, Frank. Believe me, she'd be eaten alive. His friends are, I fear, no better than he is.'

'She can hold her own in any company. She's not afraid of anything or anyone.'

'I'm sure. But, if truth be told, my son lives in an almost permanent state of chaos and intoxication.'

'Oh no. Drink?'

'Yes. And every kind of recreational drug known to western law enforcement. And, no doubt, some not known. I'm afraid I would shake in fear if the delightful Gloria were to meet my rake of a son in the flesh. He's a waster of the first order. He lives off handouts from me and has ruined his life. Probably my fault, but I can't do anything about it now.

He spends more in a minute than most earn in a year. The money he won in Monte Carlo he went and lost again. I've decided it would be cheaper if someone kidnapped him. I'd pay up as long as they agreed to keep him.'

'Oh dear. Has he always been like it?'

'He had a go at motor racing. I sponsored him, which was madness on my part. Then he had a promising career as some kind of art director and was doing fine, but it all went wrong.'

'What happened?'

'He fell in love, which is a very dangerous thing to do.'

'We've all been there.'

'Of course we have, but the more prudent amongst us – in fact, all but the very stupid – don't fall for the boss's wife. And especially not when the boss and his wife are, to all intents and purposes, happily married.'

'Oh dear. He hasn't got his father's deft touch, clearly.'

'Deft touch? Are you taking the mickey?'

'Going back to Gloria, I was thinking a trip abroad might do her good. It's all got a bit frenetic for her. She needs a break.'

'Not to meet Roane, is it?' Layne sounded genuinely concerned.

'No, I was thinking more about your philanthropic work. She's very involved with charities and maybe she could learn from what you're doing with yours.'

'She'd be very welcome here, Frank. You know that. As regards charities, well, others sort that out for me. I suppose I'm the figurehead really. But I'd be happy to introduce her to my people. She could live like an English lady if she wanted. Just not with Roane and his set. I'd be fearful of that. So if we can scotch that idea—'

'We can.'

'In a way, it's a shame. But I'm sure he'd never want an American girlfriend anyway. He hates everything about America.'

'Like his father.'

'Oh no, Frank, I wouldn't say that. Of course I'd never want to go there again unless it was for an essential environmental conference. Apart from that I'll resist the urge, thank you.'

After listening to the call, about which she suspected her father would tell her nothing, she put her head round his door and quickly informed him Ray had confirmed what señora Mencius had said about Maria giving the doctor money. As she'd expected, he dismissed this as 'slanderous nonsense'.

44

The next match, against fellow title contenders, the Flyers, was another disaster. Gloria was still injured from the incident with señora Mencius and so was ruled out. Then Dessie was injured in the pre-game warmup. Annalisa was not even in the state at the time so couldn't be asked to play, and the attack was decidedly weak with Jamie the only experienced forward. In the seventh minute one of the team's central defenders was sent off. After that the opposition laid siege to the goal to win the game 4-0. The Hummingbirds were no longer top of the league.

At the next training session, Gloria was almost back to full fitness but she felt nervous because she wondered how many of the others had heard the allegation that she and the coach were having an affair. She couldn't decide whether it was better that they hadn't heard, running the risk of an adverse reaction when they did, or that they'd heard it already and disbelieved it. Since favouritism was always a concern amongst the players, she thought the notion of them simply not being bothered by such a rumour unrealistic.

In the end, training hard enabled her to put the issue out of her mind. She often found that when there was no way to think through a problem it could turn out to be a blessing because she had to focus on the present moment. She had a good session, finding all the innocent enthusiasm of a young teenager. Her passing was perfect after following the coach's advice to practise slowing down the moment before releasing the ball.

She carried this enthusiasm into the next match, a 2-0 win against the Skyliners who were bottom of the league, but it was a nervy game. Near the end she had the chance to score. Approaching the goal with only the 'keeper to beat she looked up, saw a woman's face in the crowd, instantly thought of her nemesis Carmina Rodriguez, and scuffed the shot.

'Sorry, boss,' she said when the coach criticised the team afterwards: 'Too much complacency and lack of application. Too many missed chances. We may need those goals at the end of the season.'

Next day, she saw Barti's comments to the press: 'They always give us a tough game so I'm very pleased.' Asked about the missed chances he said, 'It happens in soccer. At least we're creating the opportunities.'

'Yeah, all we need is Annalisa back,' said Gloria. 'She wouldn't miss them.'

45

To Frank's joy he heard from Saskia again. He was always keen for any contact from her, whilst reluctant to initiate it himself for fear of being a nuisance, since she was far more busy in any meaningful way than he was. She said, 'We were so impressed by your work on the Smith Thursday company that time. Did it really not take you long? I hope it didn't because we may have something else for you.'

'Not really,' he replied. 'As I said before, when you know what you're looking for it's quite straightforward. You get a gut feeling based on experience and that puts you in the right direction.' He neglected to add that in this instance the 'right direction' had been to phone his old friend Jack Quick who'd obtained all the information for him. He suspected that if Jack could find it out, it would not have taken her own analysts much time to do so either. Clearly at some level he interested her. In his fantasies, it was a romantic interest, but he managed to keep such notions at bay.

The call ended on the most positive of notes: 'Perhaps you would care to visit me in the office. There might be other things you can assist with. Or are you too busy right now?'

'I like to have plenty to do, obviously. But I'll gladly make a couple of calls, move a few things around. No problem.'

In reality his diary was as usual almost entirely empty, his days so devoid of appointments he hardly needed to write anything down. But a man such as himself, a former – "captain" was too weak a word – general of industry should be constantly in demand, so he liked to pretend he was.

A few days later, he was sitting in the swish fourth floor reception area of Saskia's Los Angeles office. He was supposed to be meeting a couple of potential clients for his corporate advisory service then, but he had decided he did not really want them. He did not care about their asinine problems anymore. He did not want to educate them on his failures dressed up as opportunities. He hated this peddling of his past: 'Don't do what I did' and 'Look at me, I paid the price.' He did not believe he had paid a price. Price for what? He had done nothing wrong. He was not some reformed drug dealer but an honest, hardworking man with ambitions that had proved a little too big for other people. He was like someone who had loved too much and been hurt. That was the kind of price he'd paid. And like a lover it was ultimately a private thing, although a private thing that affected thousands of jobs, millions of consumers—

He was disturbed from his trail of thought by a slim young blonde in a tight grey skirt and stiletto sandals telling him the international investment star was free to see him. She had allocated him fifteen minutes. He would have liked more time, but it was a small beginning to what could be the business relationship of a lifetime. As he followed the receptionist, his daydreaming resumed. Saskia would have a bigger set of offices in future, not just a floor but a whole building full of people working for her, all necessary to cope with the investment money his personal involvement would attract.

When he arrived at her smallish, square, rather sparse office, she was on the phone. The call was clearly highly important as she completely ignored him. She looked glamorous in an exclusive and expensive blue designer dress that she'd obviously chosen for their meeting. He noticed her perfume which was subtle but seductive.

The fact she did not even acknowledge his presence did not offend him but instead added to her mystique. This was enhanced further when her face made it apparent - although to him it was clearly a pretence – she was puzzled by his presence there. Had she forgotten who he was, or merely why he was there?

But as soon as she'd put the phone down, she said, 'Frank, how are you?' Of course she'd remembered him. 'But isn't it tomorrow we're supposed to be meeting?'

'Er, no, I'm sure we said—'

'No, my calendar has it as Friday.'

'OK.' She must be right, he decided.

'Only I've got some people coming in from Seattle. I thought it was maybe one of them had arrived.' She checked her watch and then looked up and smiled at him. 'But I've always got ten minutes for you.'

Ten minutes? How generous in the circumstances, he thought. In fact, she was only able to give him three minutes because another call came in. This was time enough, however, for her to scribble on a small square of paper a company name and hand it to him. 'Just if you have anything on them. I mean, anecdotal information. Obviously, our analysts do the numbers, but they don't know the personalities. You probably do.' He nodded, then looked at the paper. He recognised the name. His mind wandered, trying to establish why it was familiar to him. She finished her call, but before he could speak the phone rang yet again.

'Frank, sorry about this but Seattle are here. Let's do lunch – soon. Have a word with Carrie on the way out.' She then left the office to greet her visitors. He followed her to reception where he was directed to the tiny office of her personal assistant situated right next to Saskia's.

Carrie's diminutive appearance was dominated by bright red lipstick, thick eyebrows, and earrings like small daggers dangling.

'Lunch?' she said. 'OK, we're looking at three months.'

'Wow. I see. Do people ever cancel?'

'If they do, she stays in the office. She only goes out once a week anyway.'

'What about dinner?'

'She doesn't do dinner. Not business anyway. Only... personal.' She looked at him like a witness assessing a participant in a police lineup. In Carrie's world could his interest in Saskia possibly be 'personal'?

'So it would have to be lunch,' she said crushingly. She put him in Saskia's diary for three months' time.

On the drive home, he decided the meeting had been 'promising'. He had spent three minutes with her, and he would have the opportunity to enjoy more of her time on another occasion when he could again impress her with his inside knowledge. His mind was already drafting the introduction of his response to her latest request. When stopped at the lights he looked at the paper again. Her handwriting was cryptic. Was that an 'e' at the end, or an 'a'? He'd read it initially as an 'e', being a company he knew of. But then most people knew it so his expert knowledge would not have been required. No, it was undeniably an 'a'.

He'd never heard of that company, so maybe she really had meant 'e'. That was it. Ah no, there was what he took as an 'o' that was probably meant to be a 'u'. Oh dear, it was a different company altogether, and he had never heard of it. It occurred to him, this time it might be a test. Maybe it was a made-up company.

When Frank arrived home, he went to Gloria's room and requested her help in investigating the company Saskia had asked about. She was reluctant but loyally acquiesced, confident she would find little. He showed her the piece of paper Saskia had given him and what he believed her scribble said. She read it differently and so arrived at another name. She told him she was hesitant to become involved without clarification.

He then asked her, 'I wonder if you've considered further the idea we discussed of moving cash to Saskia's company. I know you were going to think about it.'

'I was not,' Gloria replied firmly. 'The money is and always was, from the day you asked me to be custodian of it, intended solely for charitable purposes.'

'Of course, my dear, you're absolutely right, and I would not want it any other way. I suppose I look at it holistically, by which I mean that the investment fund could be seen - some would argue strongly - as *in effect* a charity.'

'What!? Holistically? I don't understand.'

'It has a moral purpose in bringing overinflated companies to heel.'

'That's plain nonsense.'

He decided to try a different tack: 'By the way, I couldn't help noticing you have a brochure for a particular not-for-profit on your desk.'

She picked up the document. 'What of it?'

'You haven't given them foundation money, have you?'

'I might have.' He shook his head. She said, 'Stop trying to undermine me. If I want to, I will.'

'I think even a cursory scan of their accounts and the officers' salaries will convince you it is not a good idea. Research it and you'll see exactly what I mean.'

The implication that she'd made a mistake and her normally scrupulous analysis had let her down, did not sit well with her. Seeing she was annoyed, he told her not to bother with the name on the paper Saskia had given him but focus on her charities instead.

She was disturbed by the conversation. It was clear that her dad was starstruck or lovestruck and was being bamboozled, either intentionally by Saskia or, more likely, unintentionally. He was straining to find ways to earn favour with a woman who was oblivious of him. He wasn't done, however: 'You don't believe me, do you?' he said. 'About the charity, I mean.'

'I'm struggling to understand,' she said, 'how whether I've invested the foundation's money in this or that charity, which is none of your business anyway, has anything to do with Saskia's company.'

'Imagination,' he stressed. 'That's what you need.'

'What!?'

'You need to look beyond the surface of things. Go behind what's being said. I've always told you that. Don't rely on other people's assumptions.'

'I don't.'

'Then turn some of that criticism you aim at me towards those do-gooders, however well-meaning, that are failing.'

'I'm not as easily fooled as you think. I'm tough and I think you got muddled up about the charity. I had one I was supporting – a children's charity – but I had to stop. It is sadly the case that they are not run properly and another similar not-for-profit does it better.'

'But I was right about the referee that time. The one that caused all the trouble.'

'Eh? What's that got to do with anything?'

'He booked you for diving, remember? It should have been a penalty.'

'No, Dad, I just fell over.' She did not want to admit that she cheated and didn't like the memory of it returning.

'You didn't deserve a booking. I told you that man was corrupt, and he was. Taking bribes from coaches. I was the first one to say it. And I was right. Look it up if you don't believe me.'

'OK, Dad,' she sighed.

'You see, it's about instinct. I may not understand all this internet stuff, but I sure as hell have good instinct.' He was on the point of leaving her room but paused as if something new but obvious had forced its way into his thoughts. 'By the way,' he said, 'I've been meaning to ask you: what do you invest in? I mean, where do you put the money that hasn't gone to charities yet?' She had wondered when this question would arise, having anticipated it before.

'You said that was always up to me,' she said defensively.

'It is. Having established that, you can tell me what you invest in, can't you?'

She could have denied him this information but found it hard to justify; it was charities she knew about most and she had much to learn about investments. She said, 'It's all very conservative,' and she named the funds she could immediately think of. 'And some gold,' she added. 'I thought that prudent.'

'It is. Are these all ethical funds?'

'I believe so.'

'What about the gold?'

'What about it?'

'Is that ethical?'

'Yes, it's safe, so there's more money to give to charities.'

'But that's not the point, is it? What about the ethics of things like illegal mining? What about mercury pollution? And miners with lung cancer? And money laundering?'

Gloria had no answer. He'd obviously recently seen a TV programme about it, or a newspaper article. Then he said, 'You're right: it's up to you where you invest the foundation's assets. But please don't tell me short selling is somehow immoral when you're holding gold.' With that he left her.

Talking to her father had given her a headache. But what if he was right about gold? She would have to research it, but not immediately. Instead, she wanted to check out what he had said about the corrupt referee. After Suzie had kindly brought her a strong cup of coffee and Advil, she began to investigate.

The research proved interesting. She had already thought the referee was suspicious because she was aware that a flurry of cards accompanied every game in which he officiated. Sure enough, she learned that he'd been thrown out of the league. Moreover, a very recent story, probably the one her father had seen, reported he was being investigated by the police over dodgy business dealings, specifically dubious loans which he would use as a lever to force debtors to do things for him, such as assaulting enemies of his. If the debtor complied, he was flexible; if not, he relied on the tough terms of the loan to enforce quick repayment, followed by a visit by thugs if that didn't happen.

She concluded that her father was therefore correct about the referee. The possibility he might also be right about her bullion investment nagged at her.

While Gloria was researching gold and not enjoying what she was reading, Frank was on Skype. Layne was announcing the latest idea for his estate. 'I'm getting into hardship holidays,' he said solemnly.

'You are? Aren't you a bit old and rich for that?'

'Not me, you fool. Oh, I can't you believe you're so literal. It's for holidaymakers who want to get a sense of real adventure from doing exciting things on the property.'

'Oh, I see, to help poor people like disadvantaged kids... oh, Layne, I see you in a different light. It must be your age. You're seeing your responsibilities.'

'Responsibilities be damned! Disadvantaged kids? You must be joking. Do you think I want any old hobbledehoy on the premises nicking stuff and beating up the staff? No, it's for the folks who live their pampered lives making money off others and they're bored. People like you.'

'Thanks.'

'People who want risk. I know it sounds daft, but there are people who want this kind of stuff, want to feel they're in danger, to feel fear again. I don't know what they'll be doing on the estate exactly, but the team will figure that out. Things that'll scare the buggers to death but won't actually kill them.'

'Have you thought about insurance, Layne, for all these projects?'

'Oh yes, insurance. Is that your latest racket now? Anyway, more important than this holiday thing is that I've got some oik claims he's my son. I've already got one, which is more than enough. If he's a real son of mine he's going to be a wreck. He wants me to have a DNA test.'

'Will you?'

'No way. Do you know what DNA stands for? Do Not Ask. No, he's a scammer. I'm sure of it. Anyway, please excuse me, Frank. I'd better go now. We've got Alfred's nuts to sort out.'

'Who's Alfred?'

'One of Tania's dogs – a Jack Russell-pug cross. I can't abide the revolting thing, but I agreed we'd take the Rolls. Goodbye, Frank.'

46

Gloria decided to phone Annalisa. She still felt remote from her and so took the initiative to make contact.

'Hiya,' answered her friend, itself evidence of a coolness towards Gloria because she never normally greeted her like that. And when Gloria began talking, Ant did not interject in the way she normally did. It was as though she had something to say and was going to be stiff until invited to take the chance to say it. 'Are you OK?' said Gloria, sensing this.

'I've been better. Why are you calling anyway?'

'Is this a bad time?' Gloria suddenly realised her friend had probably been crying the moment she rang her. 'I can call back,' she said.

'No, don't,' said Annalisa plaintively.

'I was phoning about that ref giving out loans. He's been fired and the police—'

'Oh, don't.'

'Did you know, then?'

'Only too well.'

'Oh dear.' Gloria wished she hadn't phoned, but she had the impression her friend was relieved. 'You can tell me if you want.'

'I know.'

Gloria suspected what her friend was about to say.

'My dad was one of the people he gave loans to,' said Ant. 'Or his business was. Dad shouldn't have been involved with it. His job's on the line. There was a rumour he'd been sacked, but it's not true... yet.'

'I'm sorry to hear about this.'

'I know you are.'

'Obviously I didn't realise, otherwise—'

'No, I'm glad you called.'

'I wanted to ask you something, Ant.'

'Sure.'

'Do you know a Carmina Rodriguez?'

'I don't know. Why?'

'Apparently she's the one who's been sending me hate.'

'Really? When?'

'There was a barrage of it. Evil stuff. I've stopped looking. I don't know why she does it. I don't know what I've done to hurt her or anyone else. I'm wondering if she's been having an affair with the coach because that's what she accuses me of.'

'Really?'

'It's the only thing I can think of to explain why she does it.'

'If it's any consolation, you're not the only one been getting horrible messages.'

'Oh no. Not you too?' She thought that if Ant was also being targeted it would create a feeling of solidarity between them. 'You should have told me,' she said.

'No, not me,' Ant said in the forthright manner of someone who believed their reputation so beyond reproach no one could even imagine such a thing. She mentioned a couple of names. Neither were team members.

'I don't know them,' said Gloria.

'How do you know this woman Carmina's behind it?'

'I have a friend in England who works on this kind of stuff. I asked her and she came back with what she'd found. She told me Carmina and Dwayne are one and the same.'

'That's crazy. Who is this person in England?'

'Her name's Mack. She's married to Lily. By the way, Dad wants me to go over there to meet his friend who's a lord. Thinks it will help me learn about charities. Plus, the lord has a son.'

'Get you, girl: "Lady Gloria".'

'I don't think so. In fact, definitely not. But I'm tempted by the idea of going away for a while.' She then told Annalisa about the man in Texas who was in love with her as Vanessa and was angry at being told Vanessa wasn't real. She mentioned that Mack had said 'Vanessa man' had Tommy's name.

'How could that possibly be?'

'I think that's Carmina too. My theory is that Carmina has been communicating with the man in Texas, pretending to be 'Vanessa'. She's then hacked into his account and changed his name to Tommy, just to get him even madder and, at the same time, drive a wedge between me and the real Tommy.'

'Wow!'

'I feel really frightened by all this,' said Gloria. 'I try not to be but it's hard. You have a nice life, and then something or someone totally irrational turns up to ruin it. But Mack and her boss will get the police involved.'

'What about your dad? Can't he talk to them?'

'I can hardly get him to talk to me, let alone the police.'

'Oh dear, Glo. All this cool stuff we've got going on; what a mess we're both in!'

47

Gloria was increasingly aware of how worries about Carmina's campaign and 'Vanessa man' were affecting her daily life. She was afraid to go on social media and worried every time her phone rang or a letter arrived. She could see how people could be paralysed by such worries. It was intolerable.

She decided, however, to tough it out. This decision itself invigorated her. She went online to look for others who were being intimidated as she was. She felt a sense of comradeship with them. She chose to believe the police would deal with 'Vanessa man', so she put that worry into a box not to be opened again if she could possibly avoid it.

As for Carmina, let her do what she wanted. Let her say what she liked. But then the thought arose: what if things Carmina said and did affected her relationship with other people in ways she was unaware of? Someone might cut her off for no obvious reason, when unbeknownst to her it was because of something Carmina had put online. It was a reasonable concern, wasn't it? But then she couldn't control her image anyway. People would think whatever they wanted, and there was little she could do about that. She could only deal with what life cast before her eyes and ears.

She became relaxed, in a state of acceptance. It was how she liked to see herself: the quiet-minded sage unmoved by events. But it was a fact of life that nothing stayed the same for long. The calmest water was soon disturbed. On this occasion, her tranquility was disrupted by an unexpected phone call. It was from Mack, and she felt immediately glad to hear from her.

'What time is it there?' Gloria asked.

'About ten.'

'How's Lily?'

'She's asleep.'

'I bet she's beautiful when she's asleep.'

'She is. Early night for her tonight. Unwell.'

'Oh, what's wrong?'

'Depressed, I think. Married life, I guess.' Mack laughed. Gloria felt slightly embarrassed and said nothing. Mack then said, 'I think it's the English weather. She wants the Californian sun.'

'Well, there's plenty of it here.'

'Oh, please send some over.'

The thought occurred to Gloria that Mack was seeking to flirt with her. Maybe the marriage wasn't going so well. Why was she even phoning? Maybe she just wanted to open up. Gloria, the counsellor. Hopefully not. She was tired of being that.

'Carmina,' said Mack.

Gloria felt a shudder. 'What about her?'

'I've found out something interesting about her.'

'OK.'

'Could she be involved with one of your charities?'

'I don't know. What do you mean?'

'Her partner was recently fired by one.'

'Partner? I don't know anything about her partner. I thought the issue was maybe the soccer coach and her seeing me as some kind of love rival.'

'It might be. I'm just saying—'

'I know you are.' She had a sudden feeling of great warmth towards Mack.

'Here's what I know. Her partner is a man called Hinks.'

'OK.' She wondered if she should know this Hinks.

'He was at a charity that works with kids and he was... putting his hand in the till, as we say here – embezzling.'

'Oh.'

'Then he changed his name and went to another charity. One that, according to your website, you support. The Alvin Trust or something.'

'Oh, I see.'

'Then he got found out. They got a tip-off. They checked his background and found out he'd been arrested and charged before but never prosecuted.'

'Why was he never prosecuted?'

'Because of a technicality. The police messed up the investigation. The case couldn't proceed. But you know how muck sticks, so being the prudent fellow he is he changed his name.'

'It was smart of the charity to pick that up, though. I recently had to tell another one I couldn't support them anymore, so this is actually reassuring.'

'Due diligence, right?'

'Sure. So Carmina thinks I'm behind it?'

'Possibly.'

'Huh! Well, I might as well be because if I'd even suspected it, I'd have been right on to them.'

'Yeah, so the question is...'

'Go on,' said Gloria.

'What do you do about it? What do we do about it?'

'We?'

'I shouldn't say that. It's just if you want my help.'

'I do.'

'I like this work. It's kinda fun.' Mack sounded excited.

'What can you do, then?'

'I can hack into her accounts if you want me to. I can disrupt her social media presence. She'll get it back, but it might worry her for a while, maybe send her into a tailspin.'

'What if she reacts?'

'But would it be any worse? I'll do whatever you want. I'm completely at your service.' She said this last sentence in an almost seductive way – inappropriate but funny. Gloria could see why Lily loved Mack so much. She herself was beginning to find her enchanting.

Gloria decided for now she wanted nothing more done. Mack sounded disappointed whilst at the same time agreeing. Of course if Carmina carried on with the campaign, that would be a different matter. Gloria then told her about her belief that Carmina had hacked into 'Vanessa man's' Facebook account and changed the name to that of her boyfriend Tommy. Mack was impressed, saying this was plausible. 'See, you don't need me at all,' she said.

'Oh, I do,' said Gloria. Even if she could do everything Mack could, which she couldn't, she would still need her support.

'OK,' said Mack, finally. 'You know where I am. I'm always here for you.'

After the call Gloria thought about something Lily told her once: Mack sounded so cute on the phone that guys would call the office just to listen to her voice. And naturally Mack liked to exploit that. Gloria could understand. 'God bless you, Mack,' she said to the empty air.

48

In the following days, Gloria could see there were more messages from Carmina but did not read them. The fact Mack said she could hack into Carmina's accounts made her feel empowered. On the pitch for the away game at local rivals the Treehawks she felt she was playing for Mack and Lily. As she looked into the crowd she did not care if there was some malevolent individual there - that middle-aged woman with the red jacket and wild hair, for example, or that young blonde behind her in the black leather jacket - willing her more than anyone to fail. She turned her back on it. Besides, the Treehawks crowd were hostile enough anyway.

Relaxed, everything seemed to fall right for her. Given a free role, she found she could work well with Dessie, setting up attacks from deep, playing one-twos with her until either was in a shooting position. Dessie was rewarded with a hat-trick, placing a neat pass to Gloria's feet for her to claim the fourth. But the Hummingbirds' defence made careless errors and the 4-4 result felt like a defeat for a team aiming for the championship. The mood after the game was ugly. The coach criticised the backs as usual: 'Stop opting out of tackles all the time. You lot are softer than melted butter.' But one or two of them were up for a row, criticising him for the formation with the lack of midfield, and the forwards not helping enough.

Gloria said nothing during the dispute. She knew when she'd played brilliantly and did not care what others thought or said. She left with Dessie. As they walked through the carpark Dessie said, 'Wow, what was that in there!?'

'Just the coach sounding off as usual. He always blames the defence. Even the one time I gave away a penalty which lost us a game, he said it was the defence's fault. And one or two of the older players have got tired of it.'

'I guess I'll be playing deeper next time.'

Gloria felt happy driving home. She knew Annalisa would need to be recalled.

There was no more abuse from Carmina over the next few days, but the row in the dressing room continued on Facebook. Gloria did not engage with it, sad at how her teammates were attacking each other and the coach. Their rivals would have loved it. She had more important things to worry about than becoming embroiled in such a depressing dispute. However conciliatory she might be, she would most likely incur the anger of all, for she'd come to understand that trying to intervene in a fight rarely ended happily for the well-intentioned non-combatant. Fortunately, there was now a break in the season and she hoped that by the time they restarted everyone would have quietened down.

She decided now was the time to tackle what she'd been putting off. She needed to investigate Carmina herself. She therefore checked out everything she could find: Facebook, Instagram. LinkedIn, all manner of public records. She could easily do this work. She didn't need Mack. It was just that her confidence had been low and she found it difficult to deal with the fact someone hated her so much. Mack was used to malevolent people from her work, whereas she wasn't. But Mack cared, and having someone to help her find out who was attacking her was a problem shared. Mack and others like her were not only investigators but confidantes and counsellors too.

She found Carmina and her partner Hinks had separated. He had been fired from the charity as Mack said, and Carmina had initially tried to distance herself from him. But when he was arrested for embezzlement she came to his defence, going online to claim: 'My former partner is innocent. Evil actors are behind his arrest. They invented the spurious allegation about his previous job in order to get him fired from the Alvin Trust. These people have too much power in charities, working darkly behind the scenes, using their financial involvement for their own ends. They pretend to work for the public good while secretly trying to destroy people they happen to dislike. Evil!' She stopped short of naming anyone, presumably because she was not so unhinged that she couldn't recognise the risk of libel claims. But it was obvious Gloria was one person she meant.

She continued investigating because she found it captivating. It was like the unravelling of a knotted ball of string. Carmina herself had a criminal record. She had been involved in fraud, changed identities several times, and been in a dispute over a former husband's will. She was an artist when it came to financial shenanigans. 'Yes!' Gloria exclaimed. 'Mack, oh Mack, how I do love you!' She had got her confidence back and she attributed this to her new friend.

She also decided to approach the woman who used to send her messages after games praising her. Was she fake too? She discovered, however, that the woman's Facebook account that generated the messages was now deactivated. This was suspicious. But Gloria was able to find a Twitter account for her and sent her a direct message: 'Thank you for your kind comments after games. They were a big boost, especially when we didn't play so well. Much appreciated.'

To her surprise the woman responded almost immediately: 'I had to deactivate my Facebook account because my son was using it to send out fan messages to you and sometimes others. He worked at the ground on match days. When the team played away, he learned the result from a friend whose sister was in the team. I think he had a schoolboy crush. No harm was meant, but I apologise for any concern. I think he stopped when he finally got a girlfriend. Best wishes and good luck to the Hummingbirds!'

Gloria thought she knew who it was - a very shy teenager. The problem was, she could not say anything to him lest he die of embarrassment. But at least he had a girlfriend now.

49

Boosted by her growing self-belief, she decided to ring Annalisa to talk about the team and whether she'd be back. She found her cold, however. 'What did you want?' she said. Gloria figured she was at her boyfriend's and so didn't appreciate the interruption.

'I'll call you back,' Ant said. Gloria didn't think she would and was surprised when she did.

'I'm sorry, Glo. Oh God!'

'What's up, Ant?'

'Ricky.'

'I thought your boyfriend was Jimmy.'

'Not my boyfriend, dummy - my cousin. He's gone crazy. He thought you calling me was his dealer.'

'What!?'

'He's paranoid.'

'Sounds like it.'

'He owes money and he's stoned and thinks everyone's out to get him.'

'Why are you even involved?'

'I'm not involved, but we used to be close. Lately, he's gotten closer again. I didn't realise the mess he's in. On the surface he's cool. Upright job and all.'

'Upright?'

'You know. He's got a smart job in L.A. He's in accountancy. But they're all on coke there – and worse.'

'Oh, Ant.'

'I know. So I'm sorry I was short with you. I heard about the match.'

'Ant, it was bad. I mean, I should be jumping for joy about my goal but I'm a team player.'

'You are. You put the team first. I wish others—'

'Do you think you'll get the call now?'

'From the coach? I don't know. Now everyone thinks I'm lazy despite all my goals.'

Gloria expected a self-serving, self-pitying speech but felt bad for thinking that way when her friend said, 'And they're right. So I've been training hard.'

'How?'

'Personal trainer. My dad got mad at me for being dropped so I told him I'd turn it into something positive. I've been watching videos of some of the top players, and I see now that I'm just a lazy, selfish brat.'

'What!?'

'You can disagree if you want. Just kidding. But seriously, if everyone including the coach thinks it, they must be right. You think it, don't you?'

'Well—'

'See, you do. And you never told me. Some friend you are. Actually, you did say it once, but you weren't exactly forceful. You're right, though. I'm going to work on my linkup play. I thought, if we're going to be champions, I deserve to be there.'

'With our defence? How can we be champions?'

'We just have to score more. It ain't that difficult. Even you can score. Oh, Glo, it would be so good to see you! Let's go to the beach or something soon.'

'Yeah, for sure.'

'I can't do today. Besides, rain's coming in, so they say. And I've got to be around for Ricky. I love him but not like this. I don't know what to do.'

'Sounds like he needs professional help.'

'He does, but he won't listen.'

'Call me anytime. And let me know when you want to get together. And let's hope you hear from the coach.'

She felt glad she'd phoned Annalisa. With Dessie and her in the same team they could still achieve greatness. Well, maybe not greatness but they could scrape their way to the championship. She wanted to let her father know about Annalisa returning. He might not be interested, but he for sure should be.

She found her father on the phone to Layne who was complaining about Tania:

'She wants me to sell the mansion. Can you believe that, Frankie?'

'Sorry to hear that. It does seem a bit quick.'

'No, you're not sorry, but I appreciate you saying it. "Quick" is an understatement if ever there was one.'

'What's the problem with her?'

'She claims it's like a house in a vampire novel. I can see that for someone of limited experience of the world that might be an easy impression to have. She also said it's not the place featured on my dating page.'

'And is it?'

'Of course not. I used the picture from some duke's palace or other. So what? My place has the essence of all that. I'm not pretty either, but you have to look behind the facade and see the potential.'

Frank made a point of turning away from the screen for a moment. 'True, I guess,' he said.

'She says it's cold and draughty—'

'I can imagine.'

'Claims it's falling down, that it's a fire risk. She even alleges it's haunted.'

'Surely not.'

'She says there's a man with no head wandering about the place with it under his arm. A man with no head, can you imagine that? Well, she's off hers, that's clear. And the latest, oh my God, is that she claims she's got a black mould infection from the place. That would explain her crazy delusions, at least.'

'Goodness me, Layne.'

His English friend then went on a rant: 'All she does is go on about the burden of being beautiful. I should have suspected something when someone who knew her contacted me before the wedding. He said I should run while I had two good legs. Well, I haven't - not even one - but you get the point. It's so tiresome. It takes her a day to get ready to go out for an hour. Her treatments, her health ideas, her diets. I can't stand all the fasting and the weird food – or lack of it. Even persuaded me to fire the chef. Living off pills, what good is that?'

'Oh dear.'

'She even does this ruddy podcast about "life in the aristocrat lane".'

'I like that.'

'Don't mock. And she makes videos about "cooking at the mansion". It's all fake. She doesn't even boil an egg.'

Layne then said that Tania had lied to him. She had pretended to be pregnant to get him to marry her. But there was clearly no baby on the way. It would have been a near miracle anyway, given their lack of intimacy. Indeed, once the marriage had been technically consummated, what intimacy there was had fallen away to nothing. However, Frank seemed to recall Layne telling her he had cancer. He was reminded of what Gloria had said: the couple deserved each other.

Poor Layne. He was beginning to feel the loss of control of the place. He couldn't trust the staff anymore. They'd all had their heads turned by her. He sounded less like the 'still young' sixty-five-year-old, as he liked to see himself, than an ancient despot prevented from seeing the true state of things by overzealous and fearful flunkeys.

The Englishman had a similar thought: 'Do you know, I feel like some antique monarch with no power, living in a world of dreams, imagining myself revered by people who secretly think I'm just part of the entertainment. I feel terribly old. But one thought gives me solace: at least my children – Roane and his sister who's estranged out in Thailand or somewhere – will never become my parents, because I'll be killed off before that happens.'

In her room, Gloria could hear her father's Skype call and stayed listening, even enjoying the odd laugh, until she'd had enough. She was then surprised by a visitor. Tommy had come to see her.

A couple of minutes later, there he was standing tall in the lounge in leather jacket and blue jeans, with his surfer blond hair, asking her if she wanted to go for a drive in the blue Cutlass convertible he'd borrowed from his dad's collection. Tommy loved the spontaneous gesture and it had been a sudden impulse to visit her. Or at least that's the impression he liked to convey. Carefree. She was used to everything being prepared in advance and in as much detail as possible, and fretting in search of perfection, but Tommy didn't fret; he just showed up when the spirit took him.

Apart from having showered she was not prepared for going out. She was dressed scruffily, her hair all awry. When she told him she should change he said, no, she looked fine. 'OK, then,' she said brightly and went upstairs to hand her still-talking father a note: 'Going out with Tommy. See you later', making a quick visit to the bathroom, a brush across her teeth, a cursory teasing of her hair. But not wasting a second lest Tommy begin to wonder what he was doing and flee in his car.

He was still standing in the same spot. As she got into his car, however, she couldn't resist speculation about who had stood him up to free him to see her. Maybe she should have made up an excuse, made him realise she was not there for picking up dishevelled and untidy just whenever he had nothing better to do. It was as though he knew she couldn't possibly be doing anything in her life more fun than going out with him at that moment.

'Relax,' he said warmly. A gentle admonition. It was as though he could hear all the gabbling voices in her head.

'I'm OK,' she said. 'Just a little surprised.'

'Don't be,' he said. 'Want to go to the beach, maybe catch something to eat?'

'Sure. I'd rather someone else had caught it, though.' A weak joke, she thought.

'Eh? Oh, you're funny. I never knew that.'

'Serious-minded Gloria.'

'I don't mind you being serious. What's wrong with that?'

'Well, nothing.'

'Exactly.'

She noticed Tommy drove slowly, slower than she herself normally did. As if feeling a need to explain, he said a friend of his had been killed in a hit and run a week ago.

'I'm sorry,' she said, affectionately touching his arm.

'Well, more of an acquaintance really.' He told her the name. She recognised it from the *Patch* newsletter.

'Did they catch the driver?'

'Yeah. The guy was loaded.'

'Booze?'

'Meth.'

'God!'

Suddenly, carefree Tommy was not so carefree. You could never be carefree for long if you were a normal sentient being. Tommy changed the subject, asking her about soccer. Her response tumbled out of her. She told him everything that was going on with the team. She was aware she was rambling and thought she ought to stop. 'Sorry,' she said. 'But you did ask.'

He smiled. 'No, I like it. I like to hear you talk. You're kinda quiet so it's nice.'

'Quiet? Oh, sorry.'

'No, no. And no more saying sorry.'

'OK.' She managed not to apologise again.

'So, do you think the new set-up will work? With this Dessie and Annalisa in the same team?'

'I certainly hope so. We need to do something. Especially the way we're leaking goals.'

'Do you ever do other sports?'

'Tennis. Wanna game sometime?'

'That's right, you have a place nearby. Maybe.'

'It's hard to get a court there nowadays. Maybe we could play somewhere else.'

'What about golf?'

'Sure. Oso Creek.'

'We could have dinner there, too,' he said, seeming genuinely enthused.

She liked the way it was going, drawing him in gradually. 'Tell you what,' she enthused. 'You can teach me golf if you play tennis with me.'

'OK.'

They went to the beach. She wanted to run around acting silly for once but he seemed restrained. He kept looking at his phone.

'Is everything alright?' she said.

'Yep.'

It clearly wasn't. Whatever was taking his attention, it wasn't her. She felt bad – for both him and her. He sensed this and put his phone away. They went to a bar and had Kolsch non-alcoholic beer with tacos. They talked about his career plans and about cars, but it felt stilted and again she began to think he was either distracted or plain bored. Or perhaps he was in turmoil over what had disturbed him before: allegations she was sleeping with the coach, and Mack saying 'Vanessa man' ostensibly had his name, and senõra Mencius screaming at him, subjects neither of them wanted to spend their time together talking about.

On the way home he took a detour and stopped the car in Crystal Cove State Park. They took in the view over the ocean and then he startled her with 'I love you, Gloria.'

'You don't know me,' she said nervously. It was meant as humour, but she was sure it sounded sinister.

'Why, you're not a killer or something, are you?'

'No!'

She had avoided needing to say she loved him, which would have been insincere, but did he say 'I love you' to a girl just because he wanted to fuck her? It wasn't the right place anyway, and even if it was, she wouldn't do it.

He surprised her with a kiss. It was deep and raw and blew any inhibition she had away. No one had kissed her like that before. No doubt, he was much practiced. She almost uttered 'I love you,' but was able to suppress it. But to be told she was loved was divine. Of course it had been said to her before, but she had never reciprocated. It seemed too easily said. Too often it later turned into 'I own you' and 'I control you'.

'Kiss me again,' she whispered, still dizzy.

He did so, but it didn't have quite the same magic.

Still thinking about the first kiss, after they'd said goodbye at her place she almost stumbled through the front door as though drunk. Her father was out and Dr Mencius' car was on the drive. If, as she believed, the doctor's relationship with Maria included sex, now would have been the perfect time. She didn't want to be proved right, however.

The only way to avoid finding out was to stay downstairs and watch TV. To waste time she made herself coffee. She sat in the lounge and convinced herself she really did want to watch the soaps. It was intolerable. She must be able to go to her room if she wanted to. She sauntered upstairs, annoyed at herself for being so affected. She was tempted to listen at her mother's door, but instead hurried past it. She picked up the sound of laughter.

Once in her room she put on her headphones to listen to the Foo Fighters and began looking at papers on the psychological theory of social exchange. Essentially a cost-benefit analysis of relationships, she thought about how it applied to her own life. She liked Tommy's company, but was he really only interested in her because he wanted to get laid? Otherwise, what did he get out of it? He surely didn't need her friendship.

50

One morning, Frank went to the short seller Saskia's office again. He didn't see Saskia herself as he had no appointment and she was in a boardroom meeting. Instead, he sat with one of her assistants, a lean young woman in spectacles, precise in appearance and manner, and conveying an impression of fierce intelligence. He talked about the information Saskia had asked him for. He'd had a lucky break because a friend of his knew something he could pass on. It was clear, however, that the assistant already knew everything he was telling her.

Perhaps it had been a subterfuge. Maybe Saskia had wanted to keep him interested for her own entertainment. He felt like a child - in thrall to someone more sophisticated and manipulated by them.

On the drive home, whilst fantasising about being in a relationship with Saskia, it occurred to him that he knew nothing about her. In the wilder reaches of his daydreaming he even wondered about hiring a private investigator to watch her movements, but he stopped exploring that notion on realising how creepy and absurd it was. He speculated about leaving Maria. Gloria was independent but needed a push to pursue her own life. Maria had no purpose for him either. Only loyalty to an earlier fairytale, mutually held, had kept them together.

While Frank was driving home from Los Angeles, Gloria had been forced to call an ambulance. Hearing his car arrive she ran to meet him. It reminded him of when she was a young girl and she would greet him enthusiastically on his return from a business trip.

'It happened when Dr Mencius was here,' she said excitedly. 'As he was leaving, he was approached by one of the new gardeners who works with Ray. They got into an argument. Then they scuffled. I heard them and came downstairs. By then Dr Mencius was on the ground. He'd hit his head on the stone steps and he was bleeding from the nose. The gardener had just left on his motorbike. Mencius was adamant he didn't want the police involved so I just called an ambulance. The doctor's in hospital.'

It was the kind of situation Frank hated; when all he wanted to think about was business-related matters and private fantasies, grubby reality intervened. To make it worse, Gloria was almost laughing as she told him about it.

He went to see his wife and found her surprisingly cheerful, although typically vague in answer to his questions. He did not learn anything additional to what Gloria had told him. Later, Maria made a rare appearance downstairs for dinner. She even cracked a few jokes at the expense of the doctor, Frank, and men in general. 'They all think with their cocks,' she told Gloria happily. 'Even when they're fighting it's all about their cocks.'

When her embarrassed father said the gardener would be sacked, Gloria told him the man should get a raise instead, which set Maria off giggling.

But unlike them, Gloria knew the reason for the incident. Or at least, she had sought and obtained an understanding from Suzie about it. Suzie had told her that she believed the young man had obtained the job solely with the intention of confronting Mencius, because he believed the doctor was having an affair with his mother. Gloria could see he was therefore a potential ally, should she need one.

51

Next morning, Gloria rang Mack. She was frustrated at still not having a handle on Mencius and his real story.

'This is nice,' said Mack

'I'm sorry if it's inconvenient. I should have checked first. I didn't think.'

'It's OK.' She sounded pleased.

'I can't find anything on this man, Dr Mencius, who treats my mother. And you obviously know your way around this stuff better than me.'

She gave Mack the background to the extent she knew it, adding that Mencius was a 'mystery man' although the picture was gradually being shaded in, citing señora Mencius' visit and the latest kerfuffle at the house. Mack said she would gladly find out what she could. Gloria was pleasantly surprised at Mack's attitude. She had expected her to be resistant to doing more than she already had. Mack seemed excited by the challenge and Gloria felt her own spirits rise.

After the call, Gloria realised she hadn't even asked how Lily was, and Mack hadn't volunteered it.

Meanwhile, Layne surprised Frank with a call to talk about investments. Layne said he had decided 'after careful thought' that he wanted to invest with Frank to get money out of his wife's hands. Frank said he had no investment vehicle of his own and instead was interested in supporting a short selling operation. He said Saskia was very skilled and he was convinced she would make good money for them both. Layne then astonished him by saying he didn't like the idea: 'I've got some morals, you know. Or at least, something that vaguely looks like morals through very dark glasses. I've got a social conscience. It's a great failing, I know.'

'What? But so does she.'

'How?'

'She's an activist. She researches long and hard and selects companies that have a share price out of whack with what they're really worth and bets against them.'

'Opportunist.'

'Rooting out bad actors.'

'I'm not convinced. I wanted to invest with you, Frank, not your floozie. After being ripped off by the last estate manager I've become cautious. Short selling sounds too much like one of his dodgy ideas.'

'This is different. This is as cautious as you are.'

'You're not selling it to me, Frank, I'm sorry. You sound starry-eyed about her. More than that, the investment itself sounds too risky. How long have you known her anyway? How many years?'

'Quite a few months.'

'It sounds like that super-ethical funny money scheme you were on about before. But is it possible she helped bring down your company, Frank? Ever thought of that? The share price crashed, didn't it?

'It did, but that wasn't because of short sellers.'

'Wasn't it? You seem pretty definite.'

'I am.' The notion had never occurred to him. It would mean Saskia had profited from his company's demise. No, he refused to believe it, but at the same time he realised he couldn't rule it out.

Layne was now rambling, sounding depressed. Frank asked him what the matter was. He replied, 'I thought having a young wife would revitalise me. Instead, I feel like a dying dinosaur.'

'Oh dear.'

'Sometimes it just feels like the end. It's not the end, of course, but if I stand on a pizza box I'm sure I can see it on the horizon. The sea's rolling in, Frank. It's already lapping at the walls of the castle.'

'What are you talking about?'

'It's a metaphor, Frank. Never mind.' He then turned into a ham actor: 'I will stand defiant and alone on this battlement until my flame is finally snuffed out. I will fight on.'

'A bit melodramatic there.'

Layne immediately lashed out: 'Call it what you will, you cur! I know what beckons me and it's not the cushy life. When have I ever had it soft and easy?' Frank did not reply, stunned at Layne's sudden fury. The old man immediately realised he was in the wrong, 'I'm sorry, Frank. It gets to me sometimes.'

'What does?'

'Everything.' He then assumed a high octave voice and gave a hushed, sentimental speech: 'Poor boy, there's always something blocking his way. Always something looks like an open window he can get through, but he can't because it's just a brick wall painted to look like the outside. Everything looking like the destination but it's just one more hard step along the way. He simply never gets there. Poor boy.' He was almost weeping now.

'Very moving, Layne,' said Frank, resisting the urge to laugh. 'But aren't we supposed to learn to enjoy the journey, rather than the destination?'

'Oh, save me from your Californian Taoist tosh! What'll it be next, a bloody sitar? You can't deny me my misery.'

'Self-pity, that's what it is.'

'And what's so wrong with that? I have a lot of self to pity. I had a lot of potential once and I never quite made it.'

'Are you seriously complaining? In your situation?'

'You bet I am. I have every right. Everyone has the right to complain about being born, for a start. Who would choose it if they were given the option?'

'As opposed to what?'

'If you could see your future life, I mean. But you don't get the chance to choose. "You have it, now enjoy it, sonny – or missy." I'm sorry, Frank. I've taken up too much of your precious time. I'll accept my fate... but I won't invest with your floozie.' With that he was gone.

52

Gloria was delighted to see Annalisa back in training and the prospect of her and Dessie in the same team excited her.

But it was not a success. In the next game Ant was clearly working harder than before, but she still didn't like running from deep and this annoyed Dessie who preferred to build up attacks from the back. The lack of cohesion spread to the whole team. Leaving the field at half-time 2-0 down, Dessie and Annalisa had a stand-up row. Gloria tried to mediate but Ant got upset with her and walked away. When the team were gathered together in the dressing room the coach was so furious at the warring pair he substituted them both. In the second half, Gloria set up a goal for the new striker, an eighteen-year-old debutante, but the game was lost 3-1 to a team near the bottom of the league. It was another shameful debacle and the players couldn't get away quickly enough from the coach's scathing criticism. Annalisa had already gone home.

A few days later, Dessie contacted Gloria, suggesting they go for coffee. Although Gloria didn't know her well, she wasn't surprised to hear from her. Dessie's half-time on-pitch row with Annalisa was all over the team's little bit of social media, with outsiders laughing about the fractious duo being subbed by the angry coach and the inevitable loss to lowly opposition.

They met in a small independent coffee shop off Irvine's main drag, with a cultivated vintage feel and potted plants hanging from the ceiling.

There was also a large TV screen on the wall that had the news on silent and a banner along the bottom constantly updated with the latest traffic developments.

Dessie said she had been 'super upset' at being substituted at half-time which had never happened to her before, but she was now over it. She said she was impressed with Gloria's speed and work rate, 'Even if your passes are a little wayward at times.'

Gloria knew this was true but it still hurt. She was tempted to defend herself but decided to be gracious. After all, it wasn't her who'd been substituted. 'I'm easily distracted,' she said.

Dessie was interested, 'Like, by what?'

Gloria hesitated. She didn't want to get into talking about the mysterious Carmina and her hurtful messages. 'Could be anything,' she said.

'I don't believe you,' said Dessie. 'You seem pretty strong-minded to me. You're sprinting down the touchline and you get distracted? How does that even happen? I mean, when you're so focused like you obviously have to be?'

Gloria was on the brink of revealing, but she merely said, 'I shut it out now; just put the blinders on, I guess.'

Dessie, sensing some deeply private wound was being opened, did not pursue it.

'I've been getting weird messages,' she said.

'Really?' Gloria was intrigued.

'Yeah. Accusing me of a relationship with the coach, as how else would I be in the team? That kind of stuff. Nasty.'

'Yeah? Does it bother you?'

'Of course,' said Dessie. 'I wouldn't be human otherwise. It's just so mean.'

'It is.' Gloria took a deep breath. 'I had that too.'

'Oh dear.'

'I don't look at it now. Like I say, I just shut it out.'

'Ah.' Now Dessie understood why Gloria got distracted.

'I had someone in England investigate.'

'Why England? That's weird.'

Gloria told her about her friend Lily whose wife Mack was a PI.

'I see,' said Dessie, puzzled.

'I couldn't figure it out, but she did. I'm pretty sure I know who's behind it and I have a theory but I don't really know why they send the messages. It's almost like a Pandora's box that I don't want to open.'

'I get it. So what do your folks say?'

Gloria explained how she found it difficult to talk to them about it, what with her mother's depression and her father's business preoccupations.

'What you're saying is, both your parents are a bit...'

'Self-absorbed, you mean? Remote?'

'I guess. Well, I don't have that. I have the opposite. They're in my business before I even know what's in it myself!' She laughed.

'Yeah?' Gloria began to perceive, perhaps as never before, what her life had been missing, although she wouldn't want quite what Dessie had.

'It can be very intrusive,' said Dessie. 'Strike that: it's *always* very intrusive.'

'So what do they say about these messages?'

'My dad's on it. He's a cop.' She chuckled. 'So I don't need to go to England to find out who's messing with me here.' She found it hilarious. 'Oh Gloria, I'm sure glad we're having this conversation. It's cheered me up no end.'

'Glad you find me so funny,' said Gloria flatly.

'Oh, honey, I'm not laughing at you. I would never.' She grabbed Gloria's arm.

'Thank you,' said Gloria, although she didn't know why she was saying it.

'Incidentally, I liked the way you tried to mediate between Annalisa and me. I mean, we were never going to hug it out, but I appreciate it. She shouldn't have bitten your head off like that.'

'She didn't like it because she thought me condescending: "Gloria gets off her saintly cloud to calm the squabbling children." That kind of thing.'

This amused Dessie and they both laughed this time.

'What's the coach going to do?' said Gloria. 'It's a mess. The problem is, Ant's dad gets so heavy with the coach. He was already mad as hell at her being dropped before.'

'I know what I'd do,' said Dessie. 'I'd play the rookie up front. She played well, I thought.'

'She did.'

'And bring Anna on as sub. Impact.'

'Oh, she wouldn't like that.'

'She's a diva.'

'Yeah, she is. Though not a diver.'

'Ha! Ha! Well, take it or leave it, I say. By the time she gets on, the game will be won, with any luck. Then they can sub me too if they want. I can't play with her.'

On the drive home, Gloria had to take a detour. She already knew why, because it had flashed up on the TV screen in the coffee bar. A five-car pile-up outside Irvine. Several injuries, three critical. It had made her think their conversation about the game had been so trivial. But it was no different to anything else compared to death, serious illness or injury, or floods and earthquakes, the latest war. One moment doing the normal things of daily life, the next moment dead. It wasn't that she didn't care about tragedies, but she had to live her own life. Live it as best she could. Alert, disciplined, caring. They were her watchwords, her affirmations that sometimes seemed so trite and yet were ultimately all she felt she could do. She could only pay attention to what she could affect and resolve to do that with the greatest diligence.

Happy at reaching this conclusion, she suddenly realised she'd almost missed a turn and narrowly avoided crashing into the cab of a Peterbilt. That would have been one critical. Or maybe two. Or even dead. After this incident she drove with the concentration of a thousand-year-old Zen monk, or what she imagined that would be like. No, that was too slow.

She was relieved to arrive home safely as she pulled into her drive. The gardeners cast a quick glance at her exiting the car – usually they stared. She recalled how her father had once told Ray that if any of his team ever made a suggestive remark to 'my beloved daughter' he would fire them on the spot. Casual leering, however, was not so easily deterred. But today they merely glanced because they were involved in a row. Ray was off sick and the two younger ones could not get along. Ray might be the 'laziest gardener in Orange County' according to Maria, but he had a calming presence on the others, and his knowledge surpassed anyone else's, giving him added authority.

The pair were in dispute over where to plant a white shrub rose, which meant it wasn't being planted. As she approached the front door the scruffier of the two hurried towards her: could she please find out where the rose was supposed to go? Gloria merely nodded.

She looked in on her mother who was in that strange habitual state of hers, lying fully clothed on her bed, neither asleep nor awake but very much in her own world. The thought occurred to Gloria that no vampire victim could have been more inanimate.

In his office her father was on the phone trying to persuade some loser why he should invest his money in his girlfriend's investment operation. He waved away Gloria's request to talk.

'For Heaven's sake!' she exclaimed as she threw her keys on her desk. If the others were oblivious, maybe she should be too – for a few minutes at least.

She put her headphones on and shut out the world. She began listening to hard Mexican rock while she looked up Dessie on Facebook. She could see the hostile posts. It was weird. Why were they targeting her? She was a brilliant player – she didn't need to get favourable treatment from the coach in return for sex. The comments weren't coming from Carmina but fake accounts that someone, perhaps her, had set up. She looked up Carmina herself. You'd think she was a primary school teacher with her neat little house and family, and the words of wisdom she posted. Gloria was always wary of people who put up such things – mindless pleasantries – on their social media pages. Invariably, the individuals concerned were full of turmoil and / or hypocrisy and could be plain nasty while writing of sheer beauty. She was tempted to send her a direct message. She would pretend to be a friend of Dessie. But she decided against it: a revenge mission might create new problems – the unintended consequence.

She was interrupted from her inner dialogue by a tap on the shoulder. It was her father.

'What the hell's been going on!?' he demanded.

The argument over the shrub rose had turned into a fight. Frank had heard it through his window and had to break off his call, which he wasn't pleased about. He'd gone out and fired them both. They'd left and the shrub remained unplanted. None critical, except maybe the rose.

'It would never have happened if Ray were here,' said Gloria.

'You're right, my dear,' he sighed.

She was annoyed with herself. She should have mediated between the fractious pair. It was what she thought she did: mediate. Even if they then turned on her.

'What will you do about the garden?' she asked.

'I'll hire a couple of temporaries 'til Ray gets back.'

She looked out and saw the white rose lying there. One in millions of such plants but she felt sympathy for it. She walked outside and found the spade and hose left on the grass. The rose was called *Carefree Wonder* and it amused her to think it could have been named after her as a joke; one thing no one would describe her as being was a 'carefree wonder'. Without further thought, she quickly dug a hole where she thought it should go and planted and watered it. Firming up the soil afterwards, she felt good. She had mud on her dress but didn't care. She'd only been caught by three thorns. None critical.

53

Over Skype, Mack reported back on Mencius. She looked so businesslike in her navy blue dress and top that Gloria felt slightly disconcerted. 'Did you really find anything on him?' Gloria asked.

'Yes, of course.'

'Then why couldn't I? OK, you're the expert on this stuff but even so—'

'That's because it's not his real name.' Gloria realised this was so obvious it was embarrassing.

'Why does he need an alias?' she said.

'Because he had someone after him. That's why there's no footprint, no trace online.'

'Who was after him?'

'They still are. Someone whose wife he was supposedly taking care of.'

'Ah. Sounds familiar. He's very persuasive. He always has an answer for everything, although a very vague one. What happened to the person's wife?'

'What do you think? She died.'

'Oh God!' Gloria's feelings of gratification at her suspicions being proved correct were overwhelmed by immediate concern for her mother. 'What's his expertise, if any?'

'Holistic healing. Treat the whole person. That kind of stuff.'

'What my dad calls New Age woo-woo. So what do you know about the person after him?'

'It's someone who apparently has some kind of mental disorder. But there's a twist. Are you ready for this?'

'Go on.'

'It was a case of mistaken identity: it wasn't even Mencius responsible, but when the guy discovered that, he went after him anyway.'

'Wait a minute. So you're saying someone's after Mencius because he thought he killed his wife, intentionally or not, through some holistic treatment, then found out it wasn't Mencius; yet the guy still decided to go after him anyway – is that it?'

'You got it.'

'That's nuts.'

'Mencius looks like the doctor who does the same woo-woo stuff, and the guy wanted someone to blame, so it was a case of "You'll do".'

'OK, so Mencius is not who he claims anyway. So who is he?'

'His name is Almero and he's a former actor.'

'Ah. We're really getting somewhere. Or you are.'

'But he did train as a doctor.'

'I want to think he's a quack.'

'He might be, although he could be genuine.'

'Please tell me he's fake.'

'I can't. But I can tell you he gave up normal medicine to become an actor, not the other way round. I'll send you what I have. Want me to carry on looking?'

'Please.'

She wondered if Mack was teasing her, holding something back, playing the mischievous disrupter. She was fun. Lily was like cold stone in comparison, but cold stone to be worshipped.

Before the call ended, Gloria told her about her new teammate Dessie receiving nasty messages. Could the perpetrator be Carmina under a different name? Mack said she would look into it. The online abuse seemed to expand all the time. Gloria told her about the row Dessie had with Annalisa but said sending horrible messages was not Ant's style. Mack accepted the new search request with apparent relish. 'By the way,' she said, 'Can I say something?'

'Sure.' Gloria suspected Mack had something serious to say, but she had no idea what. 'Go ahead.'

'I have to say thank you for saving my marriage. I mean it. Something you said or wrote to Lily shocked her. She saw you as easygoing and all-accepting, and when you criticised her morals it made her look in the mirror, and she didn't like what she saw.'

'Wow. It was just a word.'

'Well, whatever, it hit her right between the eyes. She told me she had a dream in which she was a model going to be photographed for a magazine, but her face was dirty and she couldn't clean it. And the harder she cleaned, the dirtier it got. She woke up in a panic. Lily's vain. She's forced herself to change her ways. But it all started with your criticism. So thank you.'

'Well, I don't know what to say, except that what I did was really nothing and I'm glad to hear that your marriage is safe, Mack.'

Gloria was so amazed by Mack's call it took her hours to get to sleep that night. By next morning, Mack had sent Gloria more information about Mencius. He'd been arrested for fraud but under his real name of Almero. She'd found that he had multiple identities and one of them had been the defendant in both criminal and civil litigations. He'd already had a jail sentence for fraud and been successfully sued. Plus, 'the mistaken identity' had been a distraction, merely one of his aliases he was trying to distance himself from. 'Thank you, Mack,' Gloria said happily to the laptop screen.

She went to see her father to tell him with great delight that Mencius had been exposed as a dangerous quack and fraud. Frank was unimpressed, however. 'I can't rely on internet blather, Gloria. I rely on face to face.'

'I don't believe you,' she said, stunned. 'The police have arrested him.'

He stared at her. Her reaction bothered him. Sometimes silence worked when words didn't. Frank slowly began to realise he must act.

Maria was unhappy at the news when Gloria told her. She refused to accept it. How could the good doctor be a fraud? OK, she'd had doubts about him of her own but not that. She became angry, blaming Gloria, as though what the doctor had done was her fault, not that she believed him guilty. She claimed that jealous people were responsible for his arrest. His estranged wife must be behind it.

It was the most life Gloria had seen in her in a while and, despite being unfairly accused, it pleased her. Frank then came in and asked his daughter to leave the room while he talked to her mother. For once giving his wife his full attention, to inspire himself he conjured up the feelings he had for her in their early days of marriage, and the happy times they spent together when the children were young. He was determined to make her face the truth, using a gentle, empathetic manner to persuade her. He found it difficult. He wanted to give her a good shake and tell her not to be so silly, but he tried to play the part of the caring counsellor instead.

'Stop it,' she scoffed. 'This act won't work with me. What are you and Gloria cooking up? She's become so devious lately. She never used to be like it. All this psychology stuff has made her sketchy. It's like she has some secret knowledge. It's a black art she's learning.'

'No it's not. She cares about you.'

This appeared to trigger something in her. She became pensive: 'Does she?'

'She's just the same Gloria. She's gold.'

'You always used to say that. I'm not so sure now.' She sniffed, then involuntarily turned her head to the right and back to centre to face him, indicating she had something important to say. 'Well, I hope Dr Mencius is released soon and all this nonsense is put behind him. I'm sure he has good lawyers, but if not we should pay for some.'

'We? No, I don't think so.'

Frank returned to Gloria's room. She wanted to go and console her mother, but he said it was not a good idea. 'Let her rest,' he said.

'She is my mom. I think I know her.'

He did not reply, and after he'd gone she went to see her again. Expecting she would be asleep, she was surprised to find her on the phone. She looked worried.

'What's the matter?' said Gloria.

'That bastard drained my bank account.'

'What bastard?'

'That bastard of a doctor.'

'What? How?'

'I gave him my bank details for medications so he could get reimbursed straight away.'

'What... why on Earth did you do that!?'

'He asked and I thought it made sense. I was ill anyway. I didn't know what was going on. How could I?'

'No, because you were under his medications all the time. Now that you're not, you're...' She wanted to say "normal again", but stopped herself.

'I don't know what you're getting at,' said Maria.

Gloria merely sighed and left the room.

For once, her father was not on some call or other. He noticed her down expression. 'Are you OK?' he said.

'Not great. Mencius has plundered her bank account.'

Frank was shocked. For a few moments he sat slumped forward, elbows on the desk, holding his head in his hands. Then he looked up and told Gloria to close the door. They talked about it, but quietly. He asked her, 'Did she say how much was in it?'

'No.'

He was sweating heavily. 'I bet it could have been several hundred thousand dollars. God! It really isn't what we need right now.'

'Are we OK - financially, I mean?'

'We've got reserves, but I'm not bringing in a lot these days. I'm just amazed how this could even happen. How could Maria be so stupid as to be conned by this evil man?'

'Sedatives,' said Gloria. 'Hypnotherapy, too.'

'But then, I didn't see through him either.' He looked up. 'It was you who remained consistently opposed to Mencius and his so-called "treatments". You deserve great credit for that.' She merely shrugged, whilst gratified to have been proved right. He gave her a warm hug and then went to see his wife. He remained calm as he spoke with Maria before phoning the police. The rest of the day was taken up with the issue of Mencius' fraud.

That night, a fierce storm swept through the town, causing damage to buildings and uprooting trees. A canvas gazebo blew in from a neighbour's garden. Tree branches hit the garage roof, shingles flew off, and an old leak revived. The following day, with the storm gone, once power was restored the family began repairs. One of Gloria's brothers, Tony, had arrived the previous afternoon, thereby earning the blame for the storm, and he, Gloria, and Frank did the work. Maria even joined in, passing items back and forth. They forgot their troubles. To Gloria it was a reminder of old times – times that nostalgia made better than they'd really been. Except this was a genuinely happy time, not needing nostalgia to make it so, and it would serve as a nostalgic moment for some future day. When Frank dropped a hammer on his son's foot, Tony even laughed - after the obligatory cursing.

54

A couple of days later, Frank heard from Layne on Skype again. After the Mencius debacle he was glad of the diversion into the old man's world.

'You're a necessary evil, Frank. Well, not evil, but you know what I mean.'

'I'm used to it, Layne. I should be by now. You've obviously got something big to tell me. It must be about your wife. So what's up?'

'So perceptive you are. Yes, she claims when she married me it was the equivalent of being abducted by aliens and she lost her mind. I think she's already planning her life as a divorcée. Been planning it since before we were married.'

'It's all about the money.'

'As if I didn't know.' He sounded sad and changed the subject: 'By the way, I see there's been another mass shooting. How many's that this year?'

'Give it a rest.'

'Close to you, wasn't it this time?'

'California's a big state.'

'Even so.'

'By the way, thanks for the bat pictures, Layne. Very helpful.'

'Well, I keep reading about the rabid ones over there.'

'Thanks for the concern. We do get news here. And I did know vampires were bats. But thank you anyway.'

'You're welcome, Frank. How's your week been?'

'Never better.'

'Same as ever, then. The sun's always up.'

'This is the only time I'm living, Layne. I can't change the past and the future can take care of itself.'

'Very spiritual, Frank. If I didn't know you already, I'd guess you were Californian.'

'Actually, I'm not. I'm from Oklahoma, but the Grape State adopted me. I graduated from USC and I've been here ever since.'

'But you seem a little cussed today, old boy. A little tight. Mozzies got you? I keep reading about them too.'

'As a matter of fact, we had some storm damage. A big one came through a couple of nights ago.'

'Oh dear. Bad?'

'Just some shingles. It could have been much worse. Our neighbours got hit bad, I believe.'

'I'm surprised you even know. Your house must be so big you could easily not notice it got hit. So have you got water coming in?'

'It's already fixed, Layne. That's how we do things. We pick ourselves up fast.'

'Surprised you've got power.'

'We don't wait around.'

Frank decided to raise the subject of Mencius with Layne. Suddenly the tetchy old man transformed into his patient counsellor. It felt like their roles had reversed for once. Frank gave him the full background about Maria's 'empty nest' feelings, her drift into depression, which he said he felt partly responsible for, and the arrival of the doctor.

'The great deceiver,' said Layne.

'Indeed. He called every week to prescribe the same dodgy treatments.'

'Women are faithless, though, aren't they?'

'It's not that. She was misled. Gloria knew exactly what he was up to but I wouldn't listen. Poor Gloria. She knew no good would come of it.'

'She also had her father to worry about.'

'Well, yes.'

'Where would you be without her?'

'She's been making up for her absent mother.'

'The doting father, you are.'

'I guess you could say that. But now I believe it's time for her to move on.'

'Time she found a good catch. Maybe cross the pond.'

'You're right. There must be possibilities.'

'I was joking, Frank. With her looks and undoubted intelligence she'd certainly wow the rich and famous, but aristocracy and celebrity aren't all they're made out to be.'

'She knows that.'

'Thank God she does.'

55

Mack phoned Gloria to say that she had examined the malicious posts on Dessie's Facebook and found they were from another fake account Carmina had created. But why was she targeting Dessie? Mack had found a business connection between Carmina's partner and Mr Garcia, Annalisa's dad. 'She's your friend, isn't she? Annalisa Garcia, I mean?'

'Yes. Say no more. Mr Garcia must have said something to him.'

'OK. Now for some more serious news.'

Mack said that her boss Paz Wheat had found the man in Texas who was obsessed with 'Vanessa'. He was living alone in a small town in the west of the state. A man in his thirties, he'd been in a romance with her, or so he thought, for months. She'd encouraged him, sent him intimate photographs of herself, talked about him being the one for her. Paz had been to see him to explain the truth: that a malicious person had invented Vanessa and was sending him photoshopped pictures. He found the man recalcitrant. He was already upset because someone had hacked into his Facebook account and changed his name, which Gloria had already figured out. He was angry because when he'd told people he was going to marry Vanessa they laughed at him and told him he was being duped.

He'd clung to the hope she was real in order to prove them wrong. But to have to accept Vanessa would never be his because she did not exist was more than he could bear. He threatened Paz with a gun. He said he already had all the information he needed to find Gloria, having found out her face was that of Vanessa, and was intent on visiting her, having already decided that if she wouldn't marry him, he would 'make her suffer for what she did to me'. In his eyes, if Vanessa was not real, it was Gloria's fault, and she must die. Paz then went straight to the police about it. When they called on the man there was a shootout and he was killed.

'Oh my God!' was all Gloria could utter, falling silent as she absorbed the full shock of it all. She was aware there were tears sliding down her face but was determined to continue the conversation. 'So was it suicide by cop?' she said at last.

'I'll say, no.'

'It sounds like it, though.' She felt Mack was trying to make her feel less bad. 'You can tell me,' she said. 'It's alright.'

'There's no evidence. He never shouted anything that would establish that. Of course, the cops would prefer to say it was.'

Gloria was not only stunned by the news but felt guilty about it, as though somehow she could have prevented the man's death. She told Mack this but her new friend would have none of it. It was nothing to do with her. Was she to feel guilty because her face was on the internet? Once it was there, it ceased to be something within her control. Was she going to marry this guy? Of course not. He was therefore going to kill her, and nothing that had happened to him was her fault. Or, for that matter, Paz's fault.

Gloria kept Mack on the phone as long as she could. She didn't know who she could turn to: not her preoccupied father or addled mother, not her brothers, not Annalisa, not the indifferent Tommy. Mack was the only one who understood. Mack said she and Lily were always there for her.

She decided to share Mack's findings with Dessie about the messages she'd been receiving. When she rang her, Dessie was initially amused: 'So you heard from England, then? That's funny. My dad just said it must be Annalisa and her dad behind it, but he didn't investigate it yet.'

'It's not Annalisa,' said Gloria. 'It's not what she does. She doesn't do sneaky things like that. She wouldn't have asked her father to get involved.'

'No, but she could tell him the situation in the team, knowing he'd do something. I've seen her type before. She's a devious little bitch.'

'No she's not. She does bitchy things, but then we all do.'

'No we don't. And what gives you the right to be so nice, to try and smooth things over? Why don't you just be a bitch yourself and enjoy it? You can't, can you?'

'I can be a bitch.'

'Like when?'

Gloria told her how she had tormented Trey the catfish, leading him on. Dessie was unimpressed: 'Oh, excuse me. You taught the guy a lesson. And all the time you were leading him on meant he wasn't catfishing someone else. Be kind to yourself.' Gloria then told her about the 'Vanessa man' and her feelings of guilt over his death. Dessie could not believe her ears. 'Did you ever see the pictures?' she said.

'One in a bikini I never even owned. I don't want to know.'

'Well, if you did see them, you'd know not to feel guilty. Only a very stupid person would not realise they were fake. It was a joke. Sick, maybe, but still a joke. Your head appears on at least three different bodies. One doesn't even have your skin tone. In one, Vanessa has a long neck, and in another it's short. And in one, if you look closely enough, she has three arms! That's how badly it was photoshopped. And this guy believed it? I'm sorry but Darwin wasn't wrong. How did he even get to thirty? How did he get to twelve? Some people just want to be deceived. Girl, stay as sweet as you are, but don't beat yourself up over idiots. And, by the way, thank you for calling. I appreciate it.'

While Gloria was talking with Dessie, her father was on Skype with Layne who announced that his wife had left him. 'Good riddance,' he remarked. But she was not the only one who'd left; the estate manager Todd whom she'd insisted he hire was also gone.

'You didn't trust him, though, did you?'

'No, but I wasn't expecting him to suddenly leave. Very suspicious. And there's more.'

'More? How can there be?'

'My home is gone.'

'The mansion?'

'Yes, this sacred ancestral home. She's sold it cheap for quick cash without me even knowing about it. Some sheikh bought it for his daughter.'

'Oh no! How on God's green earth?'

'Fake papers. Fake signatures. It's dastardly.' Layne explained how he believed Todd was his wife's boyfriend all along, and he had pretended to be Layne and forged his signature. 'Of course the solicitors were in on it. They had to be. How could they miss it? And there's more yet: she's drained my bank accounts. Same thing. Conned them with fake signatures, and of course the dozy bank was hoodwinked by someone who doesn't even vaguely look like me. It makes me mad because they lecture me about money laundering every chance they get and then when some fraudster comes along they say, "Here, help yourself." But I've been betrayed, Frank. It's the darkest of days. I've had a few, but this is the worst.'

Frank did not know what to say. Anything would seem superfluous, inadequate. 'I'm really sorry, Layne.'

'I know you are. You're a good man. I say wretched things to you, awful things sometimes, but you're the only decent friend I've got. All the others have gone. I fear for the future. I fear for my life now. No doubt she's taken out insurance on me. I expect to be murdered any minute.' For a few moments his voice now took on a soulful tone: 'The shadows are closing in on a life. The boy who dreamed of doing good in the world, despite all the hurdles put in his way, now sees himself about to be snuffed out like a cheap candle... But I tell you this, Frank, I go with pride. I may be at the lowest of lowest ebbs in life, but I remain fearless.'

'That's a great way to be,' Frank said blandly.

'I'm a fighter, and I'm going to punish them. When I die thanks to them, once the police and the lawyers have sorted everything out, I will return with an AI afterlife.'

'Good for you,' said Frank, although he had no idea what Layne was talking about.

'I'll find a way to be around forever to haunt them. I'll have an avatar. I'll infect their dreams. I'll destroy their days and nights with poisonous thoughts and fears. They will suffer for their evil deeds.'

Frank merely listened, letting him ramble for a while longer, then he gently ended the call before Layne's heroic stance faded and he returned to his habitual self-pity.

As soon as Frank put the phone down, Gloria rushed in and told him what Mack had said, and for once he gave her his full attention. He then held her tight and told her he would always protect her. She managed not to cry, and she asked him about his call with Layne. Afterwards, she suggested his friend hire Mack and her boss Paz Wheat to investigate the background on his wife and the dodgy estate manager. 'I thought you didn't have any time for him,' he said.

'I don't, but I'm not heartless. He clearly can't do anything for himself. Has he talked to the police yet?'

'Yes, but he's not expecting them to do much.'

'Not a man of his standing? There must be some benefits to being an aristocrat, or lord, or whatever he is.' She felt less antagonistic towards Layne now. In fact, apart from Carmina, she did not feel antagonistic to anyone since her conversations with Mack and Dessie. She felt for the deceased 'Vanessa' man's family. He was young enough to have living parents. Maybe he was even a parent himself. But, as she reminded herself, he'd wanted to kill her, and maybe the danger would persist with some crazy person feeling sufficiently aggrieved on his behalf to carry through with the man's wishes. The effect of it all would be to harden her – still seeking to be kind, but harder. She resolved not to look online to read about the man's death.

As it transpired, she didn't need to look. Mack sent her all she might have found, including the crucial fact that Paz had learned this was the fifth time he'd 'fallen in love' and been deceived in this way; Vanessa was only the latest. In killing her he would be killing all the others too. Prior to Paz's visit he'd said he would kill 'Vanessa' with five bullets, one for each of them. He fired five times at the police instead.

56

Gloria was glad of the distraction soccer training and the next match brought. She was excited because the coach had decided to follow the approach Dessie had recommended. Gloria now found herself in defence, adding pace as they built up from the back, rather than merely leading on the counterattack. Annalisa, who was uncharacteristically quiet before the game, was forced to take her place on the subs bench while her rookie replacement ran all over the pitch, something that was an anathema to Ant. By half-time the game was effectively won at 4-1. Annalisa was not introduced until the seventieth minute and had little to do. Later that day, she sent Gloria a message saying that, whether the family moved or not, she was leaving the club at the end of the season.

Apart from telling Dessie, Gloria kept the contents of Mack's call and follow-up to herself. If she resisted talking or even thinking about the subject, maybe it would fade away. She knew, however, that one day 'Vanessa' would resurface. Someone in a bar would point her out or approach her, and a friend would then ask her, 'What's with the "Vanessa"?' It could happen tomorrow or in a year's time. She would merely shrug and think about the picture with the three arms. If the issue ever became problematic for her, she would put a statement on social media making clear she was not and never had been 'Vanessa'.

57

Frank made another visit to Saskia's. He felt conflicted. He now realised that his infatuation with the hedge fund manager was absurd, as though discovering that for a while he'd become a teenager again and was now remorseful about it. Despite Frank's exasperation at Maria for allowing herself to be duped over Mencius, and at himself for not being alive to it, he could see how the latest situation had drawn him closer to his wife. He was still preoccupied with Saskia but no longer to the extent that it was affecting his judgement.

Any lingering romantic intentions came to an abrupt halt, however, after he saw her talking closely with a man in the corridor outside her office. Out of curiosity he asked her assistant who it was. Bemused by his question, she replied that it was Saskia's husband 'of course'. If that were not enough, it was obvious from the easy, relaxed affection they showed each other that the couple were happy and in love. He was relieved. He had saved himself from serious embarrassment, or worse. He'd previously imagined Saskia's toleration of the fact he hadn't contributed financially to her business was because she had a personal interest in him. He now saw that was nonsense. He thought again about what Layne had suggested: that Saskia had made money from his own company's collapse. How did he feel about short selling now? Not so comfortable. Where was the morality in it? It was opportunist. Feeling morally superior about another company was easy, but what about others feeling superior over yours? He was glad that the Saskia episode was now over.

When he arrived home, planning to take his wife out for a meal if she was up to it, he found Gloria waiting for him in the lounge and in a state of distress. 'Whatever's the matter?' he said.

'It's Mama,' she said through tears. 'She's talking about suicide. She says she's in a "pit of despair".'

'What is it with her, darling?'

'She feels guilty. She says she brought this Mencius business upon us and caused the problem over the money by being so stupid.'

'It wasn't her fault. She shouldn't feel that way. These things happen. It's only money anyway.' He noted Gloria's surprised glance. 'I mean, money's important, obviously, but it's not everything. And we'll get it back. Is she alright now? Is she sleeping?'

Sleep, the answer for everything. 'No, she's writing. She's writing it all down. I finally was able to persuade her. Or maybe I didn't; maybe she just figured it out for herself.'

'OK. So I won't disturb her; I won't disrupt her thoughts. But I will pay more attention in the future.' He was shaken, and his face was of someone chastened by events.

'To what?' she asked.

'To her, of course... and you. I promise.'

'By the way,' said Gloria. 'You were right about that ref. I looked it up. He really was a crook.'

Frank merely shrugged, happy that for once his daughter had acknowledged he knew better.

'And you were right about the gold, too. I'm not moving it because it's safe, but I will look elsewhere in future.'

'Well, nothing's perfect,' he said sombrely. 'We can aim for it but have to accept we can't reach it. No one could criticise you for trying.'

Frank was not in the mood for Layne's call soon afterwards. The Englishman was complaining because he'd seen the former estate manager Todd, Tania's boyfriend, driving about town in a Porsche.

'So what?' said Frank.

'Don't you see? You're so obtuse sometimes. Where do you think he got the money from?'

'I don't know. Maybe ask him?'

'What's up, Frank? You're a little prickly today.'

'This is a difficult time, Layne.'

'Why so? Wife left you? I can't say I'd blame her.'

'Eh? This is more serious. She's very ill.'

'Go on.'

'I really don't want to talk about it.'

'Not to your old friend? Not after you told me about that doctor. I've always opened up to you, Frank. So you should tell me.'

'Alright then. She's been talking about taking her own life.'

'Oh, I'm so sorry... Did she give any indication of this before?'

'No. She first said it to Gloria earlier today.'

'So she didn't actually try then?'

'No, but that's not the point.'

'Well, you can take some consolation from that, old boy. Most women in the same position as her would have jumped already. Just joking.'

'What!?'

'I was joking, I said.'

'Joking? This is not funny, Layne.'

'I didn't mean it. You know I didn't.'

'You're out of line.'

'Now, Frank—'

'No, I'm serious. I'm done with you.' Frank was startled at his own words, but he was not in the mood for jokes.

'Oh... Oh no. I've suddenly got a pain in my chest. Now *I'm* serious. Oh no.' Layne then disappeared from the screen.

'Stop it. Stop pretending, you jerk.'

'Oh, there it is again. It's getting worse. Oh, I hear something. What's this? A motorbike has arrived. Maybe it's a paramedic...'

'Yeah, maybe it's the postman, you self-pitying fraud.'

'Oh no, it's someone else. It's not a paramedic.'

'Of course it's not. Stop the acting.'

Frank lingered as Layne talked to the 'someone else', real or imaginary. 'Oh God! Oh, that pain! What do you want? I haven't much left now. You say you want me? No, no, not yet. Wait. No, the pain's really not so bad now. It just needs a little more time. Wrong address, hopefully. Must be. Oh, it is? It is the wrong address. Phew. OK, well, thanks for calling, I guess. The pain has definitely eased now. Just from you being here. OK, I understand: it's a reprieve. A promise of good behaviour. OK, I'll do it... Yes, I will. For now anyway. Frank, did you hear that? Were you listening? It's a reprieve, Frank. Are you still there? Did you hear what they said? Frank, where are you? You've gone. You really have gone, haven't you? See you in a week or so. Maybe not. I'll send the caller round to yours anyway. No, not yours. I didn't mean that.'

There was no answer. Frank had moved away from the screen but was still listening, shaking his head. He then left the call.

58

Gloria read in the *Patch* newsletter that more charges had been brought against Mencius. He was a serial fraudster. At the time of his arrest, it was clear from documents the police found that he was looking for a new victim. He was intending to move to Nevada with a new identity and under the guise of an accountant. He was planning to concentrate on elderly women without dependents and with not much financial nous, grateful for an 'expert' like him to invest their life savings for them.

A little later, Tommy surprised her with a visit. They sat outside in the garden sipping hot chocolate. Gloria felt almost happy. She decided not to tell him the fate of 'Vanessa man'. He said he wanted to make plans with her. What sort of plans? It was about things they could do together. They made a list: surfing, hiking, horse riding, playing tennis, golf, beach volleyball, tenpin bowling, going to Disneyland. Maybe take a trip across the border, or how about Vegas? Gloria said she'd love to do any or all of them. Or she would be happy just chilling. But Tommy was not one for chilling. He was restless. He was an outdoor guy. She wanted the outside life too but clung to the 'great indoors'. She loved literature and studying psychology, and watching TV, and she wanted to learn to cook. Tommy didn't like to be indoors and didn't seem to care much about the inner life. He perhaps wasn't conflicted like her, and yet she didn't envy him. She probably wouldn't envy herself either, but it was her inner conflicts that made her herself and she accepted that.

Once they'd completed their list, Tommy left as abruptly as he'd arrived. Maybe he was conflicted too. Maybe he detected a coldness in her. A coldness she knew was there, though she would rather be rid of it. She felt ambivalent about him. She liked him but she was not desperate.

59

Layne sent Frank a message of apology: 'I'm terribly sorry, old chap, I shouldn't have said what I did. I meant it as a silly joke but it was in very poor taste. I can say the stupidest things sometimes. Your friendship is too important to me to cause you upset, even by accident. We must talk soon, if you find it in your heart to forgive me. Currently I am too depressed to talk. The police never cease to amaze me in their efforts to punish the good citizen while the bad ones roam free to do whatever mischief their evil minds conceive. The latest is that they have raided the place on some pretext and claim to have found magic mushrooms in the disused stables and a cannabis plantation in the barn. I had no idea about this. Obviously it was one of the staff, or possibly some side business of one of the estate managers or Tania. I was hauled into the police station and browbeaten. It was humiliating, but of course my discomfort was part of their malicious and vindictive plan. I was able to persuade them I wasn't personally involved, but they could not understand how I did not even know about it. I said I knew there were some mushrooms being grown but believed they were oyster and shiitake for the vegan market, and as for the barn I never visited it after a rat tried to bite me in there once. I was able to convince the police to let me go without charge, although it took a promise to host the local force's Christmas party for free. I didn't mention to them, however, that I might not legally own the place, thanks to Tania's antics. I felt like saying, "In other countries cash usually suffices", but of course here they are supposedly "above" corruption.'

At the end of the message, Layne asked if he could phone again and Frank replied, confirming he could, resisting the temptation to add, 'Clearly the "mystery motorcyclist" hasn't returned.'

A few days later, Layne was back on Skype. Frank commented on the police raid and said, 'That must have been awful for you.'

Layne replied, 'It's just the daily persecution I've become used to, quite frankly. I can now understand how minorities feel. In fact, I'm really a minority myself. One who carries the burden of the world upon his shoulders but does so willingly despite all the brickbats and the corrupt agents of the state - the police, the tax heavies. But I am the guardian of the sacred flame, Frank.'

'You are indeed.'

Layne then gave a huge sigh. 'Do you know what the very latest is?'

'No. The police again?'

'Good guess, but no. I've discovered I've been conned by a philanthropy maximisation consultant. Ever heard of such a thing?'

'What is it?'

'He helps you with your charity choices. Or is supposed to.'

'All you need is less, isn't that what the celebrity gurus like to tell us these days? Why did you even need him?'

'I hired him after all the hoo-hah over the time I invested in a coal mine. Of course, that's a crime these days, and you know how sustainable I am, but most of the good environmentally friendly stuff I care about just doesn't work yet. Too often "net zero" simply means "net zero damned use to anyone". That's not my fault, but everyone who wants to polish their green halo piled on me about it.'

'Noblesse oblige, isn't that it?'

'Eh? You see, there's always creeps want to bankrupt me into giving all my hard-earned cash to their favourite good causes, but how would I know whether those causes use it wisely? There's simply no way of telling. For all I know, they're up to their necks in bitcoin rip-offs and every dodgy investment racket going. They'll get cleaned out by criminals and then have the nerve to come back cap in hand for more. That's what caring people like you and me, prudent with our pennies, are up against, Frank: incompetence and fraud at every level. Just providing food for sharks, that's what we're doing. So that's what this consultant was to help me with: enhancing my environmental credentials but in a cautious, prudent manner. But all he did was put me in some ethical loan scam he'd set up online and then cleared off. He was another person my wife suggested. Need I say more? I'm struggling, Frank.'

'But you're still rich, right?'

'That's harsh. I'm out of cash. I'm even having to sell all my oil industry shares. They were my hedge for the dark days and now those days have come.'

'How do you even have them?'

'I hear the word "hypocrite" left unsaid. I'll have you know, some of the greenest people on Earth are in the oil industry. It's because they care about the environment so much that there's so little pollution. Or not so much pollution as there would be. Besides, it's how my dear papa earned his fortune and his daddy made a few bob from it too. It's only through the oil industry I can do my essential planet-saving work, although I can't do much of that now. Needless to say, the evil pair stole my private planes. No more travelling to Qatar for a twenty-minute meeting on "green transitions" for me now.'

'Can I help in some way?'

'That's very kind but I couldn't ask you, dear friend. I don't want to bring you down with me. I must be prepared for my fate. I'm a recluse now. A hermit. Karma has called round and parked its fat arse on the overgrown lawn. Rich people are all exploiters, these halfwits say. Or their dads were, or their grandads, or some ancestors they don't even know about three hundred years ago. So we deserve to lose everything. People can get away with saying what they like these days. Except if you're someone like me.'

Frank felt he should change the subject. 'How's Roane doing, by the way?'

'Don't ask. Still mad as ever. Chaotic. His life is never going to be all rainbows and unicorns, but I wish he'd tone it down a bit. He says he's got an American girlfriend now. I find it hard to believe. He's never been interested in America, never appreciated it except its natural wonders. It's hard to figure out what goes on in his head. He says he's always felt an affinity for the Native Americans while practically everyone else who's gone there has been a wicked exploiter. America deserves better than them, he says, but of course he makes an exception for his girlfriend. They're pretty serious, so I think you can give up any lingering notions of him meeting your daughter which, face it, wasn't your brightest idea ever.'

It was already clear to Frank that his friend thought Gloria some kind of saint. And even if Frank had once wanted her to meet the 'countercultural' Roane, the old man would never be persuaded because he believed his son would corrupt her.

Layne said he was living in a caravan while his lawyers tried to prove he still owned the mansion. Tania and the estate manager Todd were rumoured to have set up their life together in the States, but Layne said he'd been tipped off that she might not legally be his wife. Frank suggested he hire Paz Wheat to find out for definite, saying it was someone Gloria knew from friends in England.

'I don't want some Yank,' said Layne.

'He's been over there twenty years. And he's a dual national, if you're so bothered about it.'

Instead of being grateful, Layne became irritated. He said he didn't want a PI involved and the police would find out for him.

'They might say it's not their issue,' said Frank, omitting to point out Layne's expectations of the police had shifted somewhat since the start of the call.

'I don't see why they'd say it's not for them. It's fraud, after all. But anyway, I don't want to pay for a PI.'

'Really? OK, you haven't got cash, but even so.'

'Your daughter knows about all this stuff, so you said once. She could do it, couldn't she, if I needed it? I don't think I need a professional PI to find out if my wife's a bigamist.' He then complained, 'My wastrel son's worth more than me now. Everything's gone or going from my life.'

'Everything? Surely not.'

'Oh yes. All of it. Even the bloody beavers have cleared off up the river!'

60

There was one more game to the season. The Hummingbirds, despite several humiliating defeats, were on course to become champions if they won this match. Dessie was injured in training so Annalisa was recalled to play her customary role. Although glad at her friend's return, Gloria felt sad because it was a reminder that their partnership was now ending. She told her father she was tempted to give up soccer to focus on business, but Frank, thinking this might be Mr Garcia's mischief, strongly advised her against it.

On the day it was like old times: Gloria with her runs and precision passing, Annalisa with her deadly shots. They dominated the opposition. With seven minutes to go, the score was 4-1. Ant had scored a hat-trick.

Tommy was at the game, and Gloria had been keen to impress him. She could see him, but then she couldn't. She wondered where he was. Maybe he'd gone for a drink somewhere. She suddenly heard a shout of her name. She hadn't been concentrating. She missed a pass to her, putting the defence at risk. She was more angry with herself than anyone else could be at such moments and won the ball back with a fierce tackle. She then ran for goal, but as she turned abruptly to avoid a lunging tackle she heard a popping sound, felt something in her right leg give way, and screaming crashed to the ground like a shot swan. She rolled over onto her back, clutching her knee, and her concerned teammates quickly ran towards her. The pain was intense, but after a few moments of silence she was able to make light of her predicament. 'Not long to go,' she said with a half-smile. What she meant, but managed not to say, was that with the team having used all their subs, a margin of three goals was hardly enough for their defence.

She was stretchered off and driven to hospital. In the ambulance she felt bewildered and kept thinking 'How could it possibly have happened?'

The hospital was new and sparkling, and had won awards for its design and quality of care. Not without intention, the building had the superficial feel of a shopping mall. The ambience was calm, and Gloria felt comfortable. The staff treated her like a celebrity, as though mistaking her for someone famous.

As she lay on her bed in the emergency room, desperate above everything to know the final score, she was visited by Annalisa who must have rushed from the game. Ant reported that the defence had 'held up well for them' and only conceded twice for a final score of 4-3. Their main rivals had lost and the Hummingbirds finished top of the league, something that would have seemed impossible during their temporary slump. The two celebrated winning the championship with little cups of hot chocolate. As soon as Annalisa had left to go to the team celebration, Gloria's parents arrived. Frank was surprisingly upbeat, saying how proud he was of her; Maria was more subdued, clutching her hand. As she watched them leave, Gloria thought how lovely it was just to see her mother on her first time leaving the house in months.

Next day, a young, tall, kind-looking orthopaedic specialist came to see her armed with the scan results. When he said her anterior-cruciate ligament was torn, she sighed in defeat, knowing how devastating such injuries could be - ACL the most feared acronym in women's soccer. She barely heard what he said next: that the damage was not serious enough to mandate surgery. She would need to wear a knee brace for at least six weeks and he predicted a return to fitness would take three months or so. When she realised what he'd actually said she wanted to hug him; recovery from an ACL injury could sometimes take over a year.

It was a reprieve compared to what it could have been. That's what her father said as he drove Gloria and her mother home. Apart from the injury itself, the only disappointment for her was the fact that she had not heard from Tommy.

In her room alone, depression quickly took hold. It wasn't the inconvenience of the knee brace and the need to wait patiently for recovery, but her vulnerability to the unknown, to the random, and her inevitable dependence on others. She'd sought control over her life but the incident had made a mockery of that.

She emailed Lily with her news, and her friend phoned within an hour despite the lateness in the UK. Although delighted to hear from her, Gloria soon slipped into a low mood. Lily said, 'You talk as though you'll be injured for ever.'

'It feels like it. What can I do with myself?'

'When you're fit you can come and see us. Why don't we all go to the French Riviera? Or Venice?'

'Oh, that sounds lovely, but I don't know. I'd so love to see you but won't it seem strange me tagging along with you two?'

'Not to us. Mack really likes you. She understands about you and me. Many people wouldn't, but it doesn't matter about them. Now she's got to know you a bit she's the happiest and calmest she's been since I can remember. It'll just be good fun.'

'Yeah.'

'Anyway think about it. I'd be the happiest person alive. But I'm being selfish. This call is about you.'

'No, it's good to think about these things. Something to look forward to. I was making plans with a boyfriend but he's a bit of a loser and they're not going to happen in the immediate future now. But what do I do with my time?'

'Same as before. You've got your tuition work—'

'Which I love, but there's not enough of it.'

'And your charity work.'

'Which is beginning to bore me. I don't *do* charity work as such. What I do is make decisions about who to give money to. I get tired of telling people why I can't give them money. I feel like I want to give it all away in one go. Seriously, I feel like giving it back to my dad. He wants it, too. I feel too much like a goody-goody and I don't like it. I feel like I want to get drunk and get laid.'

'You're just saying that because of your current situation. It'll pass.'

'No I'm not.'

Lily laughed. 'Well, don't follow my example. You won't have you to tell you off, like I had. God, that worked for me, whether you meant what you wrote or not!'

After the call, she thought about the French Riviera and the chance to be with Lily and Mack. But would she be a third wheel? And what if Mack fancied her? It could all end in tears, couldn't it? Always such thoughts arose to spoil everything. Tired of her rumination she forced herself to face the mirror. She said, 'Gloria, get hold of yourself. It's something to look forward to. It's going to be fun. Remember what that is?'

During her moments of depression, so many times she played that moment from the match over in her mind. The 83rd minute – for Heaven's sake, a mere seven minutes plus injury time left! Had she been lax, over-confident? She'd made three passes into the path of Annalisa that were pure gold, and the always reliable Ant had converted all of them. Every time she and Jamie ran at the opposition, their defence wilted like thirsty violets. It was fun and they could do nothing wrong that day. Carefree the moment before, then she turned too sharply, and her knee gave way in an instant. The painful horror of it! The impossibility! Nine whole minutes added to injury time because of it.

Stories trickled through to her about Tommy getting drunk and being hit with a DUI rap. There'd been a big party to celebrate winning the championship and he was there. The rumour was that he had sex with a couple of the younger players. That was about as bad as it could get from Gloria's perspective.

61

One evening, she was lying on her bed watching a corny comedy film on TV and generally feeling sorry for herself when the doorbell rang. A minute later, her smiling father popped his head through her doorway and announced, 'You've got some visitors.' In came the coach Barti with three of her teammates: 'the workhorse' Jamie, Raffie the goalie, and Micaela the young defender. After a brief chat about her progress, the coach left the room and returned with a brightly- coloured Venice Beach tote bag. He announced, 'For your work rate and dedication to the team, your goals and your league-leading assists, I'm delighted to be able to say that your teammates have voted you player of the season!' He then pulled from the bag a beautiful gold model, several inches high, of a hummingbird on a wooden stand bearing a steel plaque inscribed with her name, 'Star player of' and the year. Her parents stood in the doorway enthusiastically adding to the applause she received. Photographs were taken of her holding the award up. She was thrilled. They'd also brought her a team championship medal and the trophy cup for her to pose with. They stayed a little longer, talking and laughing about some of the highlights of the season, and then left. Frank came in and quietly congratulated her, carefully examining the hummingbird and proudly holding the medal in his palm.

Her only sadness was the non-appearance of Annalisa. The coach had said she'd been invited, but he hadn't heard back from her. She mentioned it to her father. He said unequivocally, 'You know why: it's her dad. He's upset she didn't win the award. I can hear him saying it now: "Gloria only won because she's injured. The game's all about goals and Annalisa scored most of them. It's that simple." Gloria laughed. He'd done a passable imitation of Mr Garcia's voice. But she felt sad because she'd always got on well with Ant's dad on the few occasions she'd met him.

To Gloria's surprise, the following day she received a call from Tommy. She felt cold towards him, though.

'I'm sorry I haven't been in touch,' he said, sounding contrite.

'So why haven't you?'

'I take it you heard what happened?'

'Yes.'

'I let myself down. I let you down most of all. I don't blame you if you don't want anything to do with me.'

'I don't think I do, actually.'

'Why?' He hadn't anticipated her response.

'Not after what I heard about the party.'

'I'm sorry.'

'And I hear you, but it doesn't change the situation, does it? You can't just say sorry and the hurt goes away. Look, Tommy, I can't be thinking all the time about who you're having sex with. What sort of life is that?'

'You're too good for me.'

'I don't know about that.'

'I do. But I still love you.'

'I know your type. All you want is sex. Well, that's impractical right now.'

'No. My love for you is real. I don't blame you being angry. I messed up.' He sounded almost tearful. She felt she was being hardhearted. He said, 'But if you ever change your mind...'

She merely thanked him for phoning and ended the call. It was conceivable she might change her mind, but she neither wanted to admit, nor deny the possibility to herself, let alone him. Somehow being reminded of how useless Tommy was lifted her mood. Of course she deserved better, but so did most people. Yes, her knee was busted, but it was the last game of the season anyway, and she was not seriously disadvantaged because she worked from home. She wouldn't be playing sports for a while, but she'd be back one day.

Most of all, however, he had let her down by phoning, because a real man would have turned up in person and taken the tongue-lashing he deserved.

Late one afternoon, Annalisa called round, bringing a box of Italian artisan chocolates from Valenza Chocolatier. 'Only the best for my girl,' she enthused. After talking about Gloria's progress and how she was getting on with wearing a knee brace, she asked to see the award. She gently took it from Gloria's hands to inspect it and said, 'You deserved this. It's beautiful. My dad thought I should get it but he's wrong. I should have been here for the presentation. I'm sorry I wasn't.'

Ant told her that it was now definite her family were moving up the coast to Santa Cruz, four hundred miles north, because her father was being transferred to a new office there. It appeared that her father, rather than being prosecuted for embezzlement, was being rewarded for his efforts to prevent it. He'd been involved in a sting to catch the loan shark soccer referee.

Of course, Annalisa had warned her before that she might be leaving, but it didn't really hit Gloria until now. Not only would Gloria miss her, but it meant they'd probably never play in the same team again. Gloria had talked herself into believing she'd be fit for next season but now felt her motivation fall like a broken bowstring. She expressed these thoughts to her friend who said it had been great these last few years, but everything had an ending. There was a rumour Barti was leaving and a new coach would come in. The playing style of the long pass to the front three and speed on the break they liked would probably be replaced by a 'boring' short passing game. She added that even though they'd been champions, some of the older players in defence resented the fact that as the pair who scored most of the goals, they got the acclaim. Gloria was amazed by this and even more so when her friend revealed that seeing Gloria stretchered off without even being tackled had shocked her so much that she'd even thought about giving up soccer for hockey. They discussed this and Annalisa explained there were causes and there were effects and if causes like Gloria getting injured were unexpected, then the effects were even more unpredictable and, what's more, were multiple in all directions.

Gloria looked at her friend and thought: 'Under those bangs and despite your down to earth nature, you're quite the little philosopher.'

But Annalisa was not done. She said her boyfriend Jimmy had been pleading with her not to leave and he wanted them to get a place together in nearby Laguna Beach.

'That would be great,' said Gloria, as though darkness had suddenly lifted.

Annalisa said she was tempted. 'I mean, I know I'll never be long without a guy wherever I end up, but he's a definite keeper. The only trouble is, my dad would be furious, but he has to let me go sometime. Besides, I want to see my girl fit and running up and down the pitch again.'

'This is so cool, but realistically, how likely is it you'll do it?'

'Well, I've applied for a job at the university—'

'USC?'

'Yes, Irvine. And Jimmy's started looking at rental places for us in Dana Point where he's getting a job at the harbour. So we'll see.'

Dana Point was special to Gloria, having as a child once seen a blue whale off the coast there. She tried not to hope for her friend to stay in the area, lest it not happen. Annalisa said, 'As soon as I know one way or the other, I'll call you.'

62

When Frank next talked with Layne, he found him in a rather resigned mood. 'I accept my reduced future,' he said almost apologetically. 'I see better now how the world is. My loss of wealth has closed doors to me that once, bank balance to the fore, I was dragged through. The set quietly drops those who've fallen on hard times. I should have expected that. No longer am I invited to the international events I used to attend week in, week out, so enthusiastically. I now see they were just talking shops and completely vacuous. The only things of any substance that came out of them were the banquets. I never ate so well in my life. I even took my chef along sometimes so he could learn a few new dishes. As for the talks, most of the time I hadn't a clue what they were supposed to be about. And I remembered even less.'

'This is a turnaround, Layne. What about your passion for green causes?'

'I see now that protecting the environment begins at home,' he said sagely without elaboration. 'By the way, young Roane is coming to the US with his girlfriend. He's in love, or claims he is. I don't think there's anywhere in England will have him anymore, which is very dispiriting though entirely understandable.'

After the call, Frank went to see Gloria to inform her of the latest news about Roane. He said, 'I didn't wish to worry you, but it would be worse if I said nothing and you later found out.'

She laughed out loud. 'I have never ever expressed any interest in him. That was all your idea. Besides, he's not going to be interested in me like this, is he?'

'I don't know. He might identify with you; he's pretty accident-prone, by all accounts.'

'Thanks.'

Privately, though, Gloria was not relaxed about Roane coming to the US. What if he hadn't got a girlfriend? What if she herself was the real reason for him making the trip? It was her vanity talking, though, surely. She could imagine Layne putting him up to it, perhaps as a way of getting back at her dad, jealous of the relative stability in Frank's life compared with the utter turmoil of his own.

She decided to contact Mack. She wrote to her to ask if she could keep an eye on what Roane was up to.

'Does he have a social media presence?' Mack asked in an email.

'I don't know. Probably not. I've never seen anything except an old Facebook account. Mind you, I've never really looked.'

Mack quickly came back to her by phone, saying she'd found reference to Roane in a recent blog entry, which indicated the blogger was his girlfriend and they were in California.

'Whereabouts?' asked Gloria, alarmed.

'The girlfriend said they'd gone to the "California of our imagination", whatever that means.'

'I don't know what it means either. I hope it's not anywhere near here.'

'They've been staying in a disused illegal casino.'

'Really? I guess that's original. I've never heard of one.'

'Some kind of squat.'

'OK. So are they still there?

'No. They've moved to somewhere in the northern part of the state. In the forests.'

'Let's hope to God they stay there.'

After the call, Gloria told her father that Roane and his girlfriend were now in California, but not anywhere near them.

63

Layne rang Frank. He apologised for calling at what he knew was a late hour in California, but he needed to update him on the 'Roane' situation. 'I'm afraid my son's had some kind of breakdown. He's walked out on his girlfriend and is now regrettably claiming to be interested in Gloria.'

'Where is he now?'

'In a hotel in Philadelphia. Probably with some trollop he just met.'

'When you say he's interested in Gloria, is this some kind of whim? Just something he's dreamed up?'

'No. He says ever since he saw her, she's the one he's wanted.'

'Oh no. Really?'

'I'm afraid so.'

'But you said he was in love with the previous girlfriend he had.'

'He said he was. They had the same weird ideas. Met on a flat earther dating site, if you can believe that.'

'What!? Is that a joke? Is he... Does he think the world is flat? Why would he even be on the site? Or indeed any dating site?'

'He got tired of his wild social life. But rather than become conventional or, dare I say it, normal, he's gone off in a different direction.'

'Sure sounds like it. A different kind of wild.'

'Exactly.'

'But I do think he must be pulling your leg about the dating site. I certainly hope so.'

'I've heard it all, Frank. You know that. Heard it all, lived it all. He told me he had to dump her because she wasn't who she claimed to be.'

'Not wealthy enough?'

'It wasn't about money. It was her name: Alicia.'

'Yes?'

'He became convinced that the last three letters of her name revealed her true role in life. He believed she was working for the CIA.'

'I've never heard of such a crazy idea. But why on Earth would the CIA be interested in Roane? A bit, dare I say it, narcissistic, isn't it? But maybe it's really you they're interested in, Layne.'

'Me?'

'An English aristocrat who's a passionate environmentalist.'

'I don't think so. I think you're winding me up, old chap. Not that I mind.' The way he said this made Frank realise how subdued he sounded these days, not the ebullient guy of earlier calls.

The following day, Mack phoned Gloria. She told her Alicia's blog had stopped after her latest enigmatic comment, 'All things must pass. I may be sad but at least I've got my sanity.' Since Roane was silent on social media there was nothing Mack could do now, nowhere to look.

The call prompted Gloria to ask her father, 'Has something happened with Roane, do you know? His girlfriend's blog suggests they may have split up.'

'They have,' he said. 'Layne told me.'

'And were you even going to tell me? When did you find out?'

'Just yesterday.'

'So when were you going to tell me?'

'I...I... Of course I was... I didn't want to upset you, and I wanted to think about it.'

'What's there to think about?'

'He may try to come here.'

'What!?'

'He's, er, interested in you.'

'Oh my God!'

'I was wondering actually whether we should reach out to him. That way, any meeting would be on our terms.'

She almost dropped the coffee cup she was holding. 'What are you talking about? Is this something you and Layne have cooked up? Are you two trying to fit me up with that madman? How can you even think of it? You say you want to protect me, but then you talk about inviting him and all his chaos into our world.'

'Not *into* our world. We'd meet him on the edge.'

'Yes, and he could look in and say, "Yup, that's the next destination for all my insanity."'

Afterwards, she thought about Roane from the perspective of her favourite psychological theories. From what she'd heard and from what she reasonably surmised, none of them seemed to apply to him. Apart from Englishman and graduate of wherever, there was no group that he was in, unless wayward offspring of eccentric rich aristocrats could be one. As regards any other potential groups, he would either be expelled from them, or leave almost as soon as he'd joined. As for social exchange, there seemed to be no element of fairness in his relationships: he just took whatever he could get. And regarding her cherished 'fundamental attribution error', she suspected he was quite prepared to take responsibility for the bad things that happened to him and not blame them solely on external agents. He was a natural anarchist, not by word or thought but deed. He was destructive, but in the same way a wild dog was destructive, not by intent but by nature.

In the following days, Frank heard from Layne almost daily about Roane's exploits in America. But it was unclear to Frank what had happened before he split up with his girlfriend and what had occurred after, although most of it was probably the latter because it seemed Alicia had been able to exercise some level of calming influence over him. Thus, when Frank dutifully told Gloria of the various events it was unclear what had happened when. Besides, Layne received his information from Roane himself who was hardly a reliable witness, especially as the reports were always accompanied by requests for money, which Layne had to meet from the sale of his oil industry shares. These father and son discussions had become more strained, however, after Layne discovered Roane had stolen some of the family's heirlooms to pay for his trip. The old man said, 'They're not valuable, but he's a rascal. I was so annoyed I even thought about prosecuting him. But what good would it do? My own son! But I always knew he was beyond help. Even someone like your daughter couldn't save him.'

Layne reported his son had been staying in a meditation centre in Colorado but was thrown out because he caused a fight.

'How do you get into a fight in a place like that?' asked Frank. 'It makes no sense.'

'He can get into a fight anywhere, believe me. He'd beat himself up in the middle of the desert if he had nothing better to do. I didn't ask what led to the fight this time. Now he's got sick from fake Xanax. He's just incredibly unlucky.'

'He sure is,' said Frank. 'And so's anyone who gets involved with him.' He now accepted Gloria was absolutely right about not initiating contact and wondered why he had ever thought to the contrary.

'He went to some retreat for ayahuasca, or whatever it's called. He was expecting vivid dreams and psychotherapy in a glass, and all he got was the vilest-tasting thing in the world, some kind of seizure, and thousands of dollars in medical bills.'

'But he has insurance, right?'

'He has something on his phone that looks like an insurance document but is actually a fake policy he bought from someone he found on Twitter.'

'Oh dear.'

'He's just not careful, that's all. He does his best. Well, maybe not his best.'

'Not something you or I would recognise as "best".'

'Right. I don't know why that is. He had a good education. Maybe I didn't do my bit to teach him right. Boys are difficult, aren't they?'

'Girls can be difficult too.'

'Of course. Although I think you did something right with young Gloria there, didn't you?'

'I can't claim credit, Layne.'

'Well, some do everything right and still raise an evil brat, so be glad.'

In subsequent calls Frank learned that Roane had suffered a heat stroke at a sweat lodge. Then he went to a bee-sting therapy retreat but nearly died from an anaphylactic shock. On a water fast he ended up passing out from low blood pressure and fell over and hit his head, resulting in another hospital trip. Because his insurance was a dud, Layne had to send him bank transfers to cover it. 'It's more than I can cope with, quite honestly,' he grumbled.

When Frank told Gloria about all this, she joked that any potential girlfriend could reject him on health grounds alone. Frank almost laughed at that.

64

Days later, however, Roane contacted Gloria directly via Facebook message. He wrote,
'Dearest Gloria,

I must meet you. Ever since I first saw you and heard your voice I have been in love with you. I want to make you in real life the princess that you are in my imagination. If this is not possible I need to find out for myself. But I can only be sure if I meet you. Until that time I live on the razor edge of perpetual hope and despair, Roane.'

It felt like a shadow had been cast over her again. She decided to reply, however. As always, she agonised over her words, constantly changing them. She wrote,
'Dear Roane,

I'm sorry but it is not possible for us to meet. Even if it were, it would not be wise. My heart belongs to another. I mean you no ill will, only good. If you feel love for me, as you say you do, you will leave me in peace. And if you care for me, you will care for yourself. That is my main wish. Please forget about me. Believe me, I am nothing special, Gloria.'

Although relieved at sending her message, she was more nervous than ever when she thought of him. She had a kind of ambivalence: keen for news whilst wanting to be free of the anxiety he caused her. Next, she heard from her father that Roane was recuperating amongst 'some kind of beach community doing yoga and tai chi' and was enjoying it. This was a relief. Perhaps he'd stay there. Maybe by the time he decided to leave, he'd have found someone else and lost interest in her.

On Frank's next call with Layne, he found him in a rage. He'd discovered Roane had defrauded him for the benefit of the meditation centre he'd briefly joined. He'd drained one of Layne's less used bank accounts, one that Tania had been unaware of so hadn't been able to empty it herself.

'That evil bastard!' he bellowed. 'I tell you, he is not my son.'

'Really?'

'I want a DNA test. No, I'm joking. But, Frank, I'm just so tired of it. It's like the biggest Karma manure dump ever. It's like everything I ever did wrong all descended on my head at once. He said he did it for Gloria.'

'Yeah? Where on Earth did he get that idea?'

'I don't know, Frank. I'm sure I don't. I have no idea what goes through his overheated brain.'

Frank now realised this whole scenario was the farthest possible from a joke. Roane was crazy as a drunken horse, seemed to be constantly on the move, and was obsessed with meeting Gloria.

Unfortunately, she was just about able to hear Layne before her father turned the volume on the speaker down. She felt cold inside her stomach, and when her father finished the call, she shouted out to him from her bed. He came into her room. They talked about what she thought she'd heard and what Layne had said.

'We need protection,' she said.

'I can't argue with you.'

'It's like trying to stifle the irrational,' she said. 'You can't do it, but you have to try.'

Frank phoned the local police. They pointed out that no crime had been committed against them, and no direct threat had been made to the family. In other words, they would do nothing.

Next, Layne told Frank that Roane had defrauded a religious cult, and they were after him.

'I can't keep up with it all, Layne.'

'Do you think I can?'

Frank contacted the local police again and informed them of this latest news. They told him Roane was wanted in Colorado after a knife fight following a car accident.

Gloria was now unable to rest. She was afraid to fall asleep in case Roane came in through the window and attacked her. She felt like James Stewart in *Rear Window* once the murderer realises he's been seen by him and Stewart's character can't escape because he's injured.

She was tempted to phone Tommy, but what would he do? His license was suspended because of the DUI and she couldn't rely on him anyway.

She reached out to Mack after receiving a message from her saying her boss Paz Wheat was in the US, investigating a case in which a family suspected their loved one had died from foul play rather than the coroner's verdict of accident.

'Where is he now?' Gloria asked her.

'Minnesota.'

'Can you ask him to track Roane? His dad Layne hears from him regularly but never seems to know exactly where he is and I don't think he wants to know.'

'Of course. Paz will want full details.'

Gloria told her what she knew and added, 'Please tell him everything you can think of that might conceivably be relevant, even if it seems unlikely. Please, Mack. Dad will pay for it all.'

'OK, I'll do whatever you want without question. You know by now I would always do that. Does Roane know where you are?'

'I don't know. I have to assume he does. He seems intelligent in his addled way. I didn't think he was dangerous until I heard about the knife fight. He might not mean me harm, but he still might cause it.'

Reports came in that Roane was stealing cars and abandoning them. He again contacted Gloria by Facebook message: 'I'm your Clyde, be my Bonnie. I'm coming to collect you.'

She did not reply and felt so ill she could not eat. But she did take comfort from a message from Mack confirming Paz was after him. He would surely find him, even if the police couldn't.

That night, she was able to get to rest more easily, partly from sheer exhaustion after all the wakeful nights. But she didn't stay in slumber long. She was sure there'd been a shot outside and that had woken her up. She struggled to the window, looking out for any unusual lights.

The night was clear and she took solace from looking up at the stars, a reminder of her own insignificance. She believed she wouldn't sleep for the rest of the night, but there was no other noise, so she decided maybe it had not been a shot after all. No one else in the house stirred. Eventually she returned to sleep.

65

The following morning, news circulated through the neighbourhood that a dead man had been discovered in a local swimming pool. Gloria found the social media coverage muddled and told her father one of the rumours was that the body had been found in their pool. Frank pointed out theirs was covered but he checked anyway, taking a rare walk through the garden. It transpired that the corpse was in their nearest neighbours' pool. It was all too scary to think about, but of course Gloria could think of nothing else. Friends she hadn't heard from recently were asking if she was OK. The speculation was that it was a drug dealer who'd been found dead.

She could not reply to any of them. It was too stressful. Instead, she put up a single Facebook post making it clear that she and her family were absolutely fine, and thanking people for their concern. The fact she was scared out of her wits was not something she intended to reveal.

Fortunately, the neighbours' pool was not visible from their house. She had, however, seen and heard the emergency vehicles arrive.

In the day's *Patch*, the weather promised was rain and wind with the possibility of flurries of snow on the Saddleback Mountains, but then it would turn milder. There was an item 'Woman charged over hate messages' with a picture of Carmina Rodriguez. Dessie's father must have become involved in the investigation. Carmina had claimed her neighbour's son hacked into her broadband account, but the police were not persuaded. Gloria would contact the police to tell her own story.

There was nothing in the news yet about the body in the pool. She talked to her father about it. 'It's a vagrant,' he said with an air of great certainty. They are an unfortunate nuisance, but it's a fact of life that they can show up anywhere.'

'Except in a gated community perhaps,' she said. 'Not that I want to live in one. Could the deceased have been a drug dealer?'

'Absolutely not.' Taken aback by his forthright response, she wondered whether, in his imagination, he was taking it upon himself to defend the street's reputation. 'And not some random drunk either. Not around here,' he asserted. She was tempted to point out that the neighbour himself could be a drug dealer. After all, they didn't know most of the neighbours. And those buying drugs probably had them delivered by courier.

But the corpse remained unidentified. Was he a murder victim? She didn't dare to think it, but all her friends said it must be. She asked her dad, 'Was he young or old? Could the police at least establish whether it might be Roane?'

Frank phoned Layne to ask him, 'Do you know where Roane is?'

'I haven't heard. Do you seriously think I want to? I wish he would just find some commune somewhere and stay there. Trouble is, they'd throw him out after a week.'

Frank told Gloria who said, 'Maybe it really is him in the neighbours' pool.'

'Do you wish it was?'

'Not really.'

'That's a bit equivocal.'

'At least he wouldn't be a threat to me then. But I mean him no harm, only that I be spared it myself.'

Later that day, Annalisa phoned to ask her about the body in the pool. 'I think about it all the time,' Gloria said, 'Dad says it must be a vagrant.'

'Or a crack dealer.'

'No,' said Gloria forthrightly, irritated at feeling, like her father, the need to protect the street. Realising her outright denial based on zero evidence sounded silly, she added, 'Though it could be, I guess, but I don't think so.'

'Someone on Facebook is saying the police have identified the dead person as a local rock musician. Some guy called Willie Mutch. They say he was in dispute with a car dealer. This dealer had a prison record and a reputation for violence, although no-one's saying yet that he was personally involved.'

'If I was on Facebook I wouldn't be saying things like that - especially if that guy's been in prison. Was it even a murder?'

'That's what the police are saying.'

After the call, Gloria felt depressed and nor did the promise in *Patch* of an evening of Bible sing-along songs, and even the upcoming local pizza week, lift her mood. It would be a great time to be away from home, but she had to stay there. She'd effectively told her boyfriend Tommy she didn't want to see him anymore, her parents would probably prefer it if she moved out, people in the town were at each other's throats in *Patch* about stuff she didn't care about, and some crazy English guy was determined to be with her. For a moment she envied the body that had been found in the pool. She knew that was absurd. She didn't envy anyone except herself uninjured, and maybe Annalisa. She tried her affirmations. Above all, she said to herself, she had life. All she needed, for the near future at least, was a purpose to put it to.

66

On Instagram Gloria noticed influencers were out in Dubai motivating people who were not looking forward to their winter: 'This could be you. Look at these luxurious hotels and shopping malls, look at this sheikh's superyacht, this perfect beach. Be here with all your fun-loving friends.' She said it aloud. 'Except it couldn't be you, Gloria. You are a lonely loser. You cannot go to Dubai. You are not even eligible to be a Daughter of the American Revolution, let alone the daughter of a sheikh. Confined to your room like someone in a quarantine hotel, you might as well be the body in the neighbours' pool – dead, wearing your best hat.'

On Facebook there was a report that there'd been a drowning in Lake Viejo. It was a rare occurrence, but it was always tragic and people sent prayers, and someone always asked how it could possibly happen, and they would be rebuked and told to think of the family and pray for them and not speculate about blame because the lawyers would explore that when they sued. She'd recently read how up north on Lake Tahoe a man made it his life's work to recover bodies from the cold and deep waters: murder victims, suicides, swimmers out of their depth. And there were also the victims of boating accidents: happy and carefree one moment and then the boat maybe turning too sharply and it all happening in an instant – the impossibility of it! – tipped from the boat into the jaws of death. Dying of cold-water shock. Not drink or drugs usually. Not vagrancy related. She admired the man who did this work for the desperate loved ones – his sense of purpose, his apparent serenity. There was hope in the world when there were people like him to feel inspired by.

She had been distracting herself successfully. She was brought back to Earth, however, by her phone ringing. It was her coach, Barti. 'How are you?' he said.

'Well, I've been better, but it could be worse.'

'What'll it be: three months or so?'

'Yeah. A bit more time in a knee brace and a gradual recovery. To be honest, I'm not sure yet if I want to play next season. I won't be fully fit for a while. But it's nice to hear from you. I appreciate it.'

'That's fine. And you're right. It could have been much worse. An ACL can easily take a year.'

'And often the player doesn't come back, right?'

'Yes. It's not just the inability to play when you're injured. It can mess up the rest of your life - work and everything else. So I can understand it. And maybe you're a bit depressed.'

'Honestly, I am.' She suddenly felt the desire to gush, but restrained herself. 'Anyway, I really appreciated the award and you and the girls coming round.'

'You fully deserved it. Well, I have something for you to think about and so I'll cut to the chase: I have a new coaching job at another club.'

'That's brilliant for you. Congratulations!'

'It's with the Merlins. The Bluebirds who we played against this year are their feeder team. So it's a step up. And I want you to join me there. I think you would fit in well—'

'Yeah? Oh, I don't know. They'd hate me. Remember that mass brawl?'

'Forget that. It'll all be different. You and Dessie. She's already agreed and she wants you as much as I do. And the Merlins' goalie's left so I've asked Raffie to think about it. I believe she could take a step up, too.'

'Yeah. This is great. I really appreciate you asking me. But I really don't know. I don't think I can play fast on the wing any more. Or not for a while. I will just be too... well, scared.'

'I understand. There'll be a psychologist to work with you, and I'm thinking I'd like you to play up front. But not like Annalisa.' Gloria did not respond. She liked the idea, but didn't want to criticise her friend who'd become closer since the accident. The coach added, 'She'd be a better player if her father wasn't interfering. He's convinced her it's all about goals. Well, it *is* all about goals, but you know what I mean: her goals are dependent on everyone else.'

She confirmed she would think seriously about it, adding that she was flattered at being asked. He left the call sounding happy, though not as glad as the call made her. He had not even mentioned the body in the neighbours' pool. Maybe he hadn't seen anything about it. He had other things to think about. That was the way to be. More importantly, the call had given her the idea for something that maybe she could do with her life: become a sports psychologist. This thought excited her. She began investigating online about how to become one.

As the days went by, Gloria realised her mother and father had become, in all respects, a couple again – they were even sleeping together – and this made her incredibly happy. Maria was acting like she was in a scene from one of her films: the businessman's wife doing not very much except trying to organise everyone else's life. In fact, she now had the chance to have a new acting career. She'd once played a daughter in a film and now they wanted her to play the mother in a remake of it. It was bizarre. 'At least it's not the grandmother,' she quipped as she told Gloria about it. 'But the only sad thing for me now is that you have no one special in your life.'

'Yes I do. I have someone far away who cares for me very much.' She didn't say that person was a woman and was married.

'It's not enough.'

'Yes it is.' She wasn't interested in arguing about it. Her mother could think what she liked. All those months, even years, of hardly saying anything to her, and now all of a sudden she was the expert on what Gloria needed? She'd been absent for so long that, it seemed to Gloria, there was nothing her mother could tell her that would in any way help. For a moment, she wanted the absent mother again.

She immediately felt mean having such thoughts because she was thrilled that her mother, if not fully well, was so much better than she had been before. She wondered whether Maria still missed the version of Dr Mencius with the dodgy medications and dubious bedside manner before she'd learnt the hard way that he was a crook. But at least the police had him now, the charges continuing to accumulate. The only problem was that members of her family would probably need to testify unless the old fraud pled guilty, and avoided the seductive argument that Maria and his other victims had effectively volunteered their bank accounts for him to use at his whim.

67

Layne called Frank on Skype: 'I forgot to tell you that I took up your recommendation and hired that Paz Wheat fellow. I believe there's some connection with your daughter.'

'Yes, I believe he's the boss of the wife of a friend of hers.'

'Well, I'm grateful to you and her. The fellow quickly discovered that Tania, that licentious piece of treachery, has been married before and is *still* married to that person. My so-called marriage to her is null and void.'

'That's great news, Layne.'

'It gives me more chance of getting my money back.'

'In theory, at least, and let's hope so.'

'Now, of course, for every spot of sunshine in this poor boy's life there comes up a big-arsed old thunder cloud: Mr Wheat has also discovered that she's not an heiress. The person she supposedly inherited from is still alive - and not even rich!'

'Oh dear.'

'I tell you, that boy Wheat and his sidekick - some Scottish piece calls herself Mack and a bit bohemian-looking - are damned good. They found it wasn't only the estate manager Tania brought in she was in cahoots with—'

'Todd?'

'Yes. But also the sneaky devil I employed before I met her. I trusted that creep and he steered me into all these dodgy investments—'

'I remember that.'

'But I didn't know he was also part of the gang. His role was to worm his way into my trust, then keep me so busy with his crackpot ideas that I didn't have chance to see what he was up to with my investments, earning himself juicy commissions, some of them even fake funds he'd set up himself. Then when I was looking for a new partner for this lonely boy, who was he recommending?'

'Tania.'

'Exactly. She then contrives to get him sacked and brings in her boy-friend Todd who tells me where the other fellow had deceived me. What better way to win my favour? The crooks! I tell you: no kipper was ever stitched up worse than me. And no-one deserved it less.'

'That's right.'

'I've been too trusting, Frank. It's always been my way, my failing, to expect others to have the same standards as me. But the likes of us - and I include you in this - are always going to be prey to the baser elements of society. And yet we soldier on for the sake of an undeserving mankind.'

'You're a role model, Layne.'

'Well, I've always believed, in my humble way, that when you do good it comes back to you on gilded wings. At last I've found the right person for me. That's my big news. Yes, I've a brand new girlfriend.'

'Fantastic!'

'She's reliable, that's the thing. Older than the others were. Her name's Minnie.'

'Are you sure?'

'Hey, less of the cheek! But now I feel like Henry the Eighth when Katherine Parr showed up. You know, the last one. Very intelligent. She's a biodynamic farmer, whatever that is. It's a new life for me, Frankie boy.'

'Is she the one for your old age?'

'I sure hope so. Above all, she's smart. The government pays her to grow dandelions. Even I never managed that wheeze.'

68

The next big news was from Mack when she phoned Gloria. She sounded very pleased: 'I have some good news. Paz has located Roane who's now in police custody.'

'Wow! So what happened?'

'He heard from another PI in Florida he knew that the fugitive was in the Keys. Between them they traced him to a small hotel. When they raided his room, Roane raced to the balcony and threatened to jump. He said he'd become obsessed with a woman and was depressed at her lack of interest.

'Paz was able to coax him away from danger. At one point he suggested to Roane as a joke that he should marry a rich widow. He replied that he would rather find a rich young beauty and break her heart for the sake of it. Nice guy. Once they were back at ground level, the police arrested him.'

After the call, Gloria felt a sense of relief flow through her from head to toe. She told her father, 'Thank God that saga's over!' He put his arm round her and hugged her.

With so much time alone, Gloria was thinking more about what she would like to do with her life. She decided she would definitely give the charitable foundation back to her father if he wanted it and lawyers confirmed it was possible. She would continue the tuition which she loved, and train to become a sports psychologist. Reaching this decision enlivened her and increased her determination to return to fitness as soon as possible.

But one thought continued to bother her: would she find a partner she could believe in? Was Tommy really the best she could do? Since their last conversation he, undeterred, had made an effort, sending a card and flowers, fruit and chocolates. She'd made a point of responding positively out of courtesy, but she did not allow herself to believe there was anything in their relationship. She felt she bored him, and once he'd got the sex he wanted he'd be gone. There was nothing much she wanted to talk about with him, and anyway, for differing reasons, neither of them could currently drive. And why would he want to wait for her to be fit again, when he could more easily get sex elsewhere? And yet, if that's all he'd wanted, why all the talk of making plans?

Whether or not she found the right person to be her life partner in the future, she still had her platonic relationship with Lily, and her growing friendship with Mack as well. It made her feel good to think of those two happily married. Or at least it did until she suddenly felt very lonely. She wanted someone to live with, to love, to have children with one day, just like other women. Like traditional women were supposed to live, not that she wanted to be a traditional woman. She had to accept that her mother might be right; platonic love might be the most enduring form of love but right now it was not enough for her.

She was disturbed from her rumination by an unexpected call on the house phone. A young woman's voice: 'Is that Gloria Salesman, by any chance?'

'Yes.' She thought it was probably someone selling dodgy investments, but it did not sound like a call centre.

'I have Saskia McMichaels on the line for you.' Gloria felt apprehensive. Why was Saskia phoning her? Was she enquiring about her father? Was she after the foundation's assets? Did she want to buy up its gold?

'Gloria?' It was a breathy, slightly seductive voice.

'Er, yes.'

Saskia sounded amused by the hesitancy. 'How are you?'

'OK. Apart from an injury playing soccer—'

'Oh no!'

'Yeah. ACL. Knee injury.'

'That's pretty common, isn't it? With female players, I mean.'

'Sadly, yes. But it can be minor, as with me. Just a few weeks in a brace and right now the season's over anyway.'

'Well, that's good, at least. Now, listen, your dad at one time was interested in investing in my business.'

'I'm aware of that.'

'So that's how I know him, because he approached me. He told me that you manage a charitable foundation.'

Gloria hesitated. If this was a back door approach to get at the gold it would be a short conversation. 'That's correct. But what has that got to do with anything? My dad wanted to use foundation assets for investment purposes and I flat out refused.'

'You were right,' said Saskia.

'Then what—'

'I was impressed by the fact that at your young age you're running a foundation, and I understand you're pretty tough-minded.'

'Some would say, ruthless,' said Gloria. She laughed, relaxed.

'But you study, you analyse, you research.'

'Yes.'

'OK, so you're wondering why I'm phoning. I'll get straight to it. I'm looking for a new analyst and I'm wondering if you'd be interested. You know what we do. Of course, you may not *like* what we do. Some people don't. But think about it. If you're interested in principle, let me know. We're very interested in you. We'd set up an interview on Zoom with one of my assistants, and depending on how that went I'd meet you in the office - hopefully we can get you there —'

'I'm hoping I'd be able to drive by then.'

'Great! So you'd meet the team and we'd show you more of what we do and see if we can finalise things. How does that sound?'

'Sounds brilliant. But why me?'

'Well, you're not the only one who can research and analyse, so we know all about you, Hummingbirds player of the year.'

'Oh.'

'And the cyber-bullying. I think we have a lot in common actually. Doing my kind of work doesn't make me popular with some, so you have to be resilient. And I can see that you are. So might you be a tiny bit interested in this?'

'Yes. Totally.'

'Good. So send me an email - the address is on the website - and we'll take it from there. By the way, how is your dad?'

'He's fine, thank you. Before you go, please can I ask you something?'

'Go on.'

'I'm sorry, I must ask this: did you ever bet against my dad's company?'

'No. I knew the company. The share price was inflated but it was because of hype not fraud. The companies we deal with are generally inflated because of fraud. Many of them don't even have a real business.'

'I see.'

'Does that reassure you?'

'Yes.'

Gloria was stunned by the call and its outcome. Not long ago she'd been telling her dad that short selling was immoral and now she was thinking of working for Saskia? How quickly her high-minded opposition had melted in the face of this woman's interest! The fact was, it was an opportunity too good to miss. It wasn't merely the job, however, it was the person. She understood why her father had been so attracted to her, and it wasn't merely her looks. In a world of every kind of fakery, Saskia was someone with integrity. She was authentic.

Next morning, Gloria wrote to her to confirm she would like to take the next step, though she decided she would not tell her father about it yet.

69

Bad news soon returned as it always seemed to. She received an email from Mack captioned 'Alert!' It read,

'I'm sorry to report that, according to Paz, Roane has escaped from the police. His fear is that Roane will make his way to California. He was shouting out your name when the police forced him into their car. Call me if you need to.'

That night, Gloria had a terrifying dream. An intruder was in the house and had made his way up the stairs and into her room. He had approached her bed and thrust his hand over her mouth. She could barely breathe. She could not move her hands to resist. She was sure she was about to die.

Desperate, she woke up but still could not breathe. There really was a hand over her mouth! She felt it hard on her teeth. She was now fully awake and managed to slide her mouth sufficiently to bite into one of the fingers, creating a struggle. 'Stop moving,' commanded a male voice. She smelt sweat and alcohol. 'Don't resist. It'll be fine. I only want to talk.' She tried to scream but could only manage a groan. He backed away. 'Go on, then. Scream if you must.' It was an English accent. She reached for her bedside light, but he'd disconnected it. She snatched her cane from beside the bed. She could just make out his shape.

Now in control of herself, she spoke hurriedly, telling him she couldn't help him and she didn't want him there. He should give himself up. He had no chance of escape. The police were already on their way. She did not know that, but she had to do everything she could. She sensed he was becoming frantic. She knew that he was crazed and could do anything to her. She started shouting and he became angry, insisting she shut up. He strode towards her, grabbed the cane from her, and threw it on the floor. He leaned over her, and she felt sure he was going to strangle her.

She had handled it all wrong. She should have humoured him, not upset him. What use was her psychology now?

She then remembered something she'd heard about once but had no idea if it worked. In an attempt to induce an adrenaline dump in him, she started babbling loudly: 'Have you ever been to Spain for your holidays? Is it better than France? Or Greece? I liked Athens and Crete best. What about Sicily? Or Rome?' Ignoring his ordering her to stop, she gabbled on, 'What animals did you see there? What was the pool like? Do you like skiing? Montreux? Did I pronounce it right? Or Saint Moritz?'

At that moment Roane was standing shaking beside her and he burst into tears. There was suddenly more light on the wall. She saw his head loll. He was struggling to stay on his feet. Worried he would fall forward onto her, she strained to get out of his way. To her amazement, behind him was her mother. She'd hit him on the head with a paperweight from the office and, with him confused, she managed to push him over. He fell awkwardly to the floor face down, but he was not unconscious. Then Frank came in and he and Maria pinned him down. 'How did you get in, punk!?' Frank demanded as though in a gangster movie, checking him for weapons but finding none.

'You're not letting me breathe,' Roane complained. 'I'm no threat.'

'We'll be the judge of that.'

'Let him breathe, Dad.'

Frank eased the pressure a little. Roane then gave a halting, rambling answer. From what Gloria could discern, and filling in the gaps in his story, he'd secreted himself in the building after watching the house from the garden and observing who went in and out and when. Then he'd slipped in through the front door with a fake parcel of silk flowers, so that if accosted he could say he was delivering it, couldn't make anyone hear, and was confused. He'd managed to get upstairs and hid in one of the guest rooms.

'I'm sorry,' said Roane. 'I'm totally in the wrong, I know. But please don't turn me in. I never meant any harm. I can't help it if I'm in love with you, Gloria.'

'We're not letting you go,' said Maria.

Gloria, beginning to relax, managed a weak smile, her lips sore. To her it seemed that Maria, like her father, was reliving a scene from a film, albeit one of her more low budget ones.

Satisfied Roane was no danger, Maria told Frank she and Gloria could deal with him. Gloria manoeuvred herself off the bed, found her cane, and applied its tip hard to the middle of Roane's back. Bemused, Frank returned to his room to ring Layne. The women allowed Roane up and between them told him he had to go and search for Tania and Todd who would be on the lookout for their next victim.

When he argued, Maria said, 'Listen, hot-rod, you've got one option: find your so-called mother-in-law and her lover. Otherwise, you can talk it over with the cops. See what they have to say about what you've done.'

'What's the point?' he wailed. 'Aren't the police already on their way?'

'If they're not, you have Gloria's father to thank for that. But try anything and you'll find yourself in jail for attempted rape. You already have a bunch of stolen cars and God knows what else to explain away.'

'There was no attempted rape,' he protested.

'No, there wasn't, but I was terrified,' said Gloria. 'And you did assault me. In fact, I'm thinking maybe you should go to jail. You need a lesson. You had your hand over my mouth. You hurt me.'

'I'm sorry,' he said. 'I truly am.'

'You're just a dickhead,' Gloria said. 'A menace. I hate you.'

Frank bundled him downstairs. Gloria put on her dressing gown and Maria helped her negotiate the stairs. Frank announced he'd heard from Layne that Paz, presumably with Mack's help, believed he'd found the fugitive couple but had not yet approached them. Roane was suddenly committed to the cause. He wanted to be the big hero, going up to Portland, Oregon in a stolen car to seize them. 'There's no need,' said Gloria. 'Paz will contact the police and they'll make the arrest.'

'No, let's take them on,' he insisted.

They went outside. It was a mild night. Roane wanted to talk. Gloria didn't. She wanted him to leave. He seemed oblivious. He said he'd been intrigued as to who it was his father was talking to so often. He looked up Frank's family and fell in love with Gloria's picture instantly. The more he found out about her, the more he liked. 'And then we met on Skype. And you're so much more beautiful than your picture.'

Gloria's hostility began to fade. 'What does your dad think of mine?' she said.

'He thinks you're all quite mad. He's always laughing about it.'

'Laughing? The cheek of it. All I've heard is him moaning.'

'Oh, he does that a lot. He's quite mad too.'

'OK, friend,' said Maria sternly. 'Time to be on your way. Unless you want us to press charges, that is.'

'You should,' he said sombrely. 'Charge me with being in love with your daughter. I'm guilty of that.' He then pleaded with Gloria, 'Come with me.'

'No, I can't possibly. Nor do I want to.'

'I don't want to go anywhere, then. I want to stay here.'

'No, go away,' she said.

After a pause, he said sombrely, 'I guess, if you're not coming with me, then I have no choice.'

'They'll find you anyway, so you might as well turn yourself in for all the other stuff you did. It's your only hope,' she said.

'Hmm. Maybe they'll let me off for mental health.'

'Maybe. With any luck you'll be deported.'

'Whatever happens, can I see you again? I mean, to talk to.'

'No.'

'Not even on Skype?'

'No.'

He looked so wretched, she almost started laughing. He suddenly fell to his knees, 'Marry me, Gloria.'

'What!?'

'Please marry me.'

'Get up.'

'I bet you have a queue of people lined up to propose.'

'I assure you I don't. I'm boring.'

'Boring's cool.'

'No, it's not. I live a studious life.'

'That's even cooler.'

'You must be brain damaged.'

'If that's what being in love means, then I must be.'

'Anyway, I'm already taken.'

'Lucky guy.'

'It's a woman.'

'Even better.'

'She's worth ten thousand of you. And don't get any ideas of a three-some. It's not like that. I know how your poisoned mind works. I'm not some easy English slut.' She immediately thought of Lily's infidelities and regretted her words.

'Poisoned mind? That's hard. You're really hard.' She'd hurt him. 'Can I at least hold you for a moment?' After initial reluctance, she let him approach to embrace her. He opened his jacket and, leaning on her cane, she put her free arm loosely at his back. He was bony, undernourished. In the night air, he smelt sour, but she felt a wave of sympathy for him because he was so pathetic. She almost felt she could squeeze him to death if she chose to.

'You're tense,' he said. 'Relax. This is our moment.' He was aroused. She was unmoved and felt superior to him. 'Relax,' he repeated, and he held her tighter. She immediately imagined her legs parting. Suddenly it was like a hit of pure opium, a demon unravelling her resistance. In that moment all she could think of was him. He could will her to do anything. She could easily forget her own name. He was anarchy, thrilling. She realised he was literally fucking her with his mind, and she didn't care. She didn't resist when he grabbed her hand, ran it down his face, and kissed her palm. She was now a teenager thirsty for every last drop of him. He whispered, 'The woman you say you love can have you for ten thousand hours if I can have you for just one.' He was like a teenage boy who'd prepared the words specially. It was endearing, but also funny.

It was the humour that triggered the return of reason. What could he ever offer but a moment of ultimate ecstasy followed by a life of chaos and regret? She could see why he always had a girlfriend, albeit always one about to be ruined by him. He was never going to be the kind of man anyone could possibly want to live with. He tried to kiss her on the lips, but she pushed him away. 'Fuck off,' she said. The sudden magic was all gone.

He said, 'I feel privileged to be rejected by a goddess like you.'

It sounded silly, but for a giddy moment she realised how powerful she could be – and not just over him.

It was then the police showed up in three cars. Layne had insisted they be called. Roane put his hands up in submission. He turned to look at Gloria. He was betrayed. 'I still love you,' he said.

She was tempted to tell him she honestly didn't know the police were coming, stopped herself, then blurted it out. He merely nodded.

He was so light, the policeman almost hit Roane's head on the roof of the car when he threw him into it. There was a delay in leaving; some conversation before they set off. Gloria wished she could have known what was said. She hobbled to be a little further away from her mother as they observed the proceedings. If he could have seen her standing there at that moment, he would have thought her strong-willed and yet ultimately available for him. Self-conscious, she returned to be beside Maria.

As they stood watching the cars about to leave, Gloria said, 'He is kinda cute but he's also the devil. What he really needs is a good meal inside him. We should have fed him.'

'No we shouldn't,' said Maria. 'After what he did to you? For all that talk of his, he doesn't love you at all. He thinks you're trash and you almost proved it for him. When he hugged you, there was a spark. Be careful.'

Gloria felt embarrassed, although her mother was not wrong. 'Oh no, I don't think so,' she insisted. 'No, definitely not. But I got my first marriage proposal, at least.'

'Pah! I had a hundred and fifty proposals in a month at your age.' There she was, the bragging actress.

'What would I get then?' Gloria teased.

'Three hundred,' Maria said firmly. 'You're twice as beautiful as I was. Twice as lovely. Twice as kind.'

'Stop it, Mama.'

'Don't be afraid of men like him,' Maria said. 'He's just a puppy. You could devour him. You think every man is more powerful than you and you're wrong. You don't want someone like him. Or that dick Tommy. Find yourself someone with a brain. Some shy young professor or something. Someone worthy of you. You've got plenty of time. Don't waste yourself on jerks. Find yourself someone decent. Look at your father over there.' Gloria turned. Frank was sitting on the steps to the front door, fretting about the house's security. 'He's a dick,' said Maria.

'Mama!'

'They all are. But he's a decent man and that's what counts. No, I'm serious: it's really what counts. I know he has a wandering eye. All men do but with some of them it's only their eye that wanders.'

'Is Dr Mencius a dick?'

Maria paused a moment before answering, 'Of course he is. And he conned me. You were the only one who saw through him. You see through everyone. It's a gift.'

'Sometimes it feels like a curse.'

'No, it's always a gift. By the way, what happened to that Tommy anyway?'

'DUI. License suspended.'

'Pah! If he cared, he'd crawl around here on his bare knees if he had to, even if it took him all day to get here. And there are such things as cabs.'

'You said not to waste my time on him.'

'I know, but as you are now, darling, maybe even a fool like him's better than no one for a while. But make him prove himself and don't take any nonsense. And whatever you do, don't you contact him.'

They fell silent watching the last car leave. 'We could have given Roane a shower at least,' said Gloria. They both started laughing. Then they hugged. Gloria was glad she had her mother back.

'So did you know Mencius from your acting days?'

'Of course, my dear. He was my lover.'

'What!?'

'But only in fantasy!' She grabbed Gloria's forearm, laughing even harder.

'Mama, can I ask you something? Should I leave home? Papa seems to want me to.'

'Only if you want to. You can always come and go as you please. Now I'll ask you something for you to think about. When you're well again, do you want to come to the studio with me? I'm sure I could get you a part. Ever felt like acting?'

'Oh, I don't know.'

'Only your whole life, right? Think about it.'

Gloria agreed she would, though only to please her mother. 'Mama, I want to ask you something else.' She paused. 'Do you believe in platonic love?'

'Eh? What sort of question is that, and at this time of night?'

'I know. Please.'

'I guess I can hardly complain when I haven't been here for you so much lately. So what is it anyway? It sounds like bullshit.'

'It's a deep kind of love where there's no sex involved.'

'It means nothing to me. I never knew love until I met your father. All the men wanted sex and the women were rivals. There was no love there. But, thinking about it, I guess if someone has no family love and there's no sex in their life, they must be able to still have love somehow. And you can have sex where there's no love in it at all. Sex is powerful. The most powerful thing in the world. But it's a drug and the effect wears off. So I guess a love without sex would be without strong passion, and yet it could last for ever while another love burns itself out.' She gripped Gloria's hand. 'Oh, sweetheart, if you have someone who loves you – whoever it is – and you love them, cherish it. Even if they're far away – I was wrong about that. Cherish it above everything.'

'What about self-love?'

'Isn't that what narcissists have?'

'Everyone talks about it. About needing it.'

'I don't think so. Self-respect, yes. Love is for someone else. Or something else. Something outside. So now can we go in?' Maria looked round. Frank had left the front door ajar. He was probably upstairs on the phone to Layne.

As soon as they were indoors, Maria went into the kitchen to make coffee for them all. Happy but bewildered, tired but her mind too animated for sleep, Gloria carefully climbed the stairs. Keen for a return to something like normality, she sat down at her desk, opened her laptop, and prepared to write to Lily. Before beginning, however, she checked her phone. On it was a voicemail from Annalisa:

'Hey, babe, I thought you should know: Tommy was in an accident tonight but, don't worry, he's OK. He took one of his father's cars and smashed it into a tree. He's not injured and nor's his passenger. He was out with friends at a bar. Me and Jimmy were there. All he talked about was you and how he messed up and how he regretted it. No-one's ever seen him like it before. You really got to him. Anyway, like I say, I thought you should know. I'll call round tomorrow after work.'

Gloria put her head in her hands. Poor Tommy! Instinctively she began a text to him. All it would say was 'I heard. I'm sorry. Call me.' She paused. Her mother had said not to contact him. Make him prove himself, she'd said. He'd driven into a tree, possibly deliberately, was that not proof? She thought about his kisses that could be so intense she almost lost her mind. She thought about their conversations, his interest in her, and their tentative plans. He'd been serious and Annalisa's call proved it. But then she thought about his reputation for getting drunk and the girls he'd had sex with, just in the time she'd known him, and how bored he seemed after a while in her company. He'd be bored again, he'd be unfaithful and drunk again. And anyway who was the passenger Ant mentioned?

Could someone like Tommy change? People could be changed by love, couldn't they? People could turn themselves around. Tommy was an essentially good man who fell by the wayside sometimes. There was nothing evil about him, just a certain uselessness. So could she change him? It was arrogant to think she could. She wasn't exactly perfect herself. But she did strive for good. Mack credited her with saving her marriage, all because of Lily's vanity. Lily could not bear to be thought of as a 'slut' by her long-term friend and it had made her think about herself. A single word could do that much? Gloria had sent that message by mistake. But then in her way she had helped her parents to rekindle their relationship. They now did things together, even slept together, though not every night. Maybe she had some kind of power, the power of alchemy. No, that was delusional, dangerous.

There was too much to write to Lily about. Instead a brief message would have to suffice, asking her to call. She would send a note of thanks to Mack, maybe talk to both of them on Skype. She returned to her draft text to Tommy. She was facing more time in a knee brace, but she'd soon be able to drive again, and it would be fun to make plans for when she was fully fit.

Her mother now arrived with the coffee. 'What a night!' Maria said. They both laughed. 'What are you doing?' she asked.

Gloria immediately felt defensive. 'Just writing to my friend Lily in England.'

'Oh.' Her mother's expression revealed she realised that's who Gloria had meant earlier when talking about her 'far away' love. 'That's good,' she said and gave her a knowing smile before leaving to join Frank.

Gloria took a long, grateful sip of the warm liquid and looked at the draft message again. Was six words enough to show how she felt? 'Poor Tommy,' she sighed, then she deleted the text and put away her phone.

৯৯ ৯৯ ৯ ৯

ABOUT THE AUTHOR

John Holmes has had various jobs, primarily insurance loss adjusting at Lloyd's of London.

He earned an honours degree from the Open University in social sciences with special reference to psychology.

He was accepted as a member of the Crime Writers' Association following his novel Mack Breaks The Case, and once received a distinction from the London School of Journalism on their freelance article writing course.

He actively participates in writing groups - in person and online - as well as writer support groups on Facebook and Twitter.

He has two grown-up children and lives with his whippet Ollie near the beach in Brighton, England. He would like to spend more time there.

More information on his writings, and relevant links, can be found on the website johnholmesauthor.com.

ABOUT THE CHARACTERS

Gloria's early interactions with Lily, and Lily's backstory, can be found in the novel Lily Upshire Is Winning. Mack and Frank are also major characters in the book.

The start of Mack's career in investigation, and her initial cases with Paz, can be found in Mack Breaks The Case.

Printed in Great Britain
by Amazon